The Insomniac

By Robert Gould Shaw

Chapter 1

For the last year, Steve Shawn had been drinking more coffee after dark than in the morning and was thinking of going cold turkey. The Insomniac didn't serve alcohol. During the war and the hard years that followed, being aware of your surroundings as clearly as possible had been a matter of survival. You couldn't afford to relax, so he'd never developed a taste for drinking even though he'd have some wine once in a while, and not just at Seders.

He found that he couldn't bear to drink coffee in the morning anymore. The acid was killing his stomach. the strong coffees he was drinking, from that big Italian espresso maker at The Insomniac, were rough, like what his older brother, Ignac, used to make for him when their parents were away at the lake house on Lake Balaton back in the so-called Hungarian People's Republic and they were stuck in Budapest going to class.

Before discovering The Insomniac, evenings after work had been dull, especially after his girlfriend had broken up with him. He'd drive his green Rambler from the plant in Hawthorne up to his apartment near Pico in West LA, sometimes stopping at Factor's Deli for a bowl of mushroom soup that, while good, couldn't hold a candle to what his mom used to make in the winter. He didn't miss the company of the group of guys, all single, he'd kibitz with.

Winter was something else that he missed, living in California. Winter was something you could see on Mount Baldy far in the distance. He'd watch TV to improve his English and they'd have programs with snow for Christmastime, but you could see the palm trees hidden in the background behind the prop fir trees. Weekends were even worse. Sometimes he'd go to the Museum of Art to see if he could meet any UCLA girls. He'd considered this tactic an initial success because he'd met a few girls there. His ex-girlfriend, Elizabeth, he'd met through family connections. As he'd gotten older, even though it had only been a year, the college girls seemed less interesting even as they'd become more beautiful.

It was through Elizabeth that he'd discovered The Insomniac. She was into jazz and so suggested they go to The Lighthouse down in Hermosa Beach to hear a Shelly Manne set. How could you say no to that, except that she wanted to talk, and he wanted to hear what she had to say, so after one set, they went across the street to The Insomniac, a beatnik coffee house and bookstore. Over coffee, she talked about art and he tried to pay attention, except that he was distracted by the fetching dark-haired woman all alone reading a book of poetry, or at least holding a book of poetry. Blond Elizabeth, and he usually went for blond, especially true blond Jewish girls, was no match for brunette Poetry Girl.

Poetry Girl wasn't there every night. Sometimes she'd be with the kind of guy who wore sandals and grew out his chin whiskers heatedly discussing the Bomb, but mostly she'd be by herself. For a week, he'd gone there every night just to catch sight of her.

The scene at The Insomniac didn't start until late in the evening. The serious beatniks didn't come out until after 10:00 p.m., which was hard for him to handle seeing as how he had to be up early to drive down from West LA to get to his job at Averodyne, the small defense contractor where he worked as an engineer.

Early in the evening, when the squares still roamed the Earth, if you stepped into The Insomniac, you could buy a book of poetry or the latest novels translated from French, steel band records from Trinidad, prints and paintings from local artists, and then go to the back, have a seat at one of the tiny tables, and snack on salads and baguette sandwiches.

The later it got, the more happening the place was, with slender beatchicks of the earth daughter variety and Juliette Greco's distant cousin variety were ogled by shy poets spouting cultural critiques and bongo pounders. They all amscrayed with the shutting of the gates at 3:00 a.m.

They didn't have what Steve would call real food at The Insomniac. Even Factor's offered a cottage cheese bowl. It was all effete stuff. His mom would have warned him that food like that would constipate him. If he wanted something to eat, and he was down in the South Bay, he'd go to one of the dive teriyaki joints over in Torrance or have a burger at a coffee shop. Mexican food, which seemed to be everywhere, he was too afraid to try. The chicken paprikasch his aunt made was too spicy for him even though everyone else in the family used to complain that it was too bland.

On a Friday or Saturday night, The Insomniac generated as much buzz as a Tesla coil. There was music and poetry readings, satirical skits that he never understood in part because he couldn't hear them clearly enough over the constant yammering of the crowd. Beatniks, surfers and beatnots, who were squares so square they were cubed in a factory out in Dullsville, would cram into the café space, at the little tables only large enough to hold a couple of cups of java. On those nights, especially if the cats on stage were really wailing and the place was a regular Whistleville, with all the hot chicks, Beats or Ice Cubes ready for melting on display, there was action to be had, or at least that was the way it felt to him.

It took Steve a while to acclimate to the place. At first, he couldn't understand anything that anyone said to him. When he finally got a chance to chat up Poetry Girl, she was nice and all at first, even smiling at him and complimenting him on his accent. When he asked her out, she said, "Heavens to Betsy. You're nice and all, in a murgatroid kind of way, but with the kind of groove that skips too many beats." He could tell it was a no.

On other occasions, especially after he got hip, he did a little better. The dates he went on with girls he met there never really worked out. They either lived too far, like Long Beach or Downey, or were too white bread, too mashed potatoes and pot roast, despite their adoption of Beat culture.

When he was still living in Budapest and still a student, he hadn't always dated Jewish girls. After the war, there weren't that many, and many of them were emotionally scarred in ways he could understand all too well. They'd get mad that he'd been lucky and had not gotten sent to a camp. The fear, he could understand. He'd felt it like a cramp in his soul that wouldn't go away, but he'd never been beaten. He'd escaped taking one of those trains on their way to

Auschwitz. He'd never watched as his parents were shot in the back of the head and tossed into the Danube while somehow escaping in the confusion and mayhem. His family had hidden in the countryside, in a small town on the Romanian border, until the Russians came.

The Hungarian girls had been easier, and his parents hadn't minded much. He'd even taken a couple of them home for dinner. He liked the same things as they did, had read the same books and preferred the same coffee houses even though they sometimes preferred to not eat the desserts. His favorite was a Dobos Torte, something you couldn't really get in Los Angeles, even though some of the bakeries on Pico near Overland were pretty good at marble cake and poppy-seed strudel.

He'd thought café culture would have been natural to him. He'd been going to cafés his whole life, but the beatnik cafés were different. There was music or performances you had to talk over. The cakes were boring or too sweet and cloying. In Los Angeles, besides the museum, there wasn't any other place he'd successfully met girls. He thought about taking night classes at Santa Monica City College or enrolling at UCLA for a graduate degree, but it seemed like too much work just to meet girls. The Insomniac seemed the best place; it wasn't expensive, and you got a lot for your money.

For the last month, even though he'd broken up with Elizabeth, or maybe they were just on a hiatus, a hiatus that was her choice, things hadn't been going well. He'd thought he was doing well with Averodyne despite some of the concerns he had.

His boss seemed happy to hear his concerns and suggestions. He liked his co-workers and his co-workers seemed to like him, at least as far as he could tell. Then, that afternoon, just as everyone was going to lunch, his boss called him into his office and fired him. He had to hand over his keys to the building and the keys to his filing cabinet. They let him take the small cactus he'd brought to dress up his desk and marched him out of the building.

"Why am I being fired?" he demanded, as his mind calculated how long he could make his bank account last before he was destitute.

"It just isn't working out," his boss said. Carlton Cheam was tall and still blond even though he was in his fifties. "No harm no foul. We've got your address. We'll send you your final check. Just so you don't go away mad and because I don't want to put you out, there's going to be a little bit of something extra in it. You can use me as a reference. I'm sure you'll get back on your feet. I know you don't want to hear it right now, but I respect you as an engineer."

"Then why are you canning me? You've got no right! This, this. . .this is shit!" Steve declared. He was having horrible flashbacks of when his dad was fired. One day he was a manager, in charge of a whole department. The next he was out. He had to walk home because his driver was no longer his driver. His mom tried to tell him, as he came in the door and took off his coat, that he was luckier than some, that he hadn't been arrested, that he hadn't been shot. His dad hung his hat on the hook in the foyer, looked down, and said just one word, "yet."

Mr. Cheam looked at him sternly as Steve walked away, never turning around. He spoke very calmly. "I like you, Steve. I like you, but, and I'm not joking about this and listen to me closely. Go home, take a bath, have a nice meal, maybe open up a beer or a bottle of wine, and then you can go fuck yourself."

Steve was red-faced all the way through the parking lot to his car. Averodyne had a large parking area in front of the building. The front part of the building was where the executive offices were, which had their own windows. He knew there were co-workers, former co-workers, in those offices witnessing his humiliation, which made him even more furious.

The glorious sunshine of Southern California, with no clouds in the amazingly blue sky, made him feel worse. It had been easy to feel bad in Budapest. The weather, the economy, the political and historical conditions, and the anti-Semitism, pick two and you win a prize, were gourmet ingredients for a steaming bowl of misery. When he passed Mr. Cheam's Studebaker Golden Hawk, he angrily kicked the chrome bumper with his rubber-soled saddle shoes, causing the car to shake.

Looking for a new job would have to wait until the Sunday paper came out. He could update his resume and figure out what to say when he was asked why he left Averodyne. The aerospace industry was booming in Southern California. It was like a gold rush. Getting a fat contract, and most contracts were fat, meant that he shouldn't have any trouble getting a new job in a couple of weeks or a month. Thanks to the Cold War, Uncle Sam was keen on getting ahead of the Commies and having the best. They weren't going to begin the next war with broomsticks, old destroyers and doughboy helmets. If ray guns could be invented, like something out of Buck Rogers, they would have ray guns.

His money could hold out for two months. He'd survived the Nazis and Communists; he could survive unemployment. At that moment, as he drove out of the Averodyne parking lot, all he felt like doing was having a good meal, seeing a movie and going down to The Insomniac to find a girl. He would try to milk every last drop of European moodiness Elizabeth had so liked when they first started going out. She said it was nearly as attractive as a uniform.

Steve drove down Artesia Boulevard until he got to Hawthorne Boulevard where he pulled into the large parking lot of the May Company department store and took out the paper to find a movie. If it was early enough, he could catch as a matinee.

La Dolce Vita, was supposed to be good and he'd wanted to see it with Elizabeth, but it wasn't playing in the South Bay. He'd have to go up to Westwood or see it at the Lido on Pico near his home. *The Alamo* and *Exodus* had the right subject matter for getting fired but wouldn't set the mood for landing a chick. He settled on *Where the Boys Are*. It was playing at the Fox Redondo which was not too far away. Maybe it would give him a glimpse into the female psyche.

He loved the movie, mostly because it had Yvette Mimieux. How could you not like a girl with Yvette Mimieux's name and looks? It had the kind of American happy ending that reminded him of plays by Miklós László, like *Parfumerie*. The American version, *The Shop Around the Corner*, was pretty good, especially because of Jimmy Stewart. Margaret Sullivan was pretty good too, but she was not exactly his type.

After the movie, he thought about seeing another one, maybe something at the Cove down in Hermosa Beach. It wasn't even five o'clock and the chicks didn't come out before sunset. From the Fox Redondo he walked a couple of blocks down the hill to the base of the Redondo Beach Pier to Tony's.

Johnny, the boss's son had suggested it as a great place to take dates. He took Elizabeth there but only once because just about everything on the menu was treyf, which didn't matter to him but was a boundary Elizabeth didn't like crossing.

They'd sat upstairs, with a great view of the ocean and the horseshoe pier, drinking mai tai's until their orders showed up. Elizabeth ordered linguine with without shrimp and he ordered the seafood alfredo studded with shrimp, scallops and clams. It was almost the best thing he'd ever eaten, not counting an epic horse goulash he'd eaten with his family on a cold night just after they were liberated by the Red Army and the poppy seed strudel his aunt made whenever the family got together.

That night, he was eating alone at the bar, no mai tais, just a beer, no seafood linguine alfredo, just a bowl of clam chowder and a plate of fried sand dabs and extra lemon slices. There were couples on dates; older ones who seemed happy and younger ones he imagined were on the path to happiness. The beer was too cold, in the American fashion, but the sand dabs were fantastic. He didn't know what sand dabs were. All he knew was that, at least at Tony's, they were morsels of fried goodness tart from the lemon juice.

After dinner, he drove the mile or so north to Hermosa Beach. It was still pretty early but at least the sun had set. Once you were past the harbor that was being constructed and then past the Edison power plant, you were in Hermosa. From there it was only a few blocks to Pier Avenue and the search for parking began. Parking was freely available in Hermosa especially so early in the evening, but it came with a price. The policing of the meters was more zealous than a Young Pioneer group leader. Parking was enforced twenty-four hours a day, three hundred and sixty-five days a year.

Steve drove a few blocks north on Hermosa Avenue and then up 14th Street to Manhattan Avenue and found parking that was not meter enforced and had no time limit. After parking the car, he took his briefcase and locked it in the trunk of his Rambler.

The Rambler wasn't a chick magnet, but it was what he could afford. His current dream car was a Nash-Healey. He knew someone who said he would sell his for a good price and Steve was saving up to buy a used Nash-Healey.

The Nash-Healey was a beautiful sports car and not so finicky as an MG. That car would be a chick magnet and he wouldn't have to worry about electrical problems. He'd take a picture of him standing next to it and send it to his parents back in Budapest. It made him sad to think that his brother would never get a chance to see it.

He took off his tie and suit jacket, unbuttoned his white dress shirt and put on a black Bocskai style vest, with black-corded buttons. The vest, which his mom had ordered for him the year before the Uprising, was a conversation piece and made him look as exotic as his accent sounded. The chicks seemed to dig the look: it made him seem more with it, less the poindexter he was at work.

The Cove Theatre, which was just around the corner from The Insomniac and The Lighthouse, was showing *Sink the Bismarck*. Good triumphing over evil with lots of explosions. Just what he was in the mood for.

It was just after nine o'clock when the movie let out. He went out the back of the theater and headed up the alley to the Strand, the sidewalk that followed the beach, then turned left and walked around the corner, past what was left of the old pier that was fenced off pending demolition, to The Insomniac.

The action had already started. A clean-cut, male/female folk duo, in matching Irish fisherman sweaters, were finishing a set of negro spirituals arranged for guitar and two-part harmony. A large man in a black turtleneck, bone necklace and black beret bounced on stage, sat on a chair and sang an improvised song rhyming on the names of dead poets to the beat of the bongo drums wedged between his legs.

Steven browsed the books and flipped through the prints all the while checking out the girls, especially the ones browsing the poetry books. There were girls there he'd already unsuccessfully chatted up and girls already with guys. Many of the girls were very young, possibly still in high school, clad in a chunky sweater or striped French sailor's shirt over tight black or dark blue pants.

The guys, he never paid much attention to. He didn't look like them and he didn't dress like them. Brooding European intellectual with an accent made for expounding his hard-won views of the world, even though he was too mild-mannered to excel in it, was his shtick and he was able to pull it off with girls who'd never made it out of the Pacific time zone. He was selling worldliness not tanned, fresh surfer looks.

A young woman, but not high-school young, with short dark hair who looked like a cross between Louise Brooks and Clara Bow was paging through a book of Rimbaud's poetry, in French of course, and mouthing the words to herself. She caught his eye. She was wearing black skinny capris and an embroidered peasant blouse.

He'd never seen her before and he would have remembered. Usually, he hemmed and hawed, circling his prey like an indecisive falcon. This time he approached her directly, or at least in a straight line. From where he was standing, over a small stack of Horkheimer and Adorno's *Dialectic of Enlightenment*, it was only a few paces to her. Picking up a copy of the book, he casually walked over to her and said to her in French, "Je me crois en enfer, donc j'y suis. Ô mes petites amoureuses, Que je vous hais!"

"I'm sorry, I don't speak French," the woman said as she looked up from her book and smiled.

"Just as well," Steve said. "My Hungarian is far better than my French."

"I'm sorry, I don't know any Hungarian either," she said. She blushed as he took her hand and kissed the back of it.

"And now you do. Let me introduce myself. I'm Szanto Istvan, but my friends call me Steve."

"Beatrice" the woman said, blushing, "but you can call me any time."

"We should get a table; don't you think?" Steve said, motioning towards the back of the room where the café was.

"That's one piece of furniture," Beatrice said with a wink, "but not my favorite. Keep guessing."

"Chair?" Steve said, confused.

"If you think it would be comfortable," Beatrice said, following Steve to an unoccupied table.

"I like your shirt. It reminds me of back home in Budapest."

"As long as it doesn't remind you of your mother, I'm sure we'll get on fine."

Steven pulled out the chair for her and she gracefully sat down, maintaining intense eye contact with him all the way down. "What would you like to drink?"

"Nothing. I'm drowning in the dreaminess of your eyes," she said.

A group of men dressed in black came on the very highly elevated stage. Even their guitars and stand-up bass were black.

"We're the Notional Hawthornes. I hope you like our music," the bass player said just before stomping out the beat. They played folk music versions of Kurt Weill songs, mostly taken from *The Three Penny Opera* and *The Rise and Fall of the City of Mahagonny*.

"At least I know these tunes," Steve said.

"Do you want to stay?" Beatrice asked seductively.

"No, we can go whenever you want, but I live on the West Side, just off of Pico. I had a miserable day at work and you're just the thing I needed to make the day worthwhile."

"As long as you know how to make breakfast, have more than one chair and can drive me back in the morning, we can go whenever you want."

"Have you ever had palacsinta?".

"Never when I've been sober,"

"I'll make them for you with walnuts and chocolate sauce."

"If that's for breakfast, what's for dessert?" Beatrice asked as she gently caressed his cheek.

Steve stood up and left some money on the table, even though they hadn't had a chance yet to order. "You. You're for dessert."

Beatrice licked her lips and smiled as she stood up from the table. "I can only imagine the appetizer. I'm parked on Hermosa Avenue just past the Foster's Freeze. I'll need to go to my car first and re-park it, but let me go to the women's room first."

"Not a problem. We can go out the back if you want," Steve said. "It's quicker."

"As long as you're not a moocher or a weirdo."

"Perhaps odd, but a weirdo I'm not."

"Back in a sec'," she said as she stood.

"Do you mind if we finish their set?" Steve asked when she returned. "The band is pretty good."

They walked through the back doors of The Insomniac and along Beach Drive, an alley behind the Strand. The fog had rolled in and it was difficult to see further than a short block. As they passed the rear of the Poop Deck, a dive bar on the Strand, an older man, who looked like a washed-out sailor, peed against the back wall. "There was a line," he wailed over the sound of his piss hitting the wall.

Two short blocks later, they reached the Biltmore Hotel, an old building with a salt-water plunge in the basement. There was a line starting from around the corner of high school kids in Pendleton shirts waiting to get into Stub's to see the surf bands.

"What're you waiting to see?" Beatrice asked a girl wearing an oversized plaid shirt.

"The Plungers and the Lonely Ones," she said. "They're the ginchiest. They're real surfers not like the Beach Boys."

"Yeah, the Beach Boys are a bunch of hodads," a boy standing next to her said.

They walked hand in hand along 14th Street and as they got closer to the corner, the roar of hot rods gunning their engines to show off their horsepower increased and became almost deafening.

"I'm just around the corner," Beatrice said.

"And I'm parked just up the hill," Steve said before collapsing face first onto the sidewalk. Blood seeped out of the back of his skull and from a wound in the middle of his back.

Beatrice screamed and looked around but couldn't see anyone. Steve's blood had splattered on her clothing. At first, no one seemed to hear her, but then, as the roar and rumble of the hot rods subsided, people came running from around the corner and from near the Biltmore.

Chapter 2

As Beatrice screamed, a crowd of mostly teenagers in Pendleton shirts, ran to her. Some of them bent down and looked after Steve Shawn, who was lying face down in the gutter in an ever-increasing pool of his own blood.

"The guy's toast," someone said

"Someone call the cops," another yelled.

"Did you see what happened?" a man asked Beatrice.

Beatrice was too shocked to talk. She wiped tears and blood from her eyes smearing her face red.

"Are you hurt?" a man asked.

"Give her a handkerchief," someone demanded.

The crowd around Beatrice grew larger and encircling her. She cried as she took a handkerchief someone had handed her and wiped the blood from her face.

"There's some on your forehead," a girl in a said as she handed Beatrice a pocket mirror from her purse.

"Police, coming through!" Lester Patterson barked. "Let me through!" Lester Patterson was in his early twenties with close-cropped dark brown hair. Lester had been working parking enforcement for more than a year.

He'd been in the middle of writing a ticket for a Buick with an expired meter when a woman ran up to him and yelled that someone had been shot. He scribbled the license number on the ticket, signed it, and placed it under the wipers then ran towards the screams and cries. He hadn't heard the shot, which wasn't a surprise given how many hot rods were slowly grumbling up and down Hermosa Avenue.

Friday and Saturday nights were always hopping, with cars and crowds watching the cars. The route was from Pier Avenue south to the Redondo Beach border then back up past Pier to 22nd Street where the burger place on the corner was another hangout. Some nights the rodsters would be joined by a variety of flavor of bikers, the Triumph guys, the choppers, or the older guys on their Indians.

The bikers and rodsters didn't always mix well but bikers weren't out that night, so the only strife had been between the rodsters and people trying to cross the street. The walkers would yell at the rodsters to get out of the way and the rodsters would rev their grumbly engines and snarl at anyone on two feet, unless they were a cute girl. The cute girls they'd try to get to join them in their rod.

Lester arrived on the scene in less than a minute. It was only around the corner. He hadn't seen anyone running away. Everyone was running to the screams.

There were a lot of ways to escape. There was the beach, into the crowd of kids waiting to get into the surf music club at the Biltmore, and the alleys and walk streets to the north past the bungalows that clustered the block or two between the Strand and Hermosa Avenue. A block to the south was Pier Avenue and the crowds in front of the old guy bars, The Lighthouse and The Insomniac

The body was face first. He'd been shot in the back of the head, probably from a pistol. The back of his head was blown off. Bits of his skull were spattered on the ground next to him. Unless he'd happened to have a heart attack or a massive stroke in the seconds before being shot, the cause of death was obvious.

There still had to be an autopsy. They'd take out the bullet or bullets and figure out what kind of gun they'd come from. Lester didn't even know if Hermosa Beach had a coroner. There was a small hospital on Pacific Coast Highway but it didn't have a good reputation.

The last murder in Hermosa had been a couple of years earlier. Everyone on the force still talked about it. It was better than telling old parking enforcement stories.

"Did anyone hear or see anything?" Lester yelled out. "If you have, please form a line so I can ask you questions." He took out his walkie talkie and called for backup. "While I'm waiting for backup would you please not get too close? If you get too close, you're risking becoming a suspect."

The crowd stepped back from the corpse and began to disperse.

"I'm going to have to ask all of you to stay where you are!" Lester commanded. "Even if you don't think you saw anything, you may have some piece of information that will help us solve the crime."

"That woman was with him at the time," the teenage girl in an oversized plaid shirt said, pointing to Beatrice. The girl used a tissue to try to wipe blood off of her compact.

Beatrice sat on the curb across the narrow street from Steve Shawn's body. She clutched her purse to her chest. Her mascara was smeared across her cheeks that mixed with the blood and tears. There was blood on the left side of her clothing.

Lester walked over to her. "Excuse me, Ma'am, are you the girlfriend?"

"I just met him," Beatrice sobbed. "He was walking me to my car."

"What's your name full name, address and phone number?" he asked as he took out a small notepad from his back pocket.

"Beatrice Loehner, L-O-E-H-N-E-R, 107 Kelp Street, El Porto, LIncoln 5-2298."

A couple of cops pulled up in a squad car, lights flashing and siren blaring just as Lester finished writing down Beatrice's information. Another two cops arrived from the direction of the Strand. They began to secure the scene and herd people away from the corpse. A minute later, another squad car pulled up and then a sedan, lights flashing.

Detective Sam Kappe stepped out of the sedan. He was dressed in a black suit with a white shirt and skinny tie clipped to his shirt with a gold tie clasp emblazoned with the Marine Corps logo. He put on his fedora, correcting the angle of the hat in his reflection in the sedan's window. Not bad for a guy in his forties.

Kappe strode over to Lester and Beatrice. He knew how lucky he was to have it happen on his watch. The last one had been George Albertson's to solve before he retired and they'd never found the murderer. That wasn't going to happen this time. He was going to find the murderer and not only make the charges stick but send him on a one-way ticket to San Quentin.

"What do we have here?" Kappe bellowed to Lester.

Lester stood at attention and read from his notes. "Loehner, Beatrice. She had just met the victim, Steve. She doesn't know his last name. He was walking her to her car after meeting at The Insomniac. They'd stopped to talk to the people standing in line at the Biltmore. They'd walked down this street and the next thing she knows, he's dead and she's covered in blood."

"Did you hear or see anything, Ma'am?" Kappe asked her. "Was there anything unusual about him about how he acted?"

"No, he seemed very nice. He had an accent. He was Hungarian and spoke pretty good French."

"Do you speak French?" Kappe asked her.

"Ah, no. I know a little bit of Italian," Beatrice said.

"So, how would you know his French was good? I don't think we're getting the straight story from you!"

"Well, I don't know," Beatrice stammered. "I just met him. His accent sounded good, like Louis Jourdan."

"Bring her in!" Kappe bellowed. "Put her in my car. I'll take her in myself."

Lester led her to Kappe's car, opened the rear door and showed her in.

"I want statements from everyone!" Kappe yelled out to all the cops. "Names, addresses, phone numbers! I don't want anyone leaving until every last one of them has been questioned. Get on it!"

Lester walked back to Kappe. "What do you want me to do?"

"You're doing a good job kid. What's your name again?"

"Patterson, Lester," Lester said sharply, snapping to attention.

"Your first dead body?"

"Yes sir!"

"You can help by keeping the fuck out of my way!" Kappe said quietly but firmly. "You like giving out parking tickets?"

"It's okay, sir."

"Parking tickets pay your goddamn salary and the salary of every last one of us," Kappe growled. "It's an honorable profession, no matter what anyone else thinks. It keeps that little bit of fear in the citizenry, keeps them in line, keeps them from thinking they can get away with anything. Otherwise, there'd be anarchy. You think they give parking tickets in the jungle?"

"No sir."

"That's what separates us from the savages," Kappe said with a smile. "I like you kid. If you can mind your Ps and Qs, I'll take you along for the ride, get you off ticketing and maybe make a real policeman out of you."

"Geez, that would be great!" Lester said enthusiastically.

"Watch the language!" Kappe scolded. "This ain't happy hour at the Poop Deck. If you're working with me, you better know that I run a clean operation, by the book, my way or the highway. Got it?"

"Yes sir!" Lester said, snapping back to attention.

"Now, let's see if we can catch ourselves a murderer. You said that our victim and his girl had just come out of The Insomniac? I've been wanting to raid that Commie Pinko place for ages. Listen up," Kappe yelled out to the police officers. "I want two guys to go into The Insomniac and see if any of the degenerates saw anyone suspicious. And if you see any reefers, if, so help me, you see any fucking oregano on a fucking plate, give me a squawk and we'll close the place down."

"I'll go," Lester said, raising his hand.

"Fine, take one of the Clancys and find me a witness. When you're done, meet me back at the station and we'll sift through what we've found. Has anyone found the casings?" Kappe yelled out. "One of you is going to find me the shell casings."

The sirens of the approaching ambulance and the commotion of the crowd drowned out anything that Lester could say or yell. He motioned to the two closest patrolmen to follow him. The two Johns, as they were called, were a few years older than Lester. They'd been partners since they'd graduated from parking enforcement, about the time that Lester had joined the force. They walked up along 13th Court to The Insomniac's back door.

"I don't care if you're Kappe's long lost son," John T, the taller one said. "You're still a virgin. We're leading the questioning and maybe you'll learn some real policing."

"Hey, maybe you'll get your cherry popped and graduate from ticketing," Big John, who was short and tubby, said.

John T tried to open The Insomniac's rear door and then began to pound it with his fist while Big John kicked it. From behind the door, you could hear the muffled sound of music, singing, but indistinct enough that you couldn't tell much about it.

"Can we just go around the front?" Lester asked. "You can hear that there's a band playing. They're never going to hear us."

Just then, the door opened. A man looked out, saw that they were police and ushered them in.

"Violence is always the answer," Big John said with a smile.

John T explained to the man who had opened the door, a guy with longish graying hair dressed all in black from his loafers to his turtleneck, that they needed to talk with the customers.

"But, man, Linda's on," the man said.

"I don't give a fuck if Frank Sinatra is on," John T said, "We're closing you down for the night, but nobody can leave. A man has been murdered, a guy who just came out of your rat's nest."

"Maybe if it was Sinatra," Big John said.

"Heavy," the man from The Insomniac whispered as he led them past the bathrooms and into a small room stacked with instrument cases, mostly guitars, banjos and bongos closed off from the rest of the club by a heavy purple curtain.

"That's the stage?" Lester asked.

"You could let her finish her song," the man whispered.

The curtain muffled the sound of a woman singing a folk song and someone strumming an acoustic guitar.

The two Johns looked at each other, then swung the curtain opened and strode out onto the small stage. The spotlights blinded them, causing them to shield their eyes and stumble about. Big John knocked a banjo off its stand. It clanged onto the floor causing the audience, which had gone silent when they burst onto the stage, to gasp.

"It's the fuzz!" someone in the audience yelled.

"Raid!" someone else yelled.

A third of the audience rose up and streamed to the front of the building, causing a jam.

Lester stepped onto the stage and took the microphone from a very young-looking woman with long dark brown hair.

"Everyone take a seat!" Lester yelled as loud as he could. "It's not a raid! Something happened and we'd like to ask for your help. Raise your hand if in the last half hour, did anyone see, did anyone notice anyone leaving the back of the building? If you did see someone, anyone leaving the back of the building and maybe anyone following them, please come talk with us and answer a few questions."

"You broke my banjo," a man with a goatee, said as he placed his guitar on his seat and knelt down to pick up the banjo whose neck was broken off and only attached by the strings.

"If you saw something, if you think you possibly saw something, please come up to the stage," Lester said.

A few people came up to the stage. A high school girl with long straight blond hair came up first. She was wearing a dark blue turtleneck with a dangly shell necklace and blue jeans. "Linda, you were wailing!" she yelled to her.

A young man dressed in a button-down shirt and wearing a green tweed sports coat stood behind the blond girl as she chatted with Linda.

"Did you see anything,"

"Nah, I'm just ditching my cuffs, you dig? You know, my 'rents," he said lazily.

"Did you see anything?"

The boy smiled. "In this Whistleburg? It's a real wild hootenanny, quails everywhere. You dig?"

"No, I don't dig," Lester said, annoyed to be wasting his time.

"So, real slow so you cubes can understand," the boy said. "This is chick central, a real quail farm."

"Did you see anyone, a guy and a girl, leave out the back?" Lester asked.

"Yeah, I saw them. The guy's a real murgatroid, if you know what I mean, what with that vest of his, but then somehow he's a real quail catcher and walks out with this crazy chick-a-deedle-dee. I'm thinkin' that lucky murgatroid is going to go all Sputnik before the night is over."

"Did you see anyone else leave after them?" Lester asked.

"Nah, just some stable monkey and a couple of Torrance High cubes and their wanna-be gidgets down from Valhalla to crash the scene."

"How old are you, if you don't mind my asking?"

"Almost seventeen," the boy said.

"I'm going to need your name, address and phone number, in case we need to contact you. Do you think you could remember what any of them looked like?"

"The stable monkey, I only saw from the backside and ixnay on the Vikings 'cause cubes all look alike. Cubed. The gidgets, I'd spot from a mile away, especially from behind."

"Very helpful. So, name, address, phone number."

"Well, I am trying for Eagle Scout," the boy said.

After Lester had taken down the boy's information, the two Johns came over looking annoyed.

"Complete waste of time," John T said.

"If I hear another Rimbaud or Sartre allusion, I'm going to puke," Big John said. "Nobody saw anything 'cause either they're paying attention to themselves or scouting for a date. If we had a picture of the guy, maybe that would have helped."

"I got a guy probably saw the victim leave with the girl and may have seen someone leave after him," Lester said.

"Can he ID them?" John T asked.

"Can I understand him?" Lester said exasperated. "Whatever language he's speaking, it sure ain't English. I think he said he was too busy looking at the girl's behind to notice anything else, so probably not."

"Probably not is possibly snot," Big John said. "You've got a lot to learn."

"I hate to go back to Sam Kappe empty-handed," John T said as they walked to the back of the building, past the bathrooms and then out the back door.

"He's a real hard-ass," Big John said.

"Supposedly, his butt was shot off during the war and replaced with a steel one," John T said.

"Nah, he was a desk jockey. He never left the States on account of his typing. He won the state high school typing championship men's division," Big John said.

"I thought it was because his old man was one of those Nazis that did that rally up in La Crescenta before the war," John T said.

"I thought that was a rumor," Big John said.

It took almost an hour before Lester and the two Johns were done with the questioning. All they got was that a couple of people who saw Shawn and Loehner leave out the back. Nobody saw anyone follow them or could remember seeing anyone else go out the back before them.

Sam Kappe was standing next to the body as a photographer snapped pictures with his big Graflex camera. He looked up as Lester and the two Johns approached.

"Some buttinski took it upon himself to pick up the shell casings and get his paw prints all over them," Kappe growled. "You should have seen the look on his face when I told him that he was now a suspect."

Kappe took a bundled up white handkerchief out of his jacket pocket, opened it up and showed Lester two brass shell casings. "Nine-millimeter parabellum. A Walther or a Luger, probably silenced since nobody seemed to have heard anything, though considering that most of them have done so much damage to their ears listening to rock and roll, it's a wonder that sign language isn't popular with this crowd. Walthers and Lugers are as common as the Clap. Every G.I. within ten feet of the front brought back one. What have you got?"

"I've got a wannabe teenage beatnik who says he saw them leave out the back, but didn't see anyone leave after them. I've got a couple of others who say the same thing. Nobody saw anyone follow them out."

"Not fucking good enough," Kappe snarled. "Has anyone found his car?" he yelled out to nobody in particular.

"Clearly the killer was after the guy and not the girl," Lester said.

"No shit, Sherlock, but then maybe he's a gentleman and wouldn't lay a finger on a girl," Kappe snarled.

"Do we know what car he drove?" Lester asked.

"No, we don't know what fucking car he drove," Kappe snarled.

"Well, assuming he drove and isn't from Hermosa. We can assume that it will be within a few blocks and that within twenty-four hours it will have a parking ticket on it. We can run the plates on just those cars," Lester said.

"Good work, Sherlock, except that I already thought of that. Hey, I've got an idea. Why don't you go back to writing tickets for the rest of your shift? The city's got to be able to pay our miserable salaries somehow. And maybe we'll find his car."

"If he didn't park in a metered space, finding his car is going to be a bear," Lester said.

"All we know now is that his name was Steven Shawn, that he was twenty-five and lived up near Pico, which means that he was probably of the Hebrew persuasion," Kappe said. "From the looks of his mitts, he worked at a desk. They're smooth and stained with ink and pencil lead. He was probably single, unless he was cheating on a misses, but I doubt that because he would have been home already."

Kappe showed them a set of car keys. "He's got an older car. The ignition has been replaced, or at least new keys have been made, so we can't tell which kind of car from the car keys. Here, take the keys and see if they go to any of the cars you ticketed."

Lester took the keys, put away his notepad in his back pocket and took out his ticket pad and walked his beat, up and down Hermosa Avenue and up and down Pier Avenue for the next several hours until 3:00 p.m., after the bars had closed. Nothing seemed out of place. None of the cars he ticketed fit the keys. He wondered if he should try all the hundreds of cars parked within a ten block radius.

The surf music kids in their Pendleton shirts, were the first to leave, followed by the smart-suited jazz fans from The Lighthouse and the rodsters. Without an audience, the rodsters had no reason to cruise.

Next to leave were the beatnicks. They weren't any trouble since The Insomniac didn't have a liquor license. Their clothes reeked of strong French cigarettes and reefer. After that, there were bar workers heading home after closing and the sand heads some of whom slept underneath the pier or behind the Ocean Aquarium.

Lester more than met his ticket quota, but the keys fit none of the cars. Mr. Shawn had been savvy enough to park further away from Pier and Hermosa Avenue. You didn't have to go too many blocks up the hill or north or south to get to an unmetered residential area.

When his shift was over at 4:00 a.m., he went back to the small, newly built police station. The police station, city hall, library and fire station were all either right next to each or attached. One of the other meter maids, a guy named Paul, was about to go out on his shift. After he changed out of his uniform and into his street clothes, he passed through the office. Kappe was the only one still left.

"I had all the Clancys going up and down the street looking for clues," Kappe said. "Nothing. They asked everyone if they'd seen anything. Considering how foggy it is and the fact that people barely pay attention to their own asses, it's not a surprise that we found nada. However, whoever did this was either lucky or a professional."

"What's so special about Steve Shawn that he'd be gunned down?" Lester asked.

"That's what we're going to have to find out," Kappe said wearily.

"He could have owed someone money."

"How's he going to pay it back now? You beat them up for that so they're afraid not to pay."

"Maybe the mob?"

"Dragna died in '56 and since Chief Parker came on the scene, the mob isn't what it used to be. You can't rule them out."

"Do you want me to stay?"

"Nah, you should clock out, go home and get some sleep. I'll put in a word with the chief to get you off the meters. Come in tomorrow at your usual time and we'll see what we can arrange. Maybe there's a Clancy that's fucked up recently that we can bust down to meters."

"Thanks."

"I only ask for one thing, loyalty and hard work."

"You can count on me," Lester said.

The drive back to his north Redondo Beach apartment never took long. Kappe hadn't seemed as tough as people said. Lester figured that most of it was show.

His bedroom windows faced east and even with heavy curtains, light still streamed into the room as soon as the sun rose. For months, he'd meant to black out the windows, but he hadn't had time to get around to it.

The apartment was a one-bedroom in a newish building. He was only the second tenant. The place was plain. He had just the bed he'd brought from his childhood bedroom, a dinette set that he'd gotten on sale, but didn't particularly like, a TV that got pretty good reception despite the bent aerial, a hi-fi that he could barely play because the neighbors complained, and a set of dishes and cups he'd bought at White Front.

Mary, his girlfriend, had made him go out and buy some decent wine glasses and some Revere Ware pots and pans.

His mind drifted to Mary, in all her glory. Her smile. The way her blond hair waved in the wind. Her dexterity at rolling perfectly placed balls when she lawn bowled at the club. Her body moving within her white lawn bowling outfits. The way she kissed. The way that she smoothly knocked her opponent's balls out of the way with shots that somehow also managed to defy physics and geometry.

Chapter 3

It was afternoon when Lester was woken by the ringing of his phone. The phone was on the wall in his kitchen not in his bedroom. It wasn't that far, his apartment wasn't large, but coming out of his somewhat darkened bedroom into the bright sunlit living room and then into the kitchen, was a shock. He was blinded but fortunately knew his way. All the while, the phone kept ringing and ringing.

"Lester Patterson speaking," he said after picking up the tan plastic receiver.

"You've got the keys to the car?" the voice said insistently.

"Who may I ask is calling?" asked groggily, not sure what the context of the question was.

"Sam Kappe! I'm sorry I woke you from your beauty rest, and I'll keep this very simple, do you have the keys to the car?"

"Who's car? My car? I don't understand," Lester said groggily. He looked at the clock on the stove, which read 12:03.

"What are you, a comedian?" Kappe said angrily. "What's on second, then comes I don't know. Steve Shawn's car. The stiff. The Swiss Cheese."

"Um, I don't know. I'll check. Hang on a sec," Lester said as he tried to stretch the phone cord into the living room, where his uniform pants were hanging over the back of his easy chair. As he picked up the pants, all the change and keys in his pocket fell onto the parquet tile floor with a clang. He wrapped the phone cord around the back of the chair so that the phone wouldn't fall on the floor, then knelt down and picked up his keys then the keys found on Steve Shawn's body. "Yeah, I've got them," he said, after unwrapping the phone from the chair.

"We found his car. Ran it through the DMV," Kappe said. "But, funny thing. Some imbecile forgot to leave the keys where someone can find them. I'm too polite to name names, but let's just say that said imbecile better get those keys down here so we can inspect the victim's car within, say, the next hour, or that said imbecile is going to be demoted. Funny thing is that there isn't anything below meter maid. There isn't a rank of shithead."

"I'll be there in forty-five minutes."

Lester hung up the phone, undressed and took a quick shower, then shaved as quickly as he could, nicking himself on the chin in the process. He tried to sop the blood up with toilet paper, meanwhile praying that the bleeding would stop before he got to work and that he wouldn't drip blood on his white uniform shirt. He had no such luck, so stuck the smallest bandage he could find on his chin.

The only breakfast he had time for was a wish sandwich, a slice of bread between two slices of bread, which he ate as he drove to work. The traffic was light going along Aviation and he got to the police station pretty quickly. Before he got out of the car, he peeled off the bandage and was sorry that he had. The nick hadn't closed up, so he put another bandage on it.

As soon as he got into the station, before he stopped at his locker, he stopped by Sam Kappe's desk.

Kappe looked pretty rough. It was clear he hadn't gone home since the night before. He hadn't shaved, which was a cardinal sin for anyone but Kappe. The word was that he had killed an Italian soldier his unit had captured just because the guy had asked for a smoke when Kappe was down to his last coffin nail.

"I'm here boss," Lester said as he approached Kappe at his desk.

Kappe looked up, his eyes bloodshot from lack of sleep. "Did someone try to slit your throat?"

"Nah, just a shaving mishap."

"You got the keys?"

"Yeah," Lester said, fishing the car keys out of his pocket.

"The car's out back. We had it towed. It's the green Rambler. Mr. Shawn wasn't in the money and he wasn't trying for flash. The car is in decent shape, but it's showing its age." Kappe stood up and led Lester out the side door of the station to a small lot behind the fire station that was for police use.

"Yeah, I can see what you mean." The green Hudson Rambler Super two-door was nothing fancy and didn't have any more scratches than his Ford Custom 300.

"So, let's open the baby up. I'll let you do the honors."

"Yeah, sure," Lester said as he opened the driver's side door then leaned in and reached over and opened the passenger side door.

In the front and back seat, there wasn't much there. Steve Shawn hadn't been a packrat. There were some empty food wrappers tossed onto the back seat but nothing else of interest.

"We'll take the car apart later. You've got to be thorough. Maybe he was killed because of something he was hiding," Kappe said.

"Presumably, if the killer thought he was hiding something or had something he wanted he would have followed him to his car, otherwise he might not know where the car was," Lester said. "My guess is that he killed him when he had the opportunity or just wasn't patient. Where was the car found?"

"Up the hill a bit and a few blocks away, Manhattan Avenue and 14th Street," Kappe said.

"So, close to where he was killed but not so close that you could see the car, assuming the killer knew what car he drove," Lester said.

"And, remember, the victim was killed after he left The Insomniac. He was either walking the girl to her car or to his car, but they were a few blocks away when he was shot. Let's open the trunk," Kappe said.

Lester and Kappe got out and went to the back of the car. Lester put the keys in the trunk lock and attempted to open the trunk, but the lock stuck.

"Don't break the key off or we'll have to pry it open," Kappe said.

"I'm trying not to," Lester said as he tried harder to turn the key. He finally was able to turn the key and unlock the trunk. "I got it now."

With the trunk open they could see a suit jacket that matched his suit pants carefully folded up in a corner, a box of car parts, air filters, timing belts, and a file folder closed with a large rubber band. Under a cover, there was the spare, a jack and a lug wrench, but nothing else.

They took the file folder back to Kappe's desk, took off the rubber band and looked through the papers. The papers were technical specifications for something called a flanged De Laval nozzle. The drawings showed a curvy nozzle with an outwardly flanged tip on the end. The top paper was stamped SECRET in red ink. There were other papers, mostly filled with numbers, charts and calculations that neither Kappe nor Lester could understand. Some of the papers were on letterhead that said Averodyne with an address in Hawthorne.

"I think this changes everything," Kappe said gleefully. "If I'm right, and I think I am, then what we've got here is not a murder but an assassination. A fucking assassination. Those bastards over at Manhattan PD or Redondo, they might get a murder now and then, but we've got an assassination," he said proudly.

"Let's not jump to any conclusions," Lester said cautiously, trying to restrain his excitement.

"We may have a Commie foreign national working at a defense contractor," Kappe said, counting out his points with his stubby fingers. "We do not have a robbery gone awry but a cold-blooded, shoot 'em in the back, bang, bang, assassination. Nothing was stolen and no warning was given. We have a nine millimeter, most likely a Luger or a Walther. We have a silencer, unless everyone was fucking deaf. Am I leaving anything out? Oh, yes, we have top-secret engine plans in the trunk of the victim's car, plans that maybe he shouldn't have had. We found a pink slip. Our Mr. Shawn had been fired earlier in the day."

"Why the mile-wide smile?" Lester asked.

"This is my Oscar smile. I accept the award for the best damn luck. Solve this case and we can write our own ticket, get the fuck out of this Podunk beach town and maybe even make it to the LAPD, maybe even to Chief Parker's staff."

"We've got to solve it first," Lester said.

"Halfway there," Kappe said smugly. "We've got a murder and a motive. If I'm right, and I'm usually right, this either goes all the way up the chain of command to that Commie-loving Eisenhower, in which case expect to be stonewalled, or it's some sort of spy ring. That's what makes the case so interesting. Come on, we're going to search his apartment. You know your way around Pico and Sepulveda?"

"Doheny, Cahuenga, La Brea, sure, I've been up there."

"The La Brea Star Pits. That's what I call it, what with all those Hollyweirdos. Half of Hollywood are pansies. Another half are Pinko Communists and the rest are Jews."

As they got in Kappe's blue Pontiac Super Chief, which smelled of cigarettes and had an overflowing ashtray, Kappe rolled down the windows on the driver's side. "Let a little air in," he said.

Lester rolled down the windows as soon as he closed the car door. Kappe handed him the address and a thick Thomas Guide map book.

"I've already cleared it with LAPD," Kappe said. "They've got the apartment sealed off tight just in case the FBI or the KGB come snooping."

"Should we take the 405 or La Cienega?" Lester asked.

"The 405 is fine. La Cienega is too far east," Kappe said.

It took them about forty minutes to drive up to Shawn's apartment. There was a squad car out front and a police officer standing on the second-floor balcony just outside the door. The building was on a corner, two stories, and built in a faux Spanish Colonial style with stairs on one side and that led up to the upper floor apartments. The rest of the block, except for the apartment building across the street were single-family homes, all built in the same style. Green lawns stretched the entire block.

The cop on the second floor waved to them as they got out of the car and stubbed out his cigarette under his foot. It was noticeably warmer and sunnier than in Hermosa Beach. Lester wiped sweat from his brow with a handkerchief as they climbed the stairs.

Kappe and Lester shook the cop's hand as they introduced themselves. The cop had been there for a couple of hours and was just minding the store. The detectives assigned to the case had gone off for burgers at the Apple Pan, a few blocks away.

"Do you mind if we look in?" Kappe said as he took out a notebook from his jacket pocket.

"There's not much to see," the cop said. "Bachelor, no dogs, no cats. Not much in the way of clothes, basically white shirts, long and short-sleeved, grey and dark blue gabardine pants."

"Any personal effects, pictures, phone books, little black books? Any writings that look funny?"

"Well, there's a whole shelf of books in Hungarian," the cop said.

"Those Hunks got the most gibberish of gibberish, don't you think?" Kappe said.

"I kind of liked *The Shop Around the Corner*," the cop said.

"Oh yeah, that was a good one," Lester said. "Didn't they remake that with Judy Garland?"

"*In the Good Old Summertime*," Lester and the cop said in unison.

"You girls can continue your yacking. I've got some policing to do," Kappe said sarcastically.

It didn't take long to search the one-bedroom apartment. Everything was neat and tidy, at least at the start of the search. The clothes were folded nicely. The books were in order on the shelves, with novels in one section, math and engineering books on another, and odds and ends, like an English-Hungarian dictionary and a Hungarian cookbook in another.

Kappe took each book off of the shelf and flipped through the pages, but nothing fell out. He searched through the drawers, from shirts to underwear to socks, but found nothing but clothes.

In the kitchen, the dishes were done, with a cup, a plate, knife, fork, and a saucer drying on a dish rack. The refrigerator had a carton of milk, cheeses, a half-eaten salami, a few eggs, butter, a selection of jams, half a cabbage, and some potatoes. The cupboards had cans of condensed soup, half a package of flour, salt, pepper, sugar, a can of paprika, and elbow macaroni.

The nightstand's only drawer had a diary, written entirely in Hungarian, a savings passbook showing he'd saved three hundred fifty-seven dollars and seventeen cents, an address book that had only a few addresses and phone numbers, mostly people in either New York or Hungary with either Hungarian or German sounding last names. Clipped to the address book were several scraps of paper with the phone numbers of girls. The scrap on the top had the name, address and phone number for a woman named Elizabeth Lanz who lived in Torrance.

"This place is too neat," Kappe said, "like a goddamn movie set."

"Maybe he was just uptight?" Lester said. "My mom's like that. Everything had better be exactly where it should be."

"I think we're going to have to tear this place apart. If there's a transmitter or a codebook or, it could be anywhere, disguised as anything. Do you know that the KGB and the CIA have whole departments that do nothing but come up with disguises? They can make a pen into a pistol and hide things in shoe heels. If I have to open up every can of soup, I'm going to find it if it's here."

Kappe tore the sheets off the bed and examined the mattress, then lifted the mattress and looked under the bed. There wasn't even a dust bunny. "This place is too neat, like someone had cleaned up, but just a little too good."

"Or he was a neat freak," Lester said.

"One thing I've learned in this business," Kappe said confidently, "is that murder is a messy business. Policing, that's where the order is."

The LAPD cop looked at Lester and rolled his eyes. Meanwhile, Kappe had created a pile of books, pages bend, some spatchcocked like they were chickens ready for grilling. When all the books were on the floor, he went into the kitchen, took out each drawer, poured the contents, forks, spoons and knives and kitchen gadgets onto the counter, in a cacophony of tintinnabulation. Then he turned over each drawer to inspect the bottom side, then into the cabinet's cavity. Each time when he found nothing, he was more convinced that either something had been there but was now gone, or that Mr. Shawn had been especially devious.

By the time the LAPD detectives returned from The Apple Pan, with hickory burgers, Kappe had half the contents of the closet on the bed, the pockets of the pants and jackets pulled out.

"Whoa, Nelly," one of the cops said. He was an older guy, in his late fifties and was dressed in a suit with a sharp fedora riding on the back of his balding head. "My momma always said, 'You make a mess, you got to clean it up,'" he said with an Oklahoma drawl, like Will Rogers, but with a deeper voice.

"If something's here, I'm going to find it," Kappe said, looking up from the underwear drawer.

"I'll tell you one thing that's not here," the older detective said.

"Steve Shawn," the younger detective said with a smirk. He was a little older than Lester and wore a dark blue, sharkskin suit and no hat to cover his black, movie-idol hair.

"Come on! We're out of here," Kappe said, tossing underpants and t-shirts onto the bed, on top of a pile of shirts and pants. He stalked out of the apartment and onto the balcony, then down the stairs.

Lester apologized to the other cops, gave them a generic Hermosa Beach Police Department business card with his name written on the back.

Kappe was in the car, pulling away from the curb when Lester got downstairs and across the street carrying evidence bags containing the diary and address book.

"You going without me?" Lester asked angrily.

"Get in the car!" Kappe barked.

On the ride back down to the South Bay, barreling down the San Diego Freeway, Kappe muttered to himself and threatened to arrest anyone driving too slowly.

"Wouldn't know their ass from a mule," Kappe muttered. "There's a cover-up. I can smell it and it smells like shit!"

Lester didn't dare say anything. He gripped the seat as Kappe sped up, slowed down and switched lanes abruptly. A few things ran through his mind. He might not make it back to Hermosa Beach. Kappe was either a foul-mouthed genius or blowhard asshole. They didn't seem any closer to solving the case. He tried to distract himself from his terror by closing his eyes and reviewing the case.

Steven Shawn, an immigrant from Hungary, probably from the time of the failed uprising, had worked at and then was fired from an aerospace company. He was either a terrible employee, a spy, or just an honest Janos trying to make it in the New World, Lester thought. If he was a spy, then why kill him and who would want to kill him? It seemed like the FBI would want to capture him. If he wasn't a spy, then why kill him? Maybe it was a crime of passion, a revenge killing by an ex-boyfriend of this Elizabeth. Maybe it was about money. It's hard to start anew with no family or resources.

Lester knew that all too well. Taft, west of Bakersfield, where he was from, was a small oil town in the vast sea of farms and ranches that stretched throughout the San Joaquin Valley from the Grapevine north to Redding. He left as soon as he graduated from high school, hitchhiking to Bakersfield and then traveling south by Greyhound to Los Angeles and the South Bay.

West Los Angeles was the California that Easterners thought was the whole enchilada, but to Lester it sometimes seemed half baked. Not only was it unlike his California but nobody in LA had ever heard of Taft. What was there to know about it? Not much.

He'd struggled for the first year after he came down, working odd jobs to get by and then was drafted. When he got out he had enough saved up to rent his small apartment and buy outright a cheap car. He'd given himself two years to graduate from metering otherwise he'd try something else, maybe sell cars.

This case was his big break, a way to step out of metering, that is if they solved it. He'd watched enough Perry Mason and read enough Sherlock Holmes to know that you had to go where the evidence led you.

Kappe pulled into the station parking lot next to the library, got out of the car, slammed his door shut and bounded up the stairs to the police station without looking back at Lester.

"I've got some calls to make," Kappe said as he strode through the station to his desk.

Lester ran after him. "What do you want me to do?" he asked when he caught up to him.

"Clock off! Go home and get some sleep. I'll see you in the morning."

☐

Chapter 4

There was a payphone next to the market that was across a narrow street from the police station. You weren't supposed to use the station's phones for personal business and the station was so small that whatever you said on the payphones in the hallway, everyone could hear.

The phone rang four times. He was about to hang up when a woman answered the phone. Mary and her mom sounded enough alike that he'd, unfortunately, told her mom sweet nothings that made her mom blush the next time she saw him.

This time, Mary answered the phone. "Aren't you working tonight?"

"Nah," Lester said. "I've gotten reassigned to a murder. I was the one who found the body."

"Yeah, it was in the Daily Breeze, 'Murder in Hermosa. Possible Communist Spy Network Link,'" Mary said, reading from the paper.

"We don't even know that," Lester said, exasperated. "I probably shouldn't talk to you about the case." Lester wasn't certain but it must have been Kappe talking to the press.

"My mom is calling me to supper," Mary said.

"Can you meet later?"

"I don't know. Probably not too late. I'll ask my mom if you can join us for supper?"

"I can be there in five minutes."

It wasn't often that Lester got to have a home cooked dinner. Mary's dad and his brothers owned

DixSons Supermarkets, a small chain with stores throughout the South Bay.

Mary was a freshman at UCLA studying Anthropology. They'd met when he was writing her a ticket. Her meter had just expired as she was running to her car. She tried to talk her way out of it, unsuccessfully, but he asked for her number and she wrote it on the palm of his hand.

Mary's family lived in north Hermosa near the border with Manhattan Beach, on a hill just a few blocks up from the beach. The house was a large 1920s Craftsman Bungalow with a boulder-retaining wall and a small patch of grass in the fenced-in side yard. Unlike the houses closer to the beach, the Dix's house had a yard that was only considered substantial because their neighbors had sand yards or yards covered in brick.

Lester parked on an uphill slope around the corner from their house, making sure to curb his wheels. It was a great coup to give another a parking ticket to one of the meter maids and all of them knew what each other's cars looked like.

He'd been going out with Mary for just a few months and for the whole time it never seemed like her parents were keen on him. Once they found out that he was from Taft and that he worked as a meter maid, that was enough for them. They'd never shown any interest in anything else about it, not where he lived, not what he read or if he read, not what he thought. They'd be polite and say "hi" and make sure that he knew that she had to be back before midnight. Her dad sometimes talked about sports, especially the Dodgers.

When he got to Mary's house, Mr. and one of Mary's uncles, were sitting around a long oak table while her mom brought out a roast beef. The front door led directly into the living room, which was furnished in the clean lines of Denmark. There was no chintz, no bangles or claw-and-ball feet. The walls were similarly spare, with a large painting of a bull Elk somewhere in the Grand Tetons.

"Was it on sale?" Mary's uncle said chuckling. He looked like a heavier version of her dad, in his late forties with a buzz cut and heavy black glasses.

They all welcomed Lester as he sat down next to Mary, who grinned at him and held his hand underneath the table after he sat. The dining room table was blond wood with thin wooden legs that were as sleek and slender as Mary's.

"It's a volume business," Mary's dad said.

"It's all about the turnover," her uncle said.

"Lester found the murdered spy," Mary said as she was handed a large bowl of boiled potatoes.

"I did find the victim, but you shouldn't believe everything you read in the papers," Lester said cautiously.

"It was all over the Daily Breeze," Mary's mom whispered.

"I really don't think I should be discussing the case," Lester said.

"Do you have a suspect?" Mary's uncle said, "or is it all hush, hush?" He did a one-eyed wink with each utterance of hush.

"It's an ongoing investigation. I can say that we are making progress," Lester said. He took a big forkful of beef, put it in his mouth and chewed while Mary's dad and uncle prodded him about the case. When he was done chewing the beef, he filled his mouth with a small roasted potato.

Dessert was orange sherbet served in little glass bowls. As Mary's mom passed around the sherbet bowls, Mary asked her if it was okay for Lester to come along to the Beau Rivage Lawn Bowling Club's Spring Fling.

"You'll have to wear white," Mary's mom said. "It's not white tie, nothing as formal as that, just white shirts and white pants. You'll have to wear sneakers. We don't allow any hard-soled shoes on the courts."

"I'll introduce you to everyone," Mary said excitedly.

When dinner was over, Mary excused them and told her parents that they were just going to walk down to the pier and back. Mary led them north, away from the Hermosa Beach Pier and towards the Manhattan Beach Pier, a mile away.

As they walked down to the beach and along the Strand, hand in hand, Mary talked about the Tongva and Chumash Indians who had lived on the Channel Islands and how obsidian, probably from Arizona, had been found by one of her professors on a site on one of the islands.

Lester liked when she talked about what she'd learned. When he was growing up, there wasn't much to talk about and what there was to talk about his parents wouldn't bother to discuss. His older brother had left for the Air Force as soon as he could and his younger sister married a guy who worked for the Department of Agriculture up in Merced just after she graduated from high school.

When they got to the Manhattan Beach pier, they walked out to the end. There were couples all along the pier, holding each other and looking out along the coast. You could see the lights of Santa Monica in the distance and the oil tankers of the coast of El Segundo just to the north. Occasionally, a plane would take off from the airport, a few miles north.

"I'm glad you're coming to the Spring Fling. My mom would try to pair me off with a son of one of her friends who I already know I'm not interested in." When she said this, she stopped and looked dewily into his eyes.

When Mary was like this, it was a big rush for Lester. She was the kind of girl who'd been out of his league in high school, and there hadn't been that many of them, mostly the daughters of supervisors and managers who lived in the large houses on the edge of Taft.

He was afraid that she was more attracted to his uniform than to him as a person, so he began subscribing to The New Yorker and The Atlantic to have something to talk to her about. He'd get a lot of mileage out of referring to something he'd read but felt inadequate that he'd just read it in a magazine with a classy cover.

"So, I'm reading, *Coming of Age in Samoa*," Mary said as she leaned into Lester's arms. "It's fascinating how open Samoan society is. Do you think it would be better if we didn't have so many hang-ups?"

"I'm not sure what hang-ups I have to give up?" Lester said. "What about you?"

Mary blushed and changed the subject to the finer points of lawn bowling. She'd been one of the most promising young bowlers on the West Coast until something happened at a tournament that she never wanted to discuss.

They kissed when the closest couples on the pier walked off, but stopped when another couple approached. On the walk back to her house, the fog had rolled in and was so thick that the light from the lampposts diffused into halos.

"Maybe we could go to Catalina one weekend when I'm off?" Lester said.

"My parents wouldn't let me spend a weekend with you," Mary said sheepishly. "Not even with separate rooms."

Lester laughed. He'd only thought of it as a day trip. A weekend was too much to ask for.

"Of course, we could just happen to be there are the same time, but then if anyone we knew saw us, I'd die of embarrassment. And if word ever got back to my dad, Timbuktu wouldn't be far enough away to keep you safe. I guess I'm the one with hang-ups. Sorry. I'm not always as modern as I like to think I am. See, hangups."

When they reached his car, which was around the corner and out of sight from her house, Mary pressed herself against him and gave him as passionate a kiss as she'd ever given him. "Love you," Mary said.

"Love you back," Lester said. The feeling of her firm body against his was exquisite.

His hands, which were on her lower back moved lower and for a few seconds, she allowed him that liberty, but then pulled away and sauntered up to the corner and then around to her house. He walked up to the corner and watched as she continued back to her house. As she reached the door, she turned and waved a kiss to him.

The drive back home was torture. For the first blocks, it was so foggy that he had to pay attention to the possibility of other cars turning onto Hermosa's narrow streets. The fog cleared as he drove inland on Artesia Boulevard, past Mira Costa High School. He stopped at a liquor store for a six-pack of beer and a package of peanuts and made it home in time to watch *The Bank Dick* on The Late Show.

He'd only slept a few hours the night before and could barely keep his eyes open. In the morning, he would go with Kappe to interview Shawn's girlfriend. He fell asleep thinking of the questions he would ask her, that is if he got the chance. He imagined that Kappe would interrogate her, try to trip her up, get her to confess to whatever fantasy had entered his mind.

Chapter 5

Sunday morning, Lester showed up to work early, just after six. Kappe was at his desk, in the same suit he'd worn the day before, looking like he'd spent the night at the station. Lester was wearing his one and only suit, a simple dark grey flannel number he'd scored at Bullock's downtown at their end-of-year sale.

"So, we're going over to see this Elizabeth chick, that our victim was dating, had dated. We'll have to establish the timeline," Kappe said. He had bits of an egg sandwich lodged in his teeth that he was trying to get out with his tongue.

"Do we know if she's at home?" Lester asked.

"Unless she's a tramp, she'll be at home or at church, but then she's Jewish so she should be at home."

"Well, she could be on vacation. Maybe we should call?"

"Nah, we go over and wake her up, disorient her. You get them when they just wake up and they're too groggy to make up stories. That way you get the real shit." Kappe grinned enough that Lester could see more bits of egg.

Before they left the station, Lester went into the men's room and checked to see if he had anything stuck in his teeth, something that he hadn't been able to feel. His teeth were brushed, so he straightened his short hair.

"Her name's Elizabeth Lanz," Kappe said as they got in the car. "She lives over in Torrance, just off Sepulveda."

During the short drive to Lanz's house, south through Redondo Beach and then over the hill past the Nike missile base, Kappe talked about growing up in Glendale and attending a German-language summer camp in La Crescenta.

"Really, it was innocent. My dad, who was first generation from Cincinnati, wanted me to have a connection with the culture just like he had going to summer camps in Kentucky. When the war started, that was the end of it. I got to go two summers. The camp was wonderful, all the sausage and potato salad you could eat and fish fries on Fridays. Did you ever go to camp?"

"We just didn't have the money. My family were from Oklahoma and came out during the Dust Bowl to work the oil fields of western Kern County. My mom used to like to say she'd grown up camping. She was from the Ozarks and met my dad just after they'd both got to California."

"We used to target shoot. That's what I liked the best. I got pretty good at it. We had this guy who used to be a shooting instructor in the Imperial German Army and claimed that he'd taught Hitler how to shoot."

The address was a fairly new ranch house in one of the new developments that were popping up all over Torrance. The stuccoed walls were pink and there was a carport that led to a garage in the back. In the driveway was a newish Lincoln and behind that an older Ford station wagon. It wasn't yet 8:00 a.m. and the only lights on in the house were in the kitchen.

Instead of knocking on the front door, Kappe led Lester around to the side of the house, next to the

Lincoln and they knocked on the kitchen door. It was more of a pounding than a knocking. The glass in the kitchen door rattled in its frame as Kappe pounded on the door.

You could see a couple and a young blond woman sitting around their kitchen table eating cereal. You could see them jump when Kappe disturbed their morning peace.

The father got up from his chair, milk spilling on his red tie. He was hopping mad, his face scrunched up in anger.

"What the hell do you want this time of the morning?" he barked when he opened the door.

Kappe grinned and showed him his badge. "Police. Is that your daughter, Elizabeth Lanz?"

The daughter looked embarrassed and unsure. There wasn't anything she could think of that she'd done to cause the police to pound on the door. Her parking tickets were paid up and she'd only ever gotten a warning the one time she'd been caught speeding down Hawthorne Boulevard. She was short with curly dark hair pulled back with a headband and wore a long housecoat.

"We'd like to speak with her," Kappe said.

"If it's all right?" Lester said sheepishly.

"Can I ask what's this about?" the father asked meekly.

"You can, but it's none of your business," Kappe said snidely.

"Can she at least get dressed?" the mother asked.

"Ma'am, we've seen it all," Kappe said. "We're not taking her down to the station. We just have a few questions for her. Now if you'll just step outside." He motioned for her to come out, which she did, her parents alarmed.

When she stepped outside, Kappe closed the door and led her to the back of the house, where there was a patio with a large metal table, covered by an umbrella, and several director's chairs.

"Did you know a man by the name of Istvan Szanto, also known as Steven Shawn?" Kappe asked.

"Yes, we used to go out?" Elizabeth said plainly. "Is he in trouble? Did something happen?"

"I'm sorry to tell you that he was shot and killed in the early hours of Saturday morning. You may have heard about it on the news?" Kappe said.

"That was him?" Elizabeth said, shocked. As the knowledge that her recent boyfriend had been murdered sank in, tears began to stream down her cheeks. "I'd read that someone had been killed behind The Insomniac. I can't believe it was him?"

"When was the last time that you saw him or spoke with him?" Kappe asked.

"A couple of months ago," she said. She began to sob.

Lester took out a handkerchief and handed it to her.

She wiped the tears from her cheeks and gasped. "I told him I didn't want to see him again."

"You got your wish," Kappe said coldly.

Elizabeth glared at Kappe. "He was a nice guy, just not really my type. He was kind of needy and pushy if you know what I mean, which was why I told him I didn't want to see him again. I told him that I wasn't that kind of a girl, but he never seemed to get the hint. There was something about him. He was too controlled. I can understand that he barely escaped the war alive. His family hid in the countryside and would have been caught, but the Russians got there first. You know, his brother died in the uprising. That's why he had to leave."

"How did you meet?" Lester asked.

"My grandparents and his grandparents knew each other from the old country. Our families were originally where the Austrian and Hungarian border now is. When he came, he had my grandfather's address."

"He barely knew English then," Elizabeth continued. "I was a senior in high school and he seemed exotic but we didn't start going out until a couple of years later. He started working and he'd come over for holidays. I was too young to date him but I was intrigued because he has, had, a great accent and is pretty good-looking when he actually dresses up.

"My parents liked him. He was a good guy, just real lonely and kind of damaged. And everything had to be in order, so I was surprised that he liked The Insomniac. We went there once when we couldn't get into a set at The Lighthouse."

"He was very much an engineer, if you know what I mean. I think we went out for six months and then I was feeling uncomfortable and I didn't see marrying him, so I cut it off. He didn't take the hint so I had to spell it out to him in plain English. We were just going to be friends, never anything more."

"Do you know anyone who had a grudge against him?" Kappe asked, "anyone who would want to do him harm?"

"No. He didn't really know that many people. We once went to this deli up on Pico that he was a regular at and the waitresses knew him. I know he'd meet some guys there. After that, I don't think he knew many people. He didn't ever talk about anyone. You could tell he was pretty lonely."

"Any friends, acquaintances? Any problems that he might have mentioned?" Lester asked.

"Except for the guys at the deli, none. I knew he was kind of unhappy at work, but that didn't seem strange. Who doesn't complain about their job?"

"Did he say anything specific?" Kappe asked.

"Nothing specific. He never got into details. His work was pretty secret, or so he said," Elizabeth said.

"Do you remember the name of the deli?" Lester asked.

"Factor's, though personally, I like Langer's better," Elizabeth said.

Kappe handed her a business card. "Call us if you think of anything."

"I will," Elizabeth said sadly. "Do you know who's taking care of the funeral? My mom and dad probably would if nobody else does."

"He's still at the morgue," Kappe said. "We'll let you know when they release him. Did he have any next of kin?"

"Like I said, he was here alone, but my parents probably have an address for his parents back in Budapest."

As they drove back to Hermosa Beach, Lester asked Kappe what he thought.

"Either she's the best goddamn liar in the business or she's telling the truth," Kappe said. "If she's lying, that'll mean that she's part of the spy ring. A lot of Jews are Pinkos. Common knowledge."

"At the moment, I don't see any reason not to believe her," Lester said, puzzled because she had seemed genuine.

"When we get back to the ranch, call up the LA County Sherriff's Crime Lab to see if they've got the ballistics report."

When they got back, Lester called the crime lab and was on hold for ten minutes until he got connected to the right technician.

"It was definitely a Luger," the crime lab technician said. He was munching on what sounded like cucumbers or radishes, something crunchy.

"Any match to any other crimes?" Lester asked.

"None so far. It's a common gun," the crime lab technician said. "War booty. My uncle brought some back when he was in the service and gave one to me and my brothers. It's as common as dirt. The ammunition is a cinch to get. You're talking about a generic gun that probably nobody can trace. The report says that the weapon was silenced. That's a rare thing. They're illegal in California but you can get them in if you know where to look. You can buy them in some states, but you have to have a background check."

"What do you have to know to make one?"

"If you understand the basic concepts, a reasonably good machinist could make one," the lab technician said. "It's probably a fun project, as long as you don't get caught."

When Lester thanked the technician for his help and said he looked forward to getting the report, which the technician said he would have by the end of the day, earlier if he wanted to come over to pick it up. Lester said he'd pass. Kappe was standing over him just as he was hanging up.

"Any news?" Kappe asked.

"Nothing we can use right now," Lester said. "We've got a common gun that hasn't been used in a crime before and nothing special with the ammo. Probably a Luger or a Walther. We should look into the silencer. Maybe if we can find where the silencer came from, we can find the murderer? There's also the diary. We need to find someone who reads Hungarian to translate it."

"Good thinking, but that's the hard way up the mountain. I'm famished. Let's say we make it over to the Hilltop and mow some burgers."

The Hilltop was a little greasy spoon a block from the station. The room was small with a U-shaped baby blue Formica counter and a couple of tables where there was space. The menu was short, breakfast, lunch and dinner, the usual suspects, no surprises, few vegetables that weren't boiled or crispy iceberg lettuce.

Kappe stopped them just past the barn-like market across the street from the fire station. He turned to Lester and gave him a big grin. "The bad news is that the FBI is involved. We called them in when we saw the top-secret documents. They came so fast and swept everything it'd make your head swim. Yours truly took photos of the documents or we'd be up Ballona Creek.

In an investigation, you never know what's going to be important and you got to admit that secret documents are as good a reason to get offed as any, maybe even better than a love triangle or an overdue vig."

"So, you still think the motive is espionage?"

Kappe grinned so widely that his gold crowns glinted in the sun. "Maybe we'll make a Sherlock out of you yet," he said. "Espionage is motive number one, at least that's what the FBI thinks. I'm thinking they may be right and if we're both right, and I think we are, this is going to blow the whole case wide open. Up the stakes, so to speak."

"Up the stakes?"

"There's only three things in this city that are worth anything. There's oil, planes and Hollywood. There was a guy I used to know. We came up together at the Academy. He cracked this case near Hancock Park. This woman murders her dad, you see, and the twist of it was that her dad just so happened to be the father to her little babykins. They came from oil money and somehow were descendants of old Pio Pico himself. The short of it is, he sold the rights to the story to Fox for a good five figures."

"Whoever solves this case," Kappe continued, "they could be in line for the same thing. That'd set you us up nicely. Don't worry, I'll cut you in on a share. So, our job is to get there before the FBI. The FBI's less concerned about who stiffed the stiff and more concerned about the why and wherefore. If it is the CIA, we're in a pickle and I mean full sour, not some dinky relish pickle."

They continued their walk to the Hilltop and sat at one of the tables.

"Can I get you anything?" Kappe asked. "It's on me."

"What's the surf burger?" Lester asked the waitress.

"Burger with a split hot dog on top," the waitress said. She was young, just out of high school and Mexican-American.

"I'll have that," Lester said.

"A bowl of chili with extra crackers," Kappe said.

When the waitress left for the kitchen, Kappe leaned over and whispered. "You got to watch that they don't spit in your food."

"Why would they do that?" Lester asked incredulously.

"I don't trust them, especially when they're speaking Spanish. Can you believe how many there are around here?"

Lester stared at Kappe, giving him an angry glare. "You really are a piece of work!"

"What did I say?"

"This was Mexico at one time. You do know that don't you?" Lester asked.

"That's what I'm saying. You have to watch out for them. If someone took something of yours, don't you think you'd want it back. Stands to reason. That's why I never go to Mexican restaurants. If I go into a restaurant, I want to know what they're saying. There used to be a great little German restaurant over in Manhattan Beach, Little Bavaria. I think it's a Mexican restaurant now. Them I could understand."

"Maybe we should just stick to work. I'm going to see what I can find about silencers," Lester said.

"The way I see it, we've got a motive," Kappe said. "Now it's a matter of developing leads and following them. Normally, I'd have us work together, have you tag along, but now that the FBI's involved we're going to have to work separately, get the groundwork done, otherwise they're going to lap us. We've still got a murderer to find, and they've promised, for whatever it's worth, and I don't think it's worth much, to keep us informed."

"What I want from you," Kappe continued, "is to interview all of his known associates besides the girlfriend. At the moment, we don't know any of them. The girl he was with, they'd just met, according to her. Follow up on her. See where she works, who her friends are. Maybe she set him up. He was a regular at The Insomniac, so tonight you're going to go down there and see what you can find out."

"Those Commie beatniks have fogged their brains up so much with reefer that it's a wonder if they can remember anything," Kappe said while waving his hand in a circle. "Tomorrow morning, we're going to pay a call to Averodyne and see what's what. The FBI's searching his apartment as we speak. Giving us a heads-up would have been the gentlemanly thing to do just so you know who we're dealing with. You better be taking notes because I don't want to waste my breath saying it again."

"I think I've got it," Lester said.

"Go home and change into some less conspicuous togs, something rough and ready, and mess up your hair. Dressed like that, the cats down at The Insomniac will spot you a mile away."

"You want me to go incognito?" Lester asked.

"Yeah, and bring along one of the copies of the driver's license photo. Maybe you can go as a journalist?"

"For the Daily Breeze?" Lester asked.

"Better yet, for the Herald-Examiner," Kappe said.

In the late afternoon, he called Beatrice, the woman that Shawn was with the night he was murdered, at home. She answered the phone in a professional manner. "ManageTech, Beatrice speaking. Sorry, it's a habit."

Lester introduced himself and asked how she was doing. She said she was fine but still shaken and sick of hiding out in her apartment.

"You never know," she said.

He asked if there was anything she may have remembered since they'd last spoken, anything that had seemed out of the ordinary or remarkable. Had Steven Shawn mentioned anything that he was worried about or said anything that in retrospect might be connected to his murder?

"He was charming, but then I go for the mysterious ones. He seemed to know a lot about books and spoke English pretty well even though his accent was pretty heavy. He mentioned that he'd had a bad day at work, but I thought that was a line. We were slinging them back and forth, lines I mean. He was very witty and that gets me every time. That and the accent and I was. . .I probably shouldn't say anything more."

"No, please go on," Lester said.

"Well, I hope you don't think ill of me, but I was going to follow him." She paused and took a deep breath, "follow him home, if you know what I mean?"

"Are you a regular at The Insomniac? Had you seen him there before?" Lester asked.

"I am, or at least I was. I don't think I could go back there again, at least not any time soon. It's a shame, because it's a lot closer than the Gas House in Venice and The Prison of Socrates down in Newport. I've heard that place really jumps. But who wants to drive all the way down beyond the Orange Curtain," Beatrice said glumly.

"The Orange Curtain?" Lester asked.

"Orange County, Squaresville with all those John Birchers and orange groves being bulldozed to make way for ranch house subdivisions. Where are all the people coming from?" Beatrice asked.

Lester thanked her for her help and told her that they would be in contact with her again.

Nobody was at any of the desks near him, so he called Mary's house. She wasn't home but her mom said that she would leave a message. He asked her if she wanted to meet him at The Insomniac that night. Her mom said that it was a school night so she wouldn't be able to, but that she'd let her know he'd called.

Before Lester left the station, he told Kappe the little he'd learned. Kappe said that he'd had to hand over the plans to the FBI but that he'd made sure to take photos of them. "Do you know anyone who knows any Hungarian?" he asked. "We still have the diary."

Lester laughed. "What's Hungarian for fat chance? Why don't you call one of the universities?"

"Those Commies!" Kappe growled. "It would be like giving candy to a dentist's kids. Next thing you know, the info is going straight to Moscow."

"Not all of them can be Communists. If you lived there and the Soviets invaded, you'd want to escape," Lester said.

"I'm talking about professors, college professors," Kappe said smugly. "A third of them are reds, a third of them are Pinkos and the other half are God knows what. I wouldn't trust them to throw a stick at."

"I don't think I've ever actually met a real Communist. I bet that they're as rare as a three-dollar bill," Lester said.

Kappe laughed as if Lester had said he believed in the tooth fairy. "They're everywhere and if we don't watch out, we're going to wake up one morning singing the *Internationale* with your coffee."

"So, what do you want me to find out at The Insomniac?" Lester asked.

"Just see if you see anything suspicious," Kappe said slowly. "The chief thinks that hell hole is a major den of reefer-scented iniquity."

"What does this have to do with the case?" Lester asked.

"Without being too obvious," Kappe said. "See if you can find out if anyone there has a connection to either the Communist Party of America or knows someone who can get a silencer."

Lester sighed at the ridiculousness of his assignment. At least, he figured, he'd have a relaxing evening listening to music, even though he'd rather be across the street listening to jazz. "Won't Sunday be a quiet night? It's a school night."

"You're kidding!" Kappe said. "You think those bums have jobs? If you're tired, take a nap before you go. You can clock off now if you want. And by the way, the yobbos up at LAPD questioned his neighbors. He was a good little boychik who never had anyone over, never made a pipsqueak, never annoyed or angered anyone, never had had any girls over. Nobody knew where he hung out or who his friends were. The landlord said that he always paid on time and never caused any trouble and figured he probably hung out with other Hungarian Jews over at this deli over on Pico. Sounds too good to be true."

☐

Chapter 6

As Lester drove back to his apartment, he thought about calling Mary again to see if she was home. If he was going to have any chance with a woman like Mary with a background like his, he had to win over her parents. As a meter maid, he was pretty sure, that was never going to happen. This case was the break he needed to get a leg up. Whether or not that would be enough was for the future to tell, but it couldn't hurt.

Instead of going straight to his apartment, he decided to drive over to Hawthorne to check out the Averodyne plant. It was just a few blocks from Northrop Field, just off of El Segundo Boulevard. He wasn't going to investigate, per se, just snoop around.

The Averodyne building was a large slab of industrial blankness. There was a parking lot in the front and a large flat-fronted building with the name Averodyne and their logo on the wall with a small, two-story office area attached to the front. It was difficult to see how far back the building went.

It was late Sunday afternoon and there weren't that many cars in the lot. They weren't working extra shifts. He had a friend who worked for Douglas Aircraft down in Long Beach and they sometimes worked double shifts.

The cars left in the lot were nothing special. There were a few Joe Average cars, Dodges, Chevys, Fords and then there were the hot rods. Considering that there were a lot of machinists who probably worked for Averodyne, he wasn't surprised to see hot rods. Most of the rods were nothing really fancy, works in progress, just souped-up late-model two-seaters with flashy paint jobs and exposed chromed engines.

He could imagine that the machinists were using the equipment to work on their own projects. There weren't any of the real way out ones with wacky bodywork that would make Rat Fink drool. He parked the car and went up to the gates but he couldn't see anything but the cars. The delivery bays were around the back.

When he got home, he carefully laid his clothes on the back of the sofa then laid on his sofa and listened to whatever rock and roll was playing on KFWB. As he started to fall asleep, he thought about the top-secret plans that had been in the victim's car.

He was a decent mechanic, which he had to be considering how old his car was and how low his salary was, and he knew his way around a car engine but knew nothing about jet engines besides that they were important. Most of the machine shops in the South Bay seemed to be dedicated to cars or aerospace. He tried to formulate a thought about why the plans were in the trunk but fell asleep before he was able to. There was also the diary. He had to find someone who knew Hungarian.

It was just after 8:00 p.m. when he woke up. He rummaged through his chest of drawers and his closet to find something to wear to The Insomniac. He didn't have a turtleneck or anything like that, but he did have a pair of overalls that had a patch on the knee and a red gingham snap-front western shirt that his mom had sent him for his birthday. It wasn't Beatnik, but he thought he could pass for a folkie.

In his fridge, there was only enough bread to make half a sandwich and he didn't feel like opening a can of soup. There were three options close by that were more than halfway decent. There was the teriyaki joint, the Mexican dive and Burger World. He'd eaten through the menus at each of them.

Mary didn't like the teriyaki joint because her dad had fought at Iwo Jima and she didn't like Burger World because it was too greasy but she liked the Mexican dive well enough. She liked Rosa's in Hermosa better and she was often asking him if he could take her to some place fancier for a change. They'd been to this French restaurant in Riviera Village where the food was excellent and the owners were friends of Mary's parents, but the prices were as rich as their béchamel sauce and he'd had to save up for a couple of weeks to afford it.

He settled on the Wich Stand, a new coffee shop on Hawthorne Boulevard near his apartment. As he sat at the counter and surveyed the menu, he was torn between having the golden brown spring chicken or the grilled northern halibut steak.

"Is the halibut fresh or frozen?" he asked the waitress when she came by to take his order.

"We cook it all the way through?" the waitress said. She was probably about the same age as Lester, but she seemed older, like one of his tired out aunts up in Taft just in a better body.

"Hardee har. I'm asking. . ."

"I know what you're asking," the waitress said. "Honestly, I don't know. Sometimes it is and sometimes it isn't. It depends on whether or not it's the catching season for halibut. If that matters to you, then you should get the spring chicken, though honestly, it's February, so spring has come early this year. This isn't Les Freres Taix, but still, we do a pretty good fish. I eat it every Friday."

"Never been there, but I did get to Paris a couple of times when I was in the service," Lester said. That had been a memorable weekend.

"Oh yeah? I've got a brother stationed in Mannheim," the waitress said.

"Know it well. I wasn't stationed too far away," Lester said.

"So, what are you having?"

"I'll have the top sirloin steak sandwich, horseradish if you've got it and a frosted root beer."

"I'll have to check," the waitress said.

The sandwich wasn't long in coming. It was good, maybe a little tough and he wished he'd gone for the halibut.

He thought about the kind of car he would get once he'd saved up. If he got a promotion, and the promotion might come from solving this case, he'd get a sports car, something to impress Mary. Something that they could use to drive up to Santa Barbara for the weekend, once they got married of course. If he had a garage, rather than just a parking space, he could see devoting his time to restoring something, rodding it up a bit but in a classy way, or getting something British, like an MG or an Austin-Healy.

All his plans were just idle thoughts over a thin steak sandwich eaten alone at the counter of a coffee shop. How many coffee shops were there in the Southland, from the desert to the sea, where lonely men ate and daydreamed.

Steven Shawn hadn't been so different, Lester thought. Even if he was a spy, he would still want what any man wanted, a girl, a car, a house and maybe a few kids, food on the table after a long day's work, maybe something to watch before he fell asleep next to a wife that didn't mind so much that he snored, the overthrow of the capitalist system and the establishment of a dictatorship of the proletariat.

During the drive down Artesia Boulevard to Hermosa, he ran through the questions he wanted to find answers to at The Insomniac. Did anyone know how to get a silencer? Was the place a hotbed of Communist spies? Did anyone know anything about Steven Shawn? Could they remember anything about any beefs he may have had? It seemed to him that he was being sent to fish without a hook in a dry lake, but then what did he know.

He parked his car at the station and walked the few blocks down Pier Avenue. Cars filled up every parking space and he couldn't help but check the meters to see if anyone should get a ticket. There was always one, almost one per block despite Hermosa's reputation for zealous meter enforcement. It was more crowded than usual for a Sunday night which meant that he was probably missing something really hopping at The Lighthouse.

The unit block of Pier Avenue was hopping, even though it was a Sunday night. The Lighthouse was hosting a jazz combo from Chicago that he'd never heard of but would have to check out, even if it meant just standing outside. The biker and hot rod bars were packed with greasers. A line of motorcycles was lined up alongside the sidewalk watched over by guys in jeans and leather vests.

Across Pier Avenue, The Insomniac was ablaze, with people browsing the bookstalls near the front or waiting in line to have a poem written for them by a guy who looked like he'd just come off the stage playing Prospero from The Tempest.

The fog was rolling in and it diffused the light making everything blurry as the temperature dropped. Pier Avenue smelled salty mixed with exhaust fumes from the hot rods which slowly drove Hermosa Avenue, south to the Edison Plant at the border with Redondo Beach and north almost to Manhattan Beach.

Lester spotted Jack, another of the meter maids, writing a ticket in front of the doctor's office halfway down the block. As he walked past, he lowered his head and looked towards the storefronts and away from Jack.

"Where's the hoedown?" Jack said as Lester walked past.

"Shh, I'm on the job," Lester whispered.

"Undercover metering? That's a new one. I'll be looking for your car," Jack said.

Lester ignored him and walked faster down the street then turned into The Insomniac. It was hard to know where to start or what to do. It was early-ish, so the bands hadn't come on yet. There was a teenage poet, a young girl wearing a kaftan and huarache sandals, declaiming poems on the little stage. Her audience was small but attentive. They were her age and were probably her friends.

He browsed the books and spotted a book of photos by August Sander. On the cover was a photo of three men, farmers wearing hats, dressed up for some occasion, each holder a walking stick. The men looked hopeful and ready for the evening. They were young German farmers, according to the caption, but pretty slick-looking guys with a lot of style in the summer of 1914. Too bad that history had it in for them.

"A poem for a person, a personal poem for your personality," someone behind him said.

When Lester turned around, it was Prospero. He wore sandals, loose blue sailor pants and a loose white shirt and necklace with big wooden beads. He was older and had long wild white hair.

"Only a dollar, and your poem shall begin," Prospero said.

Lester took out his wallet from his back pocket and handed the man a dollar. "Write me a poem about a silencer," he said.

The man looked at him, unsure of what he'd been told.

"For a gun, a silencer for a gun," Lester said quietly.

"Crazy!" Prospero said as he took the dollar and stuffed it into his pants' pocket. He got back up on the stool that was his normal perch. He cleared his throat and wiped his hair from his eyes.

"The rod that speaks but no one hears, from my pocket a rocket, I cock it, back to front, red, I end the story, a mess."

Lester waited for there to be more, but the poet simply smiled, so Lester walked to the coffee bar. "An espresso please," he said to the bearded bartender, "if that's not too strong."

"Cut it with milk and have a cappuccino," the bartender said. "I'll set you up. First time?"

"I'll take it black," Lester said.

The bartender nodded and pulled an espresso from the towering copper-clad espresso machine and slid the tiny cup over to him on a saucer with a slice of lemon.

Lester sipped the drink and shuddered from the bitterness.

"Suck on the lemon. It cuts the bitterness," the bartender said.

"Strong stuff?" Lester asked.

The bartender beamed. "That's the way they drink it over in Italy. Man, you've been inoculated. You're practically one of us."

"So, tell me about this place. Who hangs out here?"

"Mostly college and high school kids," the bartender said. "Do you want another one? It's on me."

"Are there any members of the Party?"

"The Party?"

"Trotskyists or Leninists?"

"Oh, that party," the bartender said, giving Lester a curious look like he couldn't decide whether or not Lester was square or cubed. "No, not that I know of. I'm sure there may be a few, but most of us don't dig politics in that way, if you catch my drift. They're here for the culture, the caffeine and the coquettes."

"Do you know anyone who might know?"

"You're not some kind of narc are you?"

"Look, I'm not into drugs."

"I know, you're a political narc, a parc. No, you're a park! I know I'd seen you before. You gave me a ticket a couple of weeks ago. I was just getting off work and the meter had just expired and you gave me a ticket anyway."

"Sorry, just doing my job," Lester said.

"What are you playing at here anyway? The city giving out tickets for hanging out?"

"It's part of the investigation of the guy that got killed. Did you know anything about him? Did you know if he had any beefs with anyone? And do you know of any place a person could buy a silencer?" Lester showed him the photo of Steven Shawn.

The bartender gaped at Lester. "That's pretty heavy. The whole thing. We try to think the little world we've built here is immune from the big bad wolves. Who are we kidding? About the silencer, most of the people here are peaceniks. I knew the guy who was killed on sight. He liked to drink what he called a mélange, which is basically a cappuccino. He'd come in and try to pick up girls. I think when I first saw him, he was usually with one girl, but I never knew her name and she dropped out of sight a few months back. Nobody had a beef with him. We're strictly vegetarians. The rodsters across the street, some of those cats are regular Bengal tigers."

"So how about that cappuccino?"

"Eighty-five cents."

"That's expensive coffee."

"We charge by the strength, but it's all on the house."

When the cappuccino was placed in front of him, the top of the foam was covered in chocolate shavings.

"Is that the way they serve them in Italy?" Lester asked.

"Never been there, but you go to any place up in North Beach up in San Francisco and that's the way they serve them."

Lester sipped the drink and smacked his lips. "Makes me wish I'd been stationed in Vicenza rather than Germany. So, you really don't remember or you don't want to remember any trouble with the guy who was murdered?"

"Turn up the stereo man," The bartender said. "The people that come here, they're looking to escape from Squaresville and all its problems, not bring them in and get knuckled by some cube dude. They don't want to be bugged if they want to swing, if you dig."

"Yeah, I dig," Lester said. As he lingered over the cappuccino, he surveyed the crowd. They looked more dangerous to strike up a conversation with, one that you might never escape from, than to murder someone. It was difficult to know what to do next. Going home was his first choice, but after the espresso and the cappuccino, he was wired.

He went to the bathroom in the back of The Insomniac, then out of the back door to the alley to retrace Shawn's steps. The alley was just an alley, with dumpsters for the restaurants and the backside of a one-story courtyard apartment building. There was only one logical path to get to where Beatrice Loehner had parked her car. They wouldn't have gone left to the Strand or right towards Hermosa Avenue. It was too far. They would have turned left and then walked the few yards to Beach Drive, which was really just an alley that paralleled the Strand and Hermosa Avenue past 13th Street and 14th Court to 14th Street.

The Biltmore Hotel was on their left and the street would have been filled with teenagers to get in to see the surf bands. Would they have seen something or someone? If they were lucky, someone would come forward. They would have been circuiting from the Biltmore to the Foster's Freeze at the corner of Hermosa Avenue.

The killer would have possibly followed them from The Insomniac and either retreated by Beach Drive or to the Strand, north around the beach side of the Biltmore, or south to the pier. The killer could easily have blended into the crowds except that he wouldn't have been a teenager and should have stood out from them, but what teenager pays attention to adults?

Where Shawn was shot, the blood had been cleaned up and there was nothing to see but black asphalt and a concrete curb. From there, he walked the short block to the beach, past the Biltmore Hotel. It was a Sunday, so the teen club was closed, and he walked over to the Strand and then down along the Strand to the pier. He stopped in at the Poop Deck, the diviest dive bar in the city, and ordered a Budweiser to take the edge off the caffeine.

The Poop Deck was filled with the high-class derelicts, one step up from the gutter, or so the other cops said. The guys who hung out at the Poop Deck were interested in Budweiser, maybe a game on the TV above the bar if there was one on, and the continuance of rambling and slurred conversations you had to be on your second pitcher to understand. These were guys who never noticed anything because they never seemed to leave the Poop Deck. Still, there was no harm in trying.

"Just a hypothetical here," Lester said, to the bartender and a couple of other guys holding up the bar. "If someone was looking for a silencer for a gun, do you know where you might get one?"

The guys surrounding him held their breath for a couple of beats until necessity forced them to exhale.

"I'm just curious. You read about them in books and see them in the movies, but I've never seen one in person. It's not like you can go to the gun store and buy one," Lester said.

"It depends on the state you live in, but sure, not in California," a man with short brown hair holding a half-empty glass of red wine said. The man was wearing a blue button-down shirt, unbuttoned at the neck with his red tie loosely tied. "Your best bet is to make one. If you're a machinist, then that's not so hard. The materials are easy to get. It's the design that's hard, especially if you want it to effectively silence, or really make the gun less noisy."

"I knew a guy once who made one in shop class in high school," a man in his mid-twenties said. The man wore grey work pants and a shirt from a 76 gas station.

"Do you remember his name?" Lester asked.

"Nah, I didn't pay much attention in class. He was just some guy I went to high school with over in Hawthorne. The teacher was royally pissed, made him take the thing apart and kept the pieces. He couldn't flunk him though because it was a real piece of art, or at least that's what I heard. That was, like, six years ago."

"Do you think you could recognize him if you saw his picture in a yearbook?"

"Sure, but like I said. I only heard it. He was bragging about it for a week, like he was some rebel without a cause."

Lester identified himself as a police officer, assured everyone that he was investigating something and wasn't trying to get anyone in trouble. He took down the name, address and phone number of the guy who'd claimed he'd known of someone who'd made a silencer. After thanking them all, he finished the rest of his beer and headed out onto the Strand.

As he reached the pier, half a block away, he had a terrible urge to piss, so made his way onto the beach and headed for the underside of the derelict pier. The pier had been closed for years and was supposed to be torn down, but the demolition kept getting put off. On the south side of the pier was a large faded blue building that had housed the Ocean Aquarium across from the Sea Sprite Motel.

There was a party going on at the Motel's pool which spilled out to the bricked front of the small, 1920s apartment building next door.

What was left of the pier was falling apart and so going under it you risked a slab of concrete or an old timber falling on you, which is something Lester felt he could do without. On the other hand, nature was calling in a very loud voice and the underside of the pier was convenient. There was a chain-link fence around it to keep people out but the fence was in worse shape than the pier. There were public bathrooms not far from the pier, but he was never ever going in there, especially after dark. He'd heard rumors about those bathrooms, rumors involving scarlet hanky panky. The worst of it was probably going to be the smell. He felt sorry for the city staff who had to clean it, assuming someone did.

The coast was clear as he peed against the old aquarium. At least he thought it was clear. Just as he was finishing, a man began to sing, strumming an acoustic guitar and accompanied by a full rock band.

He looked around, but facing the wall, it was difficult to see anything. He was sure he didn't see anyone and nobody was close enough to see him, unless they were directly behind him. With overalls, he was particularly vulnerable. You practically had to take the things most of the way off just to go.

When he was done, he pulled up his overalls, fastened the straps then wiped his hands on the backside, where there was a patch from when he'd accidentally leaned against a barbed wire fence and gotten stuck. The music was coming from underneath the pier.

He crouched down and tried to hide behind the pier's crumbling concrete supports. He rested his hand on one of the supports to brace himself as he peered around it. Chips of concrete crumbled off into his hands as if it were chalk or sandstone.

Far underneath the pier, there gathered a group of a couple dozen kids, none of them much over nineteen. The guys were wearing shorts and jackets with the names of various surf clubs embroidered on the backs, Kahanamokus, the Skegs Royale and the Goofy Feet. The girls were wearing bikinis partially covered by sweaters and sweatshirts with the names of local high schools, Mira Costa, Redondo Union, and Bishop Montgomery.

The rock band was playing next to a fire pit that everyone was standing around. The dancing shadows caused by the flames against the guys and the girls as they swayed to the music were menacing. Also, the possibility that chunks of concrete could fall off and kill them never entered their minds, but was something that Lester was keenly aware of.

The band's singer, a blond kid wearing a sweater, strolled around the fire strumming his acoustic guitar and singing a song about lost love until the chorus kicked in with the bass and drums and rhythm guitar and the singer switched to an electric guitar handed to him by someone in the crowd.

As soon as the band started rocking out the kids started dancing wildly, somehow avoiding the fire. Lester thought the music was good to dance to but nothing he'd ever buy. It was bacchanalian, and he preferred music that was contemplative. If that made him a square in the eyes of these kids, who were only a few years younger than he was, he would gladly accept that divide.

"Hey farmer John, wanna' dance?" a girl with long bobbed black hair asked him as she dragged him from his hiding place and into the dancing throng. She was gorgeous and vivacious, and it was difficult for him to say no to a half-dressed girl, especially since in high school he'd always had trouble getting girls to dance with him.

Dancing on the sand was difficult. He took off his shoes and stuffed his socks into one of them. The rave-ups the band played drove the kids wild. They'd bump into each other and sometimes they'd knock each other over. They'd get back up and start all over again until the band paused between numbers.

After a bit, Lester was pooped but also wired, feeling the effects of the caffeine. The girls he was dancing with asked him if he was okay and said that they could go somewhere if he wanted to. He said sure and then searched for his shoes. They'd been buried in sand and even with shaking them out and banging them against one of the concrete pier supports, he wasn't able to get the sand out. As they stepped away, a small chunk of concrete fell where they had been standing.

"Let's vamoose," the girl said. She took off running out from under the pier with Lester running after her.

"Can I give you a ride home?" Lester asked. As soon as he said, it he knew it wasn't the best idea.

The girl hugged him and kissed him passionately. Her breath smelled of cheap beer and cigarettes, not at all like Mary, whose breath smelled minty and whose skin smelled of vanilla.

"I'll take that as a yes. But I'm parked up by the police station."

"I know where it is, next to the library and across from the post office."

"Maybe we could stop for a drink or a soda?" Lester stopped and turned to her. As he thought about where he could take her, with the best possibility being either the supermarket on Pier Avenue near a few doors down from The Lighthouse, she kissed him again and wrapped her body around his. Between kisses, after it occurred to him that one of his co-workers might spot him, he asked her how old she was.

"Old enough to know to know that you're a great kisser," she said.

He pulled away from her, which made it worse since as he looked down at her, her cleavage stared back at him. "What high school do you go to?"

"Mira Costa. I'm a senior."

He pulled away and said, "Whoa, isn't it a school night? Aren't your parents wondering where you are?"

She frowned, giggled and said, "They don't even know that I'm not at home. I'm eighteen. I've been eighteen for a couple of months."

He asked her if she lived far, concerned that her house could be closer than his car. She lived a couple of blocks away and just up the hill on Bayview, so he walked her home. As they walked, she berated him for acting like her dad or her older brother. Lester ignored her complaints and kept watch for broken glass and rock. When they got to her house, he knocked on the door. Her dad opened the door and she slunk in, squeezing past him.

"I'm with the Hermosa PD. Your daughter's not in any trouble, but she was at a party under the pier. It's a pretty dangerous place considering that it's falling apart."

Her dad was wearing a short-sleeved white button-down shirt with a tie still tied tight and a pocket protector filled with pens. "Thanks for bringing her back," he said while shutting the door. When the door had closed, Lester could hear the dad yelling at his daughter, the daughter yelling back and the mother yelling for both of them to tone it down so the neighbors couldn't hear.

It was just after 10:00 when Lester made it home. The apartment was stuffy, so he opened the windows in his bedroom, stripped down to his skivvies and flopped on the bed. He got up, blundered in the dark to the bathroom, brushed his teeth, went back to his bedroom and flopped back down on the bed. As he lay on his stomach, his side, and then his back, he was exhausted but couldn't keep his eyes closed. The world spun clockwise making him ill, but not ill enough to have to make it to the bathroom, but ill enough to be uncomfortable.

Chapter 7

Lester's alarm rang from across the room. To turn it off, he had to get out of bed, which was an old trick his dad had taught him. He'd been in the middle of a wonderful dream. The surfer girl from the night before had come home with him. The dream girl had breasts that would have made Gina Lollobrigida jealous and was fresher than any girl he'd ever met not counting the girls at the soldier bars in Heidelberg.

In his dream, he heard someone taking a shower. He looked around and saw a pile of his clothes on the floor next to his bed. There weren't any panties or other signs of female companionship. He couldn't remember bringing someone home, but the dream had been so vivid. Just before the alarm went off, he was taking off her bikini as he kissed her neck, salty from sweat and the ocean.

There was sand in his bed, underneath all the sheets and especially at the foot of the bed. He carefully stripped the sheets off his bed, trying not to get sand more places than it already was. His toes were covered in sand and so he set the sheets onto the floor and tried, as best as he could, to brush sand off of his feet and out from between his toes, which was an impossible task without a hose.

It was disappointing that his apartment was empty and that there wasn't a cute girl to make breakfast for. The shower sounds were from the apartment of one of his neighbors. His girlfriend, Mary, had never stayed over and had rarely been to his apartment. Her parents didn't approve and she hadn't yet succumbed to his charms, assuming that he had charms that were succumbable.

He was beginning to think that he didn't have any charms. Sometimes they talked about going somewhere for the weekend, San Diego, Catalina Island, maybe even Santa Barbara. She'd even bring it up, showing him ads for hotels by the shore from the *Sunday LA Times*. She imagined moonlight strolls and dinners at restaurants serving filet mignon. He imagined other things equally delicious. She'd never propose or agree on a specific weekend and he'd rarely try to pin her down. The times he had tried to pin her down, she'd scrambled out of his grasp saying, "Not now, not yet."

One time he made a crack about going to Neverland. The scowl she gave him was so withering that he feared she'd break up with him. Later, she snuggled with him and thanked him for his patience with her. He wondered how patient he would be if some surfer girl really might want to follow him home.

There wasn't much in his fridge to have for breakfast, so he stopped at the Donut Garden on Artesia Boulevard and had a cruller and a cup of weak coffee. When he first started working the night metering shifts, he'd stop by on the way home from work. It was one of the only places open where you could get a bite that didn't involve a sit-down meal.

The Donut Garden wasn't much, just a small building with a counter and a small seating area. Most of the building was taken up by the donut bakery. He'd stopped coming regularly when he bought a bathroom scale and discovered he'd put on a few pounds. He didn't recognize any of the staff. The cruller was good as always because it was overly glazed. Bits of sugar glaze fell leaving a small but noticeable stain on his dark red tie. When he got to the station, he went to the locker room and tried daubing the stain with some water to get it out, leaving a big dark blotch on his tie.

"Morning," Lester said as he sat down at his desk.

"What's wrong with your tie?" Kappe asked.

"Just a little stain. I think I can get it out," Lester said.

"Get the fucking thing dry cleaned. You've got a spare? I've got a spare if you need one."

"Let me just wait until it dries and I'll get back to you."

"How did it go at The Insomniac?" Kappe asked.

"I think that's a dead end. Nobody knew anything or saw anything. I'm pretty sure I believe them."

"You would," Kappe said snidely.

"I've got a line on a guy who may know how to make a silencer."

"So what? I'm sure I could find a couple of dozen in a couple of hours. We're looking for a murderer not a machinist."

"So, do you want me to follow up on that or not?" Lester asked.

"Or not. No, fine, do what you want. If your gut tells you to walk off a cliff, would you do it? I'm not going to stop you. Just help me out a bit on some real policing. We're going back up to Pico Boulevard to interview some possible fellow travelers at the deli up on Pico."

"Is this just speculation?" Lester asked.

"Okay, known associates," Kappe admitted.

"Do I have to come? The killer had to have mixed with the surfer kids hanging around the Biltmore. Unless he was an amazing shot, he'd have to have been pretty close. It seems unlikely that nobody noticed an older guy."

"Good call. We just have to canvas every high school five miles around and ask them if they noticed someone that looked like their parents armed with a pistol," Kappe said.

"Or go there the next time they have a concert," Lester suggested. "I bet a lot of them are regulars. I recognized quite a few of them. I've probably given parking tickets to half of them."

"You like corned beef or pastrami?" Kappe asked.

"Corned beef but I can go both ways. What are we going to do until then?"

"I'm going to meet with the FBI and see what I can find out about suspected spies and spy rings in the area. Something productive. You can do what you want, just so long as you meet me at Factor's Deli at 6:30. And when it comes down to the wire and I catch the guy, if you're not standing right next to me, I'm going to look right through you and act like we never met."

Lester scowled. "You ride me and ride me and you think you're a big man but you've solved as many murders as I have. None. What about the Hungarian diary? What about talking to his girlfriend again or the girl he was with? What about going to Averodyne?"

Kappe smiled. "The difference between you and me is that I don't give a fuck what you think or if you think. I just care that you're good police and not wasting my time. If you don't like the way I'm handling the case, then go back to metering."

Lester walked away. He was close to punching Kappe in the nose. It wasn't worth it.

"Pussy!" Kappe called out.

Some of the other officers looked over at Kappe and the backside of Lester as he stalked down the hall to the locker room.

"He's a pussy. The guy needs to be toughened up," Kappe said to no one in particular.

Lester heard all of it. His first instinct was to let it ride. He stopped in the doorway to calm himself, but then he heard Kappe yell out, "Pussy! Meow! Meow!" He spun around and strode confidently back to Kappe.

"Better to be a cat than a dog," Lester said calmly.

"What the fuck's that supposed to mean?" Kappe growled.

"When you figure it out, keep it to yourself," Lester said.

Kappe shrugged and looked to the other cops in the room but they looked back at him.

"Miles ahead of you. Miles ahead," Lester said as he sauntered out of the room.

When Lester got to the door, he stopped and turned back to Kappe. "Factor's at 6:30. I'm going to the

May Company to pick up a new tie and then to Averodyne to interview his boss and co-workers. Do you want to come along?"

"FBI," Kappe growled. "Give me a full update later and take good notes."

Lester was elated as he walked out of the office, down the hall and to the locker room. He checked his tie in the mirror. The water he'd dabbed on the tie had dried and you could barely see the stain. It wasn't one of his best ties but it was cleaner than his two others.

Driving east on Artesia, he decided to stop at his apartment before buying a new tie and then drop off his ties at the dry cleaners around the corner. If he was going to impress Mary and especially her parents, he was going to have dress better. His inclination was to be thrifty, though not as much as his uncle Jed, who stuffed newspaper in his shoes when he'd worn a hole through the sole, or his mom who had a stash of used wrapping paper that went back to when she was a child in Oklahoma, before the family lost the farm in the Dust Bowl.

The May Company was so modern. When it first opened he went a lot, treating himself to date-nut bread at the lunch counter in the basement and browsing the furniture department fantasizing about going there with Mary to choose dining room and living room sets. In Hawthorne and Lawndale, you could get a house for a decent price with a yard big enough to play catch in if they were lucky enough to have children. The men's department was on the second floor, but instead of going there, he went downstairs to the sale section and found a striped tie that was thirty percent off.

The South Bay Center was one of the new shopping centers that were springing up, including the new one in Torrance. He resisted the temptation to make a quick stop at the Wallach's Music City across Hawthorne Boulevard. He'd been to the one in Hollywood and dropped a Jackson and some change on jazz records he didn't know he needed, mostly small combo stuff out of New York and Europe. Having a Wallach's so close was going to burn a hole in his wallet, but in the sweetest possible way.

There wasn't much traffic. He passed by El Camino College where he'd taken some classes. He had plans to get a BA, but didn't have the time, not with his metering schedule. Mary thought he should transfer to UCLA, where she was going. He didn't have the luxury of not working. She said he could get a job on campus. He was mulling it over, but didn't see how it was possible until he got off the night shift. He'd promised her he'd look into it and she'd promised to get him some brochures, but she hadn't yet delivered.

The Averodyne parking lot was full as were the parking lots of the other companies to the right and to the left which had names like Gistec, Plessner Fabrication, AspaTech and others that gave no hint as to what their business really was.

Lester thought the cars were a tell. At Averodyne, there were some hot rods, some fully tricked out and some in progress. You had to figure there were machinists there. At Plessner, there were station wagons, which implied older workers. At AspaTech there was a Simca, a brand-new Saab, and an Austen-Healey Sprite which made him think that young designers or engineers worked there, people who were gear-heads but not wrenchers. Gistec's parking lot was empty, so maybe it wasn't in business any longer.

He parked in one of the visitor spots near the front office, a two-story building attached to the front of the large, windowless factory. He was afraid that he hadn't thought through his questions enough, that he'd let his mind drift to other things on the drive over. He was going to have to wing it, stick to the who, what, when, where and how.

He'd start with the boss and then work his way down to Shawn's immediate supervisor, his co-workers and then everyone else. Did he have any friends? Why was he fired? Did he have any enemies? Did people like him or was he cold? Shawn had been fired the day he was murdered. Was that a coincidence, a cause or tangentially connected? He felt like he had a lot to learn but he was going to try not to show his greenness.

As he got out of the car, he checked to see if his Paper Mate ballpoint pen wrote by scribbling on the last page of his notebook. He wrote down the day's date and Averodyne at the top of the page. He checked to see if his shoes looked all right, his new tie was straight and his hair was in place, not so tough when you sport a crew cut. Everything was a-okay as he locked his car and went up the couple of steps to the front door.

Just inside the front door was a room with a receptionist sitting behind a desk to the side of a closed door. The room was spare but fancy, like the showroom of a Swedish furniture factory, all clean lines with black upholstery trimmed in chrome. There was a maple, lima-bean shaped coffee table with aircraft industry trade publications, hot rod magazines, the tasteful kind not the kind with buxom broads on the cover leaning over a Deuce Coupe, and golfing magazines neatly stacked on top.

"May I help you?" the receptionist said as he entered the building. She was young and wore a blue dress with a grey cashmere sweater overtop, too warm for the room due to the excessive air conditioning. She was blond and tanned and looked like she'd spent a bit too much time in the sun. Crow's feet were just starting to form even though she couldn't have been much older than twenty-five.

"Excuse me. I'm from the Hermosa Beach Police Department," Lester said. "I'm here to ask questions related to the murder of one of your former employees, Steven Shawn."

The woman frowned and wrote down something in a notebook. "We were very sorry to hear about his death," she said coolly. "Do you know who did it?"

"That's what we're investigating," Lester said. "I'd like to start with Mr. Cheam, and then work my way through the company. Is Mr. Cheam available?"

The receptionist frowned again and looked down at her notebook. "I'm afraid this isn't a very good time. We're in a crunch right now trying to get orders out."

"What was your opinion of Mr. Shawn?"

The receptionist smiled broadly. "I loved his accent. All the girls loved his accent. It was like listening to Peter Lorre' but without all the creepiness. Other than that, he was an engineer, if you know what I mean?"

"I'm not sure I do." He took out his notebook and made some notes. "Can I ask your name?"

"Yes, I'm Loretta."

"Pleased to meet you. Lester Patterson."

"Likewise."

"So, what do you mean by his being an engineer?" Lester asked.

"Well, what I mean by that. . .and don't take it in the wrong way. . .Without engineers the world wouldn't go 'round, would it? So, what I mean, is that your typical engineer has the dress sense of a high school math teacher, a sense of humor only other engineers or accountants can appreciate, and the orneriness of a librarian on a bad day."

"So, did you like him? Did people like him?" Lester asked.

"Oh, yeah, sure. He was a swell guy," Loretta said with an honest smile. "The other engineers liked him. He was one of the gang as far as I could tell, though I don't normally hang out with guys who wear more than one pocket protector."

"Do you know if he had any enemies?"

"Not that I know of."

"Do you know why he was fired?"

Loretta leaned over. Lester could see a bit into the top of her dress, so he forced himself to look her in the eyes. She whispered, "the story I heard was that he was caught spying, not that I know that to be true."

"Is a lot of the work that Averodyne does secret?" Lester whispered.

"Well, it's a secret to me. We make these gizmos that are supposed to do I don't know what and the government pays us and I get an income and we all go home happy, right? Well, except for poor Mr. Shawn." Tears welled up in her eyes and she dabbed them away with a tissue she pulled from a box on her desk.

Lester thanked her for the information and asked if he could see Mr. Cheam.

"I'll see if he's available." She picked up the phone, pushed a button and whispered into the phone, shielding her mouth with her hand. "He'll come out in a minute. Can I get you some coffee?"

"Thanks, but no, I'm running on a full tank."

"The bathroom's down the hall."

"I'm fine." Lester sat down on one of the chairs and wrote some notes in his notebook. After ten minutes, he glanced up at the receptionist.

"I'm sure he'll be only a minute," Loretta said before going back to typing.

A dozen minutes later, the door behind the reception desk opened and Carlton Cheam stepped out. He was wearing a sharkskin suit and had a gold pinky ring on his right hand. His blond hair was slicked back and parted and with just a little grey coming in on the sides. His narrow tie was kept in place by a gold tie clasp with the stars of a five-star general.

Lester stood up and shook at Mr. Cheam's well-manicured hand. "Nice tie clasp you got there," Lester said.

"A gift from Eisenhower during the war," Mr. Cheam said, beaming. "You don't mind if we get down to business?"

"Lester Patterson, Hermosa Beach Police Department," Lester said formally and at attention.

"Detective Patterson?"

"Mr. Patterson is fine."

"Mr. Patterson, can I get you anything. Has Loretta taken care of that already?"

"Yes, I'm fine."

As Mr. Patterson opened the door to the back office, he said to Loretta, "Hold my calls, would you?"

"Sure thing Mr. Cheam," Loretta said through the intercom.

Mr. Cheam led Lester down a hall with closed doors to an office at the end. The office was uncluttered, with neatly stacked papers on the large Danish modern desk. There were golf balls from all the golf courses he'd played at in a case on the wall next to photos of him with various politicians, including Vice President Nixon. There was also a parliament of glass and ceramic owls all neatly lined up as if on parade.

"I can get his employee records if you don't mind waiting," Mr. Cheam said as he sat down behind his desk.

"I understand that Mr. Shawn was fired on the day he was murdered. Can you tell me why he was fired?" Lester asked as he sat down in a chair across the table from Mr. Cheam.

Mr. Cheam smiled and leaned back in his chair. "I suppose I could have saved myself the trouble," he said chuckling. "Don't mind me, just a little black humor. That's how we dealt with things in the war."

"So, why was he let go?" Lester asked.

"Mr. Shawn was let go for two reasons, officially. He didn't get along well with the other staff and we suspected, though we couldn't prove, that he was a spy, working for the Russkies. But hell, he could have been spying for one of my competitors and I would have canned him just the same. You really can't be too careful and with government secrets, the nation can't be too careful."

"How do you mean he didn't get along well with others?"

"He was always pointing out things he thought weren't right, making the machinists do things over, running through a lot of time and material."

"Do you think he was a good engineer?"

"Oh yeah, he was fine all right and pretty sharp, maybe a little too sharp if you know what I mean?" Mr. Cheam said coldly.

"Could you explain?" Lester said, looking up from his notebook.

"He caught on quick. He was always asking questions, trying to learn all the ins and outs of the business, things that weren't within his job description," Mr. Cheam said snidely.

"Would you say he was nosy or just curious?" Lester asked.

"Nosy. He always wanted to know about projects he wasn't working on. We do a lot of hush hush, high-level work for the Air Force, mostly, things that not a lot of people are supposed to know about, especially if their names are Ivan or Boris. Plus, they caught him with papers, confidential papers in his car. He wasn't supposed to have them, and by the way, we'd like them back ASAP. What was he doing with them if he wasn't a spy? He didn't work here any longer and by the way, we have a strict policy about taking sensitive documents home. Don't! I was right to fire him. I should have fired him sooner, not to speak ill of the dead."

"Did you happen to report your suspicions to anyone, the police, the FBI?" Lester asked.

"Like I said, they were suspicions, though I think we know now don't we?" Mr. Cheam said with a wide smile.

"We're not assuming anything," Lester said.

"I didn't call anyone until later, the day after when your boss, Detective Kappe, called. Now it's in the FBI's hands, isn't it?" Mr. Cheam said.

"They've got their part and we've got ours. I think I'm done with you for now. Thank you very much, sir, for making time for me. I'd like to speak to his supervisor, his co-workers and some of the other employees, and if you could show me a copy of his employee file, that would be great."

"It's not a big company, though we hope to grow. I was his supervisor," Mr. Cheam said as he stood. "Let me show you around."

"How did he take getting fired?" Lester asked.

"I think he was shocked. Nobody ever sees it coming and if they do, they find a way to ignore it until it slaps them in the face. I've always thought that you're better off staring your problems in the face," Mr. Cheam said as he looked directly at Lester.

Lester stood and followed Mr. Cheam out of the office and down to one of the closed doors. When the door was opened, there were several men in short-sleeved white shirts, with pocket protectors filled with pens and mechanical pencils. They were hunched over technical drawings. There were slide rulers on every desk. The men were startled and looked at each other.

"We don't get many visitors," Mr. Cheam said. "Hey gang, let's put away whatever we can put away, if I'm not interrupting at a bad time. Mr. Patterson is from the Hermosa Beach Police Department. I know we're all on edge. Please cooperate with him and answer all his questions to the best of your ability."

"Can I speak with them individually?"

Ah sure, if you don't mind using the breakroom. They'll show you where it is."

One by one, the five other engineers and draftsmen came into the breakroom. They sat awkwardly as they answered his questions. They were all in their mid-twenties. There were five of them and each one was nervous when asked about what they thought about Steve Shawn. They liked him and thought he was a good engineer but one who could be bossy especially when he detected a mistake.

"He'd yell at us sometimes," one of them said, "when we'd make mistakes. He was a little older than us and not really in charge, but kind of put himself in charge, if you know what I mean. He said that engineers couldn't afford to make mistakes; that people's lives depended on them doing their job correctly. He was always on time and always happy to help other people with their projects."

Lester asked them if they were surprised that he was fired, they all said that they weren't, that he'd been feuding with Mr. Cheam and especially his son Johnny.

None of them would say what the feud was about because they'd been told that the subject was secret and confidential beyond that there was a basic difference of opinion. None of them had ever spent time with Mr. Shawn outside of work.

They knew he lived a bit away, up near Pico, and wasn't interested in baseball, football or the fights. None had ever met his ex-girlfriend, Elizabeth, though they'd known that he'd had a girlfriend.

Some of them didn't think that Shawn could have been a spy given how much he talked about what the Communists had done to his family. Others thought that he could be a spy but had never seen anything that had made them think.

"You never know," one of the engineers said. "If you thought they were a spy, then they weren't a very good one. If they were a good one, then you wouldn't suspect that they were a spy. James Bond, have you read Ian Fleming? I don't think that's anything like what real spies are like."

The machinists were a different sort. They looked like rodsters, with their greased back hair and short-sleeved shirts showing off the tattoos they'd gotten in the service. The sound of the machine shop was terrible, a screechy whine that was almost as bad as fingernails on a chalkboard. There were stacks of little metal parts out of what looked like aluminum but was probably titanium or something exotic like that. The purpose of the parts was a mystery to Lester; little pieces of flanged metal all looking the same, all looking like they had a serious purpose.

When he entered the machine shop he went over to the closest machinist, who was wearing an apron and goggles. It took a while for him to get the man's attention. There were about twenty stations, with millers and drillers and grinders. He didn't know much about machinery or carpentry or any other RY beyond buffoonery, or at least that's what his brother would say. It's probably why he became a policeman.

As he tried to talk with the first machinist, another one, a tall blond man, came over and yelled at him over the din.

"Johnny Cheam! You're the Dick?" the man said with a big grin, but you can call me Johnny Wayne."

Johnny didn't shake Lester's had so much as crush it, with a big fat grin.

"I'm going to ask you and your staff some questions about Mr. Shawn."

"I always thought he was probably a spy," Johnny Cheam said confidently.

"Why's that?"

"It figures. He was a Jew and a Communist, or at least raised a Communist. You put two and two together and that spells S.P.Y., spy."

"Did you ever see any evidence of spying?" Lester asked.

Johnny laughed. "It's not like they show themselves."

"So beyond the idea that he was Communist spy, what else did you think about him?" Lester asked.

"And he was a busybody. Anyone here could tell you that. He always thought he knew better and, yeah, sure he's got the degree and all, but that doesn't mean he knew shit about jet engines."

"So, why was he hired?"

"You'd have to ask my dad, but I'm guessing that he thought he was a pretty good engineer. He probably thought he saw something in him, at least at first. That's how my dad is. He's a sentimental guy, but a tough as nails businessman. He's not afraid to make a decision. I just wish he'd listened to me and made it earlier."

"To fire him?" Lester asked.

"Damn straight to fire his ass! He was a liability and God knows what secrets have been passed on to the Russkies."

"Do you mind if I talk to some of the other machinists?"

"Sure, go ahead," Johnny said as he folded his arms and didn't move. His arms had bulging muscles and the veins on his forearms popped out, like he was a souped-up late model hot rod. He towered over Lester by a few inches even though Lester was nearly six-foot himself.

"How about we take it outside?"

He could see the muscles on Johnny's arms tense and flex and he could hear the beginning of a growl.

Lester laughed. "No, I mean, why don't I go outside with your guys and interview them there and the rest of you can get back to business. Oh, and by the way, and this is for another case entirely, but since you're a machinist, I thought I'd ask."

"Yeah, what?" Johnny asked impatiently.

"Well, I was wondering if you knew anyone who could make a silencer? I mean for a gun. I was at the Poop Deck, down in Hermosa, the other night and this guy was bragging that he knew some kid in high school that'd made his own silencer for shop class and turned it in as his class project."

Johnny glared at him but otherwise didn't change his expression. "Those things are illegal," he said. "Must have been a real numbskull."

"Yeah, that's what the guy at the Poop Deck thought, but you know, kids do some stupid things all the while thinking they're pretty smart. My dad says that there's nothing stupider than a guy who thinks he's smarter than everyone else."

"Well, I hope you find what you're looking for," Johnny said calmly. "I'll send the guys out one by one. There's a picnic bench right outside the backdoor if you don't mind using that as an office."

"That'll work. And if you wouldn't mind asking around about someone making a silencer. I'd rather stop trouble before it starts," Lester said.

"I like to finish trouble quickly," Johnny said coldly.

"Sometimes that's not a bad policy."

Lester shook Johnny's hand and gave it a good hard squeeze, which was a mistake because Johnny squeezed back so hard that Lester felt like his bones were being crushed.

The machinists had a low opinion of Mr. Shawn, but more as a person than as an engineer. They didn't mind him making changes that meant they had to scrap work already completed. That was part of the job. What got them was his manner, the way he'd tell them, which was brusque. Even if he'd been the one who told them to do something a particular way in the first place, he'd act like it was their fault.

"Man, we're just the hands of the engineers," said one of the machinists.

"He was under a lot of pressure," another said, "but then so are we. There's no reason to act like a dick."

The machinists were all sad that he'd been killed and none of them knew who might have had a beef with him.

"There's nobody he pissed off more than anyone else," one of them said. "All the engineers are like that. He wasn't so special. At least he wasn't a screamer, more of a scowler. Some of them act like they're the only ones who can do math and know how to put things together. We've got guys here who could build a car from scratch, not counting the tires. Machine the whole damn thing."

Lester asked about making a silencer. All of them said that it wasn't particularly difficult technically, but none of them would admit that they'd made one.

"I know a guy who claims he made one in high school. Likes to brag about it, I don't know, to intimidate people or to just show off that he was some kind of badass."

"Would you mind telling me who that guy was?"

The machinist laughed at him. "I'm not some fucking snitch!"

Lester handed him a business card. The card was a generic one for the Hermosa Beach Police Department. He scribbled his name on the back, handed the card to the guy and said that if he changed his mind or knew someone else who might know something, that they could call him at that number. The guy thanked him and crumbled it up and stuffed it in his back pocket.

When he was done with the interviews, Lester went back into the building and found Johnny standing next to a lathe talking with its operator.

"I'm going to need to speak with your dad again."

"My old man is a busy guy," Johnny said before turning his back on Lester.

"I'm not asking. I'm telling, if you don't mind. A man has been killed and you're treating it like an inconvenience," Lester said indignantly.

"Up the stairs and down the hall," Johnny said. "I'm sure you can find your own way out. I don't give two shakes about some Commie spy. If you ask me, the only good Commie is a dead Commie."

Lester wrote in his notebook that Johnny was aggressive and barely cooperative.

Johnny glared at Lester. "You can write all that down in your little notebook. It's a free country thanks to guys like my dad. I can speak my mind, especially in my own place of business."

"No doubt," Lester said as he walked off to find Mr. Cheam. "You're what makes American the great country that it is."

"Damn straight!" Johnny said with a big grin.

It wasn't hard to find Mr. Cheam. As soon as he entered the office, he could hear Mr. Cheam down the hall in his office yelling at some poor Joe, telling him he must have gone to Stupid U. When he got to the office, he peaked in the open door and saw Mr. Cheam red-faced sitting at his desk glaring and yelling at two of the engineers.

"David, when you work with Jack over here, have you ever noticed that he's so incompetent that he couldn't screw in a lightbulb?"

David, who was one of the engineers, didn't say anything and sat stiffly, like rigor mortis had overtaken him. Mr. Cheam hadn't noticed Lester until Lester cleared his throat. Jack stared straight ahead expressionless.

"Get the fuck out of my sight before I fire the both of you!" Mr. Cheam yelled. His face was bright red all the way up to the tops of his ears.

David and Jack, who were in their early twenties and dressed in grey slacks, white shirts and skinny ties, got up from their chairs and rushed out the door and down the hall.

Mr. Cheam took out a handkerchief and wiped the sweat from his brow, put it back in his pants pocket and ushered Lester into his office. "I don't like to, but sometimes you've got to light little fires under people's behinds to bring out the best in them," he said calmly.

"You think that works?" Lester asked as he entered the office and sat down on a chair.

"How do you think Patton beat the Nazis? You know, I served under Patton," Mr. Cheam said. "They only made one of them. If he'd have lived, he'd have made a better president than Eisenhower, I can tell you."

"I don't want to disturb you any more than I have to, Mr. Cheam. I've interviewed your employees. I can't say yet whether or not I've made any progress. Just one more thing. Do you have Mr. Shawn's personnel file?"

"Yes, I mean, no. I'll have Loretta get it for you."

"That would be great," Lester said. "I think I can find my way out. If you think of anything, you can call me at the Hermosa Beach Police Department. Leave a message if I'm not there." Lester wrote down his number on the back of a business card and handed it to Mr. Cheam.

"I'll do that. Keep up the good work. It's a shame what happened to Mr. Shawn, even if he was a spy. There's due process and all that."

"That's the way it's supposed to work," Lester said as he stood.

Mr. Cheam leaned over and punched a button on his intercom. "Loretta, please pull out Steven Shawn's personnel file and make a copy of it for Mr. Patterson." Mr. Cheam turned off the intercom and looked up at Lester. "We've got this new copying machine that they just came out with," he said proudly. "A word of advice. Invest heavily in Xerox. I promise you that you won't be sorry."

Lester thanked him and walked down the hall. In the side offices, engineers and other workers were busy at their desks. Jack was quietly talking to David wiping tears from his eyes with his handkerchief.

At the front desk, Loretta was waiting for him with a narrow folder in her hand. "It won't take long for me to make the copies. The Xerox is wicked fast and it's almost exactly like you have the real thing."

It took a surprisingly short time for her to return with a manila envelope filled with a copy of the personnel file, a half-hour at the most.

As he waited, Lester looked over his notes. It seemed to him that Steven Shawn wasn't well-liked but also that Averodyne's culture was aggressive rather than collegial. Both of the Mr. Cheams seemed to be bullies. It wasn't hard to see that it was pretty easy to get fired at Averodyne.

Chapter 8

Lester left Averodyne feeling he'd made progress. He had more information about Steven Shawn and an idea of what kind of place he'd worked at. Mr. Cheam was a nasty boss, but then that wasn't anything unusual. Half the people on the planet had a nasty boss.

Maybe Shawn was a spy. He couldn't rule that out. Averodyne was a defense contractor with secrets that might be worth killing for. He made a note to see if he could find anyone to decipher the plans they'd found. Still, it nagged at him that if the plans were important to the killer, then the killer had failed, unless he just wanted to stop a spy and he didn't know about the plans. Maybe the killer didn't know about the plans.

Rather than go back to the station, he decided to have lunch and then go to Hawthorne High School to see if he could talk to the machine shop teacher.

The Wich Stand wasn't far away. He'd thought the food there had been pretty good. He was disappointed that the same waitress wasn't on duty, but he was there to eat and work. He asked if he could have a booth that was close to the window.

He ordered the northern baked halibut, which was pricey but he felt like he deserved it, and a frosted root beer. While he waited for his order, he spread out the copies of the personnel file and sorted through them, careful to keep them in order.

There was a copy of Steven Shawn's resume, which showed that he had been educated in Hungary. His Hungarian name was in parentheses at the top of the page, Szabo Istvan. The notes on the resume, presumably by the elder Mr. Cheam, showed check marks next to his degree and there were notes that he had a familiarity with aircraft engines, including jet engines. There was also a note that his English was pretty good even though he had a heavy accent. At the top of the page, someone had written, "Hire."

There were three job reviews, two annual and one from last Friday. The first two reviews were positive. He'd been given raises both years. Only the last review was negative. He was accused of taking confidential papers home, a violation of company policy, of various undescribed acts of insubordination, and of sloppy work habits. This review was dated only a couple of months before the last one. It didn't seem like someone would go from a good and valued employee to a terrible one.

Maybe breaking up with his girlfriend, Elizabeth had changed him. Maybe the work had changed somehow or the Cheams had become nastier, which didn't seem likely. People like that never changed, they were always jerks and bullies. It was possible that he'd hidden his bad qualities for a couple of years and been found out, but that didn't seem likely because Mr. Cheam seemed to be a more than a hands-on boss and the company was small. It seemed more likely, especially with the insubordination charge, that Mr. Shawn had somehow angered Mr. Cheam enough that firing him wasn't enough.

The rest of the papers were insurance forms and forms for the pension plan. There was no indication in the files that they thought he was a spy, beyond the accusation that he was taking papers home. Lester thought that if he had a spy working for his company, he would contact the FBI and then maybe use the spy to send fake information to the Commies, but what did he know beyond watching *Dragnet* and reading a couple of mysteries every year.

It was after 1:00 when he finished lunch. School let out sometime after 2:00. He wasn't sure the exact time. He was keen on getting there before the teachers left, which he figured was just after the final bell rang. That was at least when he'd left when he was in school. Unless he'd gotten detention, he'd never stayed longer than five minutes past the bell, which was just enough time to get to his locker, grab his stuff and go home or hang out with his friends at the Foster's Freeze.

Thinking about Foster's Freeze reminded him there was one near Hawthorne High. He could stop, hang out, check out the girls before driving up to West LA to meet up with Kappe.

It was pretty easy finding the shop classrooms. Kids were working on rebuilding a car, an old Dodge station wagon that had probably been a family car.

The teacher walked over to him as he entered the shop. He was a short guy about his dad's age wearing clean blue coveralls. Lester introduced himself and he'd only been working there for a couple of years, so he didn't know anything firsthand about a student making a silencer.

"I'd heard about it, rumors anyway. It wouldn't surprise me," the teacher said. "Better than the pipe bomb some numbskull made at my old school or maybe a zip gun."

"I didn't know school could be so rough," Lester said incredulously.

"A new generation. Sometimes I think they put the boom in the baby boom."

"Where were you before?" Lester asked.

"I moved down from Oxnard and the guy I replaced moved down to Anaheim, I think. That's what I'd heard. The office can probably tell give you his address if you need it."

The office gave him the ex-teacher's name and contact information. They weren't sure if it was current but it was what he'd given them when he'd left. One of the secretaries typed up the contact information on an index card and handed it to Lester. The teacher's name was Gerald Connors. He lived in what was probably an apartment in Anaheim and there was a phone number.

"Is it possible for you to tell me if there was any student in the last ten years who was expelled or otherwise in trouble for making a silencer for a gun?" Lester asked the secretary.

"Not off the top of my head," the secretary said. "I'll have to look into it. I can call you when, or if, I find anything. I'll give you my phone number if you want to call me." She wrote a phone number on a slip of paper and handed it to Lester.

"Is this a direct line?" Lester asked.

The secretary blushed. "It's my home phone," she whispered. "I'll be home later. My roommate is on vacation in Hawaii. Do you like roasted pork? I went to Hawaii once and all I seemed to eat was roasted pork with pineapple."

Lester blushed as he carefully folded up the phone number and put it in his wallet. "Agnes?"

"But you can call me Angie."

"Lester." He left her a business card with his work phone number written on the back. "Call me if you find out anything."

"I'm really not supposed to give out confidential student information," Angie whispered.

"Well, I am the police and it may be a matter of life or death."

Angie's eyes bugged out and she leaned over, closer to Lester. He could see down her dress and into her bra, which was distracting and enticing enough that he seriously considered calling her later. He felt guilty about betraying his girlfriend, Mary, at least in lust if not yet in deed. "You really think so?" she asked.

Lester leaned over and whispered in her ear, "I do."

Angie shuddered and blushed then sat back quickly when a student entered the office and rang the little bell at the counter. "I need to go. Please call me later."

"Please call me later when you find that information."

"Oh, I surely will," Angie said with a wink.

The school bell rang just as Lester was leaving the office. He hadn't expected school to be so sexy. He thought about the slip of paper with Angies' number in his wallet and worried that somehow Mary would find it there and call him on it, not that she'd ever looked through his wallet or even had a chance to. It's not like they were married or even engaged.

Now that he was further along in his career, albeit just a couple of days further along, it was something he had to consider.

Mary was smart and beautiful and came from a well-off family. If only he could earn enough to support both of them, not to mention provide the kind of living standard that she'd grown up with. There wasn't much chance of that on a policeman's salary, unless he made captain or chief of police and that was getting far ahead of himself.

Teenagers bumped into him in the hallway in their mad dash to an afternoon of freedom, at least until they started their homework, but he only noticed when they were cute girls. A few of the girls caught his eye but he quickly admonished himself because they were all jail bait, which was the last thing he needed.

He drove the few blocks to the Foster's Freeze on Hawthorne. The parking lot was full of high school kids sugaring up. There was a pile of bicycles leaning against a fence, a few older hand-me-down cars with dents and fading paint jobs and a couple of hot rods. The hot rods were magnates to the guys and the guys were magnates to the girls, who were competing with chrome, shiny engines and flashy flame paint jobs.

There was a long line of kids waiting to get to the order counter. Lester had some time to kill and was hankering for a vanilla malt so he braved the line.

He wasn't much older than these kids, he thought, but he felt a lot older, like they were from a different generation. He was born at the end of the Depression and they were born near the end of the war. They were loud and boisterous. One of the hot rods had their stereo blaring out a song with a heavy guitar line and no singing that sounded kind of like snake charmer music. It was an interesting sound, which Lester found too raw but hard to ignore especially when played at full volume.

A gorgeous girl in jeans and a tight pink sweater cut the line in front of him. The guy she joined didn't mind but the girls now behind her were pissed off.

"What's the big idea? Aren't you supposed to be at the library?" one of the girls said.

The gorgeous girl smiled and said, "That's what I told my old man. I've got his T-bird until he gets home from work. Until then I'm going to have fun, fun, fun."

"Till he takes the T-bird away?" the guy asked.

"No, until I give it back," she said.

"What are we, in kindergarten," another girl said.

Later, as Lester leaned against his car and slurped the last of his shake, he was startled by the roar of a car engine and the squeal of tires as the T-bird convertible, top down, beautiful in powder blue, roared out of the parking lot and down Hawthorne Boulevard. It's a wonder she didn't cause an accident, Lester thought.

He looked at the hot rods with their proud teenage owners and thought about his meager car. It was sobering to think that there were a lot of high school kids better off than he was, and this was Hawthorne High, not even a fancy school like Beverly Hills. He was just a regular guy from Taft feeling adrift as he threw his empty shake cup into the trash can.

On his way back to Hermosa, he drove west on El Segundo Boulevard, under the freeway overpass being constructed, before turning left at Sepulveda at the enormous Chevron refinery and into Manhattan Beach.

Sand dunes were being turned into nice houses. Intersections were sprouting small shopping centers, with a liquor store and a dry cleaner, or gas stations uniformed attendants ready to fill 'er up and wash your windows.

At the station, nobody had seen Kappe the whole day and he hadn't called in, which hopefully meant that his talk with the FBI was productive.

From his jacket pocket, he took out his notepad and flipped it open to the page with Gerald Connors' phone number then took out Angie's phone number from his wallet. He placed it on his desk and stared at it, daydreaming about spending the night with her, then he crumpled it up and tossed it in his trash can. He looked down into the trash can and seriously thought about taking it out and calling her but then an image of Mary, his beautiful Mary came to him and instead he called Gerald Connors. If he needed to get ahold of her, he'd just call the school and ask for her.

The phone rang and rang and rang without it being picked up. It was frustrating that there was no way to leave a message. If only there could be some way to leave him a message without driving all the way down to Orange County.

Lester reminded himself of one of the things his mother always said to him. "Patience is a virtue but the Lord ran out when he made you." He'd have to try later when he got back from meeting up with Kappe up on the Westside.

It was going to be a drag to drive up there Lester thought as he got in his car and headed north on Sepulveda.

He took Sepulveda all the way just so he could see what was playing at the movie theaters in Westchester. Traffic flowed so smoothly, making all the lights, that he was going too fast to check out the theater marquees without rear-ending someone.

He made most of the lights and even in Culver City, everything was smooth. He ended up getting to Factor's Deli by 5:45, almost an hour early.

He headed to the newsstand over at Westwood and Pico next to Junior's. They had out-of-town newspapers, often a day or two old from as far away as New York, but never from Taft or even Bakersfield. There were magazines and a little section hidden away with naughty magazines like Playboy which he'd glance at from time to time. He had a stash of them hidden in his apartment, but not too many because he didn't want to seem like a perv if Mary ever found them.

He bought a copy of *Downbeat* and the latest *Playboy*, which he carried back to his car in a plain paper bag and put in the trunk.

He found Kappe standing by his car, parked down Pico a block from Factor's Deli. Lester had parked around the corner on a residential street. Kappe was looking jubilant as he leaned against his car and picked at his nails with a pocket knife.

"You think you can keep me waiting?" Kappe snarled as Lester walked up to him.

Lester looked at his watch and saw that it was only 6:25. He was five minutes early. "I'm early. Why give me a hard time?"

"You think criminals give a shit about niceties? Are you some kind of wilting flower?" Kappe demanded.

"I'm early!" Lester snapped. "Stop with the shit! Did you learn anything from the FBI?"

"The world's filled with Commie spies and their Pinko sympathizers. What else is new?"

"I've got a handle on maybe identifying someone who built a silencer in the past."

Kappe didn't look impressed. "Meanwhile, I was doing some real policing. The FBI has given me the names, addresses and phone numbers of some of the pinkest of the local Pinkos. Any one of them could be our killer. I haven't figured out why but I can figure that out once I catch the bastard."

"So what's our plan here?" Lester asked.

"This delicatessen is a hotbed for Pinko Communists and mobsters. If you knew how many Communists and mobsters are Jews, it would make you sick."

"So, you're basically saying that Jews are Communists or hardened criminals or are you saying that Communists are Jews?" Lester asked, annoyed. He was tired of Kappe's tirades.

"Did I ever tell you about how my dad signed me up for the Hitler Youth?"

Lester stared at Kappe. He wasn't surprised.

"Before the war, my dad, who was a real old country Kraut even though he was from Cincinnati, signed me up for the youth wing of the German American Bund. I can tell you it was fantastic. I was in their drum corps. We'd march around in our uniforms and I'd beat the hell out of the drum they gave me. Went through a couple of heads."

"Meanwhile down on the farm," Kappe continued, "the point is that, don't get me wrong, I don't have anything against Jews. They mind their business. I mind my business. But when they're plotting to overthrow the American government and threaten the American way of life, that's when I get my dander up. These guys in there, the ones we're going to meet, they may seem all fine and dandy, with their horned-rim glasses and pastrami sandwiches, but they'd just as soon overthrow mom, dad, and apple pie as ask for extra mustard on their rye bread. We're going to show them whose boss and keep at them until they've answered all our questions. Capisce?"

"Capisce," Lester said reluctantly.

"Now that we're on the same page," Kappe said, "I'll let you in on the info that I got from the FBI. That J. Edgar is the sharpest peg in the whole damn government. Practically everyone else is either full Communist or half Communist, right on up to the President of the United States, Dwight David Eisenhower," Kappe declared. "I keep up with the times no thanks to the *Los Angeles Times.*

"Kennedy's the President now."

"No shit, Sherlock," Kappe snapped. "Ask Mindszenty over there in the United States Embassy how much Eisenhower went squishy on the Commies."

Lester was getting annoyed. He looked at his watch and tapped his feet as Kappe went on an extended tirade about Communists in the movies and in Washington.

"Yeah, I can see you're a patriotic American concerned about the erosion of freedom," Kappe growled.

"I served my country and I did it without yammering. Get to the point!"

Kappe's face turned red. It was clear that he was steaming. If it weren't for the young family walking down the street past them, he might have knocked Lester's block off. "To the moon!" Kappe growled.

"Look, I've had a long day," Lester said calmly. "Just tell me how you want to play this, what it is we're trying to do and I'll play whatever part you want."

"Let's get one thing straight," Kappe growled. "If I tell you to play Juliet, you'll play Juliet, otherwise you're going to play Yorrick."

"Yeah, I get your drift."

"Okay, hunker down for a sec," Kappe said as he leaned over towards Lester and began whispering. "The FBI has been bugging this deli for the last year. They think it's a big drop site, meeting place and watering hole. One of the regulars, Paul Hess, is supposedly also a mug with Sam Scozzari's crew and maybe had something to do with the Cohen hit. This they don't know for sure. His brother, Manny is the Red. I guess you could say that they have all their bases covered."

"So, what do you want us to do?"

"We're going to talk with Manny and his Kaffeeklatsch and see what's what. If we have to take one of them in, we'll take him in."

"What if he doesn't know anything?" Lester asked.

"One of the lessons I learned a long time ago, and a lesson you're going to have to learn, is that if you squeeze them like an accordion, they'll tell you everything you want to know. You just have to know their buttons and once you do, man, it's like playing a top of the line Titano or Excelsior. It's a beautiful thing."

"But what are we going to ask them?" Lester asked.

"Just follow my lead. I tell you, they're involved or my name isn't Sam Kappe."

Kappe led him into the delicatessen, which had a bakery counter filled with rye bread in the back and cookies in the front below where the cashier stood. There was a counter along one of the walls and black vinyl booths filling the rest of the space.

"Remind me to pick up a corn rye on the way out," Kappe said.

Kappe strode through the restaurant to the back and stood in front of a booth in the back where three men in their late twenties and early thirties sat eating pastrami sandwiches stacked high with meat. As they would take a bite, bits of pastrami fell on their hands and plates. The men were dressed in shiny grey suits with dark ties and looked like they'd just gotten off work from an accounting firm.

"Sorry to interrupt boys," Kappe said cheerily, "but one of you wouldn't happen to be named Manny Hess?"

"Depends on who's asking," the men said in unison. Lester could see the men tense up as they slowly put down their sandwiches and wiped their hands clean with their napkins.

Kappe whipped out his badge from his coat pocket and flashed them a wide grin. "Now I'm going to ask again and I expect you to mind your manners this time. Starting with you," he said, pointing to the man on his left, "what's your name?"

"Gestetner, Joe," the first man said nervously

"Are you stuttering or is that just how you speak?" Kappe asked.

"G-E-S-T-E-T-N-E-R," he spelled.

"Brody, Mel," the second man said.

"Yeah, I'm Manny," the third said coolly. "Do you mind if we continue eating?"

"My mama told me it wasn't polite to talk while you eat," Kappe said threateningly. "Tell me what you know about Steve Shawn." He reached down and picked up Manny's sandwich and took a big bite out of it, chowing it down with his mouth open so bits of bread and pastrami fell onto his chin.

"He was a good guy," Joe said. "It's a real tragedy what happened to him. To go through the war and escape from the Soviets and to come here all alone and try to build a new life and to have someone gun you down, it's a real shanda."

"That guy had the luck, which I guess he used up," Mel said. "His girlfriend was a real looker, but she dropped him. He was a mensch, I thought he was a mensch. To end like that, he didn't deserve it."

"If you want my opinion," Manny said, "he'd still be alive if he could have kept his mug shut."

"That too," Joe said.

"Biting the hand that fed him," Mel said. "He had standards. You could say that about him."

Kappe put the remains of the sandwich down on Mel's plate, not much more than a bit of bread and the fatty ends of pastrami stained yellow with mustard. "That's exactly my theory," Kappe said. "He pissed off a commissar and he was whacked. But you wouldn't know anything about that, would you, comrade Hess."

Manny Hess grimaced then laughed. "I don't know what you're saying, but I categorically deny it."

"He wasn't a Communist. He was as anti-Communist as the President of the United States!" Mel said.

Kappe grinned and nodded. "Your words, not mine."

"His family somehow managed to survive the Nazis, thanks to the swiftness of the Russian advance at the end of the war. For that, I suppose they were grateful, but then his brother was killed fighting the Soviets when they invaded in '56. He told me his story once and I can tell you it wasn't pretty," Joe said. "There was a calm before the storm and they were doing okay, but then things went from vermisht to tsuris, if you catch my meaning, and he had to leave. If he was a Communist, then my mother is a schiksa."

"He was having trouble at work," Manny said. "He wasn't getting along with his boss and his boss wasn't getting along with him."

"Do you know they fired him the day he was killed?" Kappe said. "Why would they knock him off too?"

"I didn't know that," Manny said. "I'm not surprised. He was going to quit anyway, at least that's what he told us."

"Did he tell you why he was unhappy?" Lester asked.

"He said he couldn't say," Joe said. "His work was top secret, all hush hush."

"But, he did try to hint that things there somehow weren't kosher," Mel said.

"And?" Lester asked.

"And, he wouldn't say any more," Mel said. "It was all hush hush and he kept his lips zipped tighter than a nun's blouse."

"He wouldn't," Joe insisted. "If there was a secret to keep from the Communists, he'd keep it."

"He knew how to keep his mug shut," Manny said. "He never talked about his work. We didn't want to know about it anyway. Sometimes he'd talk about his co-workers and boss. You know, the usual complaints. They're stupid. They don't respect me."

"Yeah, and now he's got lockjaw, permanent like," Kappe sneered. "The cure for everything, except for the poor schmo with lead poisoning."

Manny scowled and stood quickly. "You've got the wrong end of it! He was our friend. We'd meet here for dinner 'cause none of us has a family yet, ess, kvetch and kibbitz and then go home to our lonely apartments. When he had a girlfriend, we saw less of him and then a couple of months ago, he shows up again all regular like. He complains about his love life again just like the rest of us. He kvetches about his job. There's nothing unusual about that. Next thing we know, he's dead."

As Manny spoke, Kappe fumed. "I smell a rat. I can't prove it yet, but I know the smell. There's something you're all hiding and believe me, when I find out, I'm going to nail each and every one of you to that big wooden chair up at San Quentin."

"We're straight with you," Manny said. "If you don't want straight then we can't help you."

"You're as crooked as your brother," Kappe sneered.

"My brother's business is his business. I don't know anything about it and that's the way both of us like it," Manny said.

"Does he know you're a Pinko?" Kappe asked.

"That's your opinion," Manny said.

"And a fairy?" Kappe growled.

Joe and Mel tried to stand up in the booth but they were blocked by Lester on one side and Manny on the other. They were enraged but Manny was calm.

"If you think words are misspelled swords, then ouch, I'm dying," he said sarcastically.

Kappe wound himself up to clobber Manny but was held back by Lester, who grabbed his arm and tugged him back.

"It's not worth it," Lester whispered in Kappe's ear. "Half the deli would testify against you."

"My brother's a personal injury lawyer," a man at an adjacent table yelled out.

"Ambulance chasers," Kappe grumbled as he pulled away from the booth and shook off Lester's hand on his arm.

"Before we go, can I get your names and phone numbers just in case we have to contact you?" Lester asked as he pulled a piece of paper off of his pad and handed it to the men along with his ballpoint pen.

They wrote their names and phone numbers down on the piece of paper one by one with Manny the last to sign. As he handed the paper back to Lester, Manny said, "It's been a pleasure. I hope we've been helpful."

"I really hope you find the killer," Mel said.

"What happened to Szanto shouldn't have happened to a dog," Joe said.

"We'll do our best," Lester said, taking the paper, folding it and putting it into his jacket pocket.

"Do you want to get a bite?" Kappe asked as they walked to the front of the deli.

"Do you want to eat here?" Lester asked.

"Sure, why not. The pastrami is pretty good," Kappe said as he sat down at the counter.

Lester sat down next to him. Kappe ordered the pastrami while Lester ordered the corned beef. While they waited for their orders, they reviewed the case.

Kappe was adamant that he didn't believe anything the three guys had said, including their tears. Whispering, he talked about learning from his FBI contact that there were dozens, if not hundreds, of Communist sympathizers many of whom were probable Comintern agents. These agents, according to Kappe, had been placed at all levels of society and in important jobs. They were a fifth column ready to take over the country.

When Lester described his visit to Averodyne, Kappe blew up at him, calling it a waste of time because they had no motive to kill Steven Shawn. Lester talked about trying to contact the shop teacher who reportedly had a student who had made a silencer. Kappe thought it was a good idea, but didn't see the connection with the case, explaining that the Communists had plenty more ways to get a silencer than to buy one off of a high school student.

They hadn't noticed Manny, Mel and Joe leave, but they were gone by the time Lester and Kappe had finished their dinners. Kappe bought two loaves of corn rye bread, one for him and one for Lester as they paid their bill. The air was cool but not windy as they walked separately to their cars.

Lester drove home with the windows down as he drove along the coast, past the airport and the oil refinery and into Manhattan Beach. The fog had come in heavier than usual.

As he entered El Porto, the little strip of unincorporated land just north of Manhattan Beach, he thought about Beatrice, the woman whom Steve was with the night he was murdered.

As he waited at the light at Rosecrans Boulevard, he thought about Mary and how nice it would be to see her, but it was after 8:00, too late to come calling on a school night, so he drove home instead. He thought about Angie and half wished he hadn't thrown away her phone number.

He felt like they weren't making any progress. Maybe Kappe was right and his angle was wrong. He didn't think so, but then he knew that he didn't have the experience to be able to tell. Parking at his apartment and walking up the steps to his place, he reminded himself to call Mr. Connors again if it wasn't too late. Kappe may have more years on the force, Lester said to himself, but they'd both worked the same number of murder cases.

Sitting at his small dinner table, he wrote out the questions he wanted to ask Mr. Connors. The call was going to be long-distance and he didn't know if he could get the cost reimbursed. His ballpoint pen ran dry, so he had to search around in his apartment for another. There was another one in the drawer of his bedside table but it was also dry. He found a dull pencil in one of his kitchen drawers and whittled it sharp with a penknife.

Before calling Mr. Connors, he finished writing his questions and then reviewed them. The phone was attached to the wall, so he had to dial from there. He untangled the long cord so that it could stretch far enough to reach the dinner table. The phone rang five times before someone picked up.

"Hello, may I speak with Mr. Gerald Connors please?" Lester asked.

The person on the other line cleared his throat and with a grumbly, cigarette scarred-voice said, "Whatever you're selling, I don't want any!"

"I'm not selling anything," Lester said calmly. "Is this Mr. Gerald Connors?"

"Who wants to know?" the man on the other end of the line growled.

"I'm Lester Patterson with the Hermosa Beach Police Department."

"What? Do I owe for a parking ticket? I haven't been there in a year. You people are vultures! It's why I moved down to Orange County. A man can park in peace."

"No, I don't think you owe for a parking ticket, but don't quote me on that. I'm calling about a former student of yours," Lester said.

"Whatever he's got to say about me, I didn't do it. Those punks will drive down our standard of living. Mark my words," Mr. Connors said angrily.

"No, nothing like that," Lester said.

"My supper's ready, so I hope this won't take a while."

"I'll try to be quick. Do you remember if anyone in one of your classes, and this would have been in the last five years, if anyone had made a silencer, for a gun?"

"This is exactly what I'm talking about. To think that my generation sacrificed our lives, our bodies, our blood for little shits, pardon my French, so that some juvenile delinquent could make a silencer. They're still wet behind the ears. They don't know what killing is. Were you in the service? I've seen some things. I've seen what a bullet or a shell can do to the human body." Mr. Connors began to weep.

"Are you okay?"

"No, sorry. I don't think I can talk about it. Sometimes, I get these memories coming back to me, things that a human being shouldn't ought to ever see."

"So, do you remember any students making a silencer?"

"Sure, but ask me if I remember his name and I can tell you no."

"Would you remember him if you saw him, a picture maybe?" Lester asked.

"Sure, that I could do," Mr. Connors said reluctantly.

"I'll come down to you. How about tomorrow night?"

"Sure, no problem. You've got my phone number; do you have my address? I'm not that far from Disneyland. You get to Disneyland; I'm a mile away towards downtown, near the high school."

Lester wrote down Mr. Connors' address and promised to meet him at his apartment at 7:00. He figured he could get an old yearbook from the school. He just had to hope that the guy had shown up for school on picture day. He'd have to bring a couple of years just to be sure he'd covered everyone.

When he was done writing up his notes from his call with Mr. Connors and updating his list of things he had to do, he pulled the phone cord so it stretched to his couch. His apartment was sparsely furnished, with few decorations. It wasn't that he wasn't interested, but he just didn't have the money. He hoped he could expense the long-distance call he'd just made.

His dining room set was bought new, which he was still paying off. The couch was something he'd found at the Goodwill. The cushions were fine and the fabric was in great condition. He'd only had to fix the legs, which were wobbly. The décor wasn't much and certainly not what Mary was used to, but he figured that once he got himself established, they'd have some money to decorate.

It was 8:55 when he called Mary's house, just within the time it acceptable to call.

"Nix residence," Mary's mother said.

"This is Lester. Can I speak with Mary please?"

"Whether or not you may speak with Mary is up to her. She's working on a paper."

"I promise not to take up much of her time,"

"A promise I expect you to keep," Mary's mother said sternly.

In the background, he could hear her mother call for her and Mary answer and come to the phone. There was no such thing as privacy on a phone call. The phone in Mary's house was in the kitchen and there was an extension in her dad's study, but she wasn't allowed to use it.

"Hi!" Mary said brightly. "How was your day?"

"Long, but I don't want to keep you. I just wanted to hear your voice before going to sleep. What are you doing a paper on?"

"We had to read *Argonauts of the Western Pacific*. It's about the Trobriand Islanders."

"Interesting?"

"It's sort of the founding of modern anthropology. Malinowski's second book is kind of scandalous, I can't even say its name," Mary whispered.

"Maybe you can tell me about when I see you again."

"Lester Patterson, you're making me blush," Mary whispered.

"You're making me blush too and I don't know what we're blushing about," Lester whispered.

"I've got to go, love you," Mary whispered.

"I can't see you tomorrow. I have to go down to Anaheim for a case."

"Then Wednesday, but definitely at the Spring Fling on Saturday."

Chapter 9

Lester woke up half an hour before his alarm rang. Lying in bed in the half-light, he thought about the case. The trip up to the Westside, to Factor's Deli, had turned up nothing but an excellent sandwich.

He was pretty sure that Angie at Hawthorne High would be able to rustle up the yearbooks he wanted. If that cost him a lunch, maybe a dinner, the price wouldn't be too high as long as he took her out to a place Mary or any of her friends would never ever spot them at. If all went well, he'd be able to get an ID from Gerald Connors on the guy who made the silencer and be back in time to call Mary.

Even if he got an ID that just meant that he knew the name of someone who had, years before, made a silencer. There was nothing in that to connect the silencer maker to the murder. He could have sold the silencer, thrown it away, put it in a drawer or taken it apart. Or, it could be a dead-end.

As he put on his robe and walked outside to collect his newspaper, he wondered if he had what it took to be a real detective. He'd put his eggs in one smaller, flimsy basket, but he didn't see many other avenues. There was the silencer. He could see if he could find out more from Steven's ex-girlfriend, Elizabeth. There was the Communist spy angle, which was a possibility. There were the plans and papers they'd found in Steven's trunk. Those hadn't been examined. The diary seemed to be a bust unless they could find someone who knew Hungarian.

The cover of the Los Angeles Times, below the fold, had an article titled "Communist Spy Ring Implicated in South Bay Murder." The article didn't name the source, but Lester knew it was Kappe. Who else could it be?

He was mad enough about the article to want to tear the paper to pieces, but restrained himself, counting to ten to keep his cool. He read the article and didn't see anything in it that was based on evidence. Kappe was hijacking the investigation, or he really knew what he was doing.

So far, Kappe had let him do his own thing, but that was only because he thought everyone but him was an idiot. The risk he was taking was that, despite everything, Kappe was right, like a stopped clock at just the right time of day.

Breakfast was a couple of English muffins and a cup of instant coffee. The Dodgers had lost but were ahead in the series. Everyone was raving about the new stadium, except for some of the people who'd been forced to move out of Chavez Ravine, where the stadium was built. Mary had talked about going to a game, but they hadn't yet scheduled it.

Kappe wasn't at the station when Lester got there before 8:00 a.m. and nobody had seen him. Lester walked down the street to the Hill Top Café but Kappe wasn't there. What a partner, Lester thought as he walked back into the station and Kappe still wasn't there. He left a note on Kappe's desk saying that he was out interviewing Elizabeth again and would probably be back before lunch.

It took about twenty minutes to get to Elizabeth's house through the fog until he went over the hill past the Nike Missile base and into Torrance. The sky cleared abruptly, and he had to turn down the visor to keep the morning sun out of his eyes.

He was lucky that Elizabeth was at home. Her dad had already gone off to work and her mom was in the kitchen cleaning up from breakfast.

"Sorry to bother you again," Lester said as Elizabeth led him into the house and they sat down in the living room.

"Would you like some coffee? I don't have much time before I have to go to work," Elizabeth said.

"That would be great but only if you have some ready. I don't want you to go to any trouble."

"Mom, coffee!" Elizabeth called out.

"I'm on it already!" her mom called out from the kitchen.

"Sorry about that," Elizabeth said.

"I'm sorry to bother you again, but I wanted to ask a few more questions." He wasn't sure where to begin so he looked about the living room. There was a needlepoint framed on the wall with a picture of an old man with a long beard looking over a scroll.

Elizabeth's mom brought in the coffee on a little tray. She was wearing a blue housecoat and slippers. "I can get you some milk if you want it. There's some sugar if you want."

"Thanks," Lester said, "I'll take it black, if you don't mind."

"Why would I mind?" Elizabeth's mom said. "He wasn't quite a mensch, but who could be with all that he'd gone through? A cursed life, if you ask me."

"Mom!" Elizabeth exclaimed.

"Can't I have an opinion? I liked him, what can I say. I was sad when you two broke up. I can understand why you did, but I was still sad."

"Why were you sad?".

"He was stable," Elizabeth said wistfully. "He was interesting, had that cute Hungarian accent going. He had a good job, not a doctor or a dentist or a lawyer, mind you, but he would have been a good provider. I know you need a spark. A spark is good at the start, but ask me in twenty-five years and two kids, if there's still a spark."

Her mom left the room and went back to the kitchen.

"What did you do together. . .on dates, I mean," Lester said.

"We used to go to the movies, foreign movies up near where he lived," Elizabeth said. She wiped tears from her eyes but began to smile as she reminisced. "He'd meet me after work and we'd drive me all the way up to the Westside or Santa Monica, then drive me all the way back home afterward. We'd stop at a deli. He liked artier movies than I did. He'd rather have symbolism than action. I'd rather have more of a story. He said he'd had enough real action in his life, which I can understand. He'd survived the Nazis. He'd survived the Communists and the Uprising. He just wanted to have a quiet life, raise a family and forget about the past. He loved my mom's goulash, but even still wanted her to make it a little different," Elizabeth said. She stopped to wipe her eyes.

"He didn't want it too spicy," her mom called out from the kitchen.

136

"On the weekend, he'd play soccer, pick-up games over at a park in Santa Monica."

"Soccer?" Lester asked.

"It's this the European game where they kick a ball a lot," Elizabeth said.

"I remember seeing it when I was stationed in Germany. Did he have a regular team?"

"I don't think so. When I went to watch him play once, it didn't seem like any of them really knew each other. They were from all over, Argentina, Mexico, England, Italy. Afterward, they'd just go home. I don't think they would really hang out afterward. Sometimes they couldn't even really talk to each other. They just somehow knew what to do," Elizabeth said.

She paused and sighed. "He told me that after the war, a day or so after the Germans left Budapest, they went back to their apartment and it was stripped bare. Even the wallpaper had been torn out. They'd hidden in the countryside near the Romanian and Ukrainian border and had managed to escape being sent to a concentration camp because the Russians advanced so quickly."

"What about after the war?"

"During the Uprising in '56, he said he was at a house they had on Lake Balaton outside of the city but his brother snuck back into Budapest and threw Molotov cocktails at the Russian tanks before he was arrested and they executed him. Steve thought his brother was pretty stupid but his parents were worried that he'd be marked too as an enemy of the state, so they arranged for him to escape to Austria."

"Do you think he was a Communist?" Elizabeth laughed. "Not a chance. He loved the

U.S. and was on his way to becoming a citizen. He wanted to marry me to speed up the process."

"But you didn't want to marry him," Lester said.

"I didn't and that's why I called it off. I enjoyed his company, but I just didn't see marrying him. He was super orderly, almost too orderly, definitely too orderly."

Elizabeth looked at her wet handkerchief and twisted it anxiously. "He had to have everything his way. If we went to see a movie I wanted to see but he didn't want to see, he'd say it was too comic booky and refuse to go. He'd say I could go see it and he'd wait around somewhere until it was over. He wanted me to learn Hungarian, which isn't the easiest language, because Hungarian was the most romantic language in the world, according to him. He said that he couldn't really tell me he loved me in English."

"Do you know anyone who speaks Hungarian? What about your parents?"

Elizabeth laughed. "No, just a couple of swear words."

"What about his job?" Lester asked.

"When I first met him, he seemed to love it, but over the last six months and especially after we broke up, he hated it. He said that they were idiots and cheats, but he couldn't tell me anything about it because it was secret."

"Did he have any friends from work?"

"Not that I know of. I never met any of them."

"Did he say anything about his bosses?"

"He hated them, but doesn't half the world hate their boss?" Elizabeth laughed but then began to sob.

"Probably," Lester said, trying not to smirk. "Do you know anyone who had a grudge against him?"

"No, he didn't know enough people for that to be a problem. I suppose the Communists wouldn't like him, but do you really think they'd come all the way over here to kill him?"

"There are a lot of refugees, especially Hungarian ones. They'd have a long list but I can't rule it out," Lester said.

"What if what he was working on was dangerous to them?" Elizabeth asked.

"But why him and not the whole company? He was just an engineer and the company fired him."

"Maybe they didn't know that," Elizabeth said.

"Yeah, maybe they didn't." Lester didn't like the speculation. He needed fewer avenues and not more. Actually, he needed the right one.

Before going to the station, Lester drove up Hawthorne Boulevard, past empty lots, tank farms, newly built shopping strips and housing developments, to Hawthorne High School. Angie was at her desk in the front office and smiled when she looked up and saw Lester.

"I was hoping you'd call last night, but this is even better, sunshine," Angie said as she got up from her desk and came over to the counter.

"Well, I knew I must have forgotten something," Lester said as he leaned across the counter and gave her a big smile.

"I hope it was me," Angie whispered.

"You? How can I forget you? What I forgot is that I need copies of yearbooks going back the last five years, if you can manage that."

"The last five years?" Angie frowned with disappointment.

"I wouldn't ask if it wasn't necessary. And, maybe we could go out sometime. I could take you to dinner."

"You don't have to take me to dinner. Come on over and I'll cook for you," Angie whispered.

Lester blushed. "It's hard when I'm on a case to keep to a schedule."

"A moment's notice. That's all I'd need," Angie said.

"I can get them back to you maybe as early as tomorrow, Friday at the latest when I bring back the yearbooks."

Lester left with the yearbooks, which were a heavy load in his arms, and a promise to set a date for dinner when he returned them. It wasn't a bad thing to think about. As he drove back to Hermosa Beach, along Artesia past dry cleaners, corner stores, donut shops and Mexican restaurants, and then left on Aviation up over the hill and then down past the middle school, he thought about all the possibilities.

He couldn't really afford a nice dinner. Some of the seafood places on the pier in Redondo Beach were classy but too close to home. All he needed was for one of Mary's friends to be there on a date too. Angie seemed very delicious, that was a step too far and he hoped that he was strong enough to resist taking that step because he was only human and with Mary they'd barely gone past appetizers.

Kappe wasn't at the station, but he'd left a message saying that he should meet him again at 4:00 p.m. near Factor's Delicatessen where they'd met last time and to be ready for a stakeout also that the diary was a bust. It had been translated and was just a lot of moaning about girl troubles and loneliness.

Lester groaned and thought about how he'd already arranged to go down to Orange County to meet with Mr. Connors. He called Mr. Connor's high school and left a message for him with the office that he wasn't going to be able to make it and that he would try again the next day.

It was only 11:00 a.m. It might be possible to drive down to Anaheim and then back up to West LA by 4:00 p.m. It was a fer piece, as his dad liked to say. Even if he could make it, there was no telling that Mr. Connors would have the time to look at the yearbooks. It wasn't worth the risk. Instead, he went to lunch, driving down Pier Avenue to the beach and having a taco burrito at the taco stand right on the Strand and across from the closed aquarium.

Hermosa Beach during the week was quiet, a small town like any other without a beach. The pier was closed and slated for demolition. The Biltmore Hotel, by far the tallest building for miles, was partially derelict, a once-grand resort with a saltwater plunge in the basement that never really took off. The bar that now hosted teen dances had been busted as an illegal casino only a few years before.

On the weekends, the town lit up, but not always in a good way, with bikers mixing with rodsters and the beatniks. The surfers kept earlier hours and were generally no problem. The morning fog was burning off and you could see as far as Catalina Island, down to the Palos Verdes Peninsula and up the coast to Malibu.

Hermosa didn't have any industry beyond surfboard manufacturing and no real purpose beyond housing the families of local aerospace workers. It could be a nice place to raise a family, Lester thought. He just needed a family to raise. You could get a house for pretty cheap. Even if it didn't have much of a yard and was so close to the houses next door that you could reach out your window to touch them, you had a view and good schools.

When he got back to the station, there was no sign of Kappe. He typed up his notes from that morning and the day before. He still didn't have a clue whether or not he was on the right track. Maybe it was the perfect crime and they'd never solve it. When he was done typing up his notes, the receptionist patched through a call for him from Gerald Connors.

Lester told Mr. Connors that he was sorry that he wouldn't be able to come down to Anaheim that night and wondered if he would be able to come by the next day. Mr. Connors said it was okay but told him that it would have to be early, between 4:00 and 6:00 p.m. because he had dinner plans that evening. Lester told him that he would be there between 4:00 and 5:00 p.m.

"By the way, do you know anything about engines?" Lester asked.

"I was a mechanic in the Army during the war. That's where I learned to be a machinist. We had to be able to make our own parts sometimes when the supply lines were disrupted. Why, do you got car trouble?"

"No, my car is running fine, knock on wood. I was just wondering if you could look over some plans for me and see if you can make any sense of them."

"I can give it a try, but I've got to be out of the house by 6:00."

"No problem, I've been neglecting my girlfriend too."

After speaking with Connors, Lester took all copies of the plans and technical papers found in Shawn's car, put them into a large manila folder and took placed them in a box in the trunk of his car next to the yearbooks, which he'd placed in doubled-up paper shopping bags. He had an hour to kill before he had to head up to West LA so he reviewed the crime scene photos and the rest of the evidence.

With a pistol in the dark, the killer had to have been close to hit him. He had to have known that Shawn would be there, unless it was a random killing, and that didn't seem likely since most murders are committed by people who know the victim.

His ex-girlfriend, Elizabeth, didn't seem a likely killer. Sure, Shawn was with another woman at the time he was killed, but jealousy didn't seem a likely motive unless she was a fantastic actress.

He knew guys who he hung out with at the deli, but why would they drive all the way down to the depths of the South Bay when they could more easily kill him near where they all lived?

A spy would kill him wherever he got the chance, so if that was the case, the location of his death had no importance.

His workplace was fairly near and he'd had a beef with his employers, but they'd fired him so there was no reason for them to kill him. They'd already won. That left a beef with one of the employees, but he had no evidence that there was a beef with any of them, except for his bosses.

If the spy angle didn't work out, then they'd have to interview his co-workers again. There was also the possibility that there was an aspect of his life that they didn't know about.

The Insomniac seemed a good place to meet chicks, especially ones who might be attracted to a guy with a foreign accent. There might be a drug angle but there wasn't any evidence of that even though The Insomniac was a den of drug dealers, junkies and potheads according to local lore.

Lester waited around the station for half an hour trying to think of something to do before he had to meet Kappe, but couldn't think of anything beyond berating himself for being such a lousy detective. On *Dragnet*, everything always fell into place with one clue leading to another and the crime solved with a confession and contrition.

While he was there, the cops came and went with no haste. They typed up their paperwork and handled calls from people annoyed at their neighbors. There were few robberies and most of the assaults happened on weekend nights. The only department that saw a lot of action was parking enforcement. They paid for the whole shebang, and not just the police department but a good part of the city government. Nevertheless, parking enforcement was on the bottom rung.

Lester called Mary's house and left a message with her mom that he wasn't going to be able to get together that evening, but wanted to know if she could go with him to see a concert at The Lighthouse the next night if she didn't have too much schoolwork. Mary's mom took the message. "Her schoolwork is important to her. I'll give her the message," she said and hung up before Lester had a chance to say it was important to him too.

He decided to take the coastal route, through Manhattan Beach and along Dockweiler State Beach. The wind was low and you could see Malibu clearly. The ocean was glassy and it looked like paradise at least until a plane flew overhead taking off from the airport.

By the time he got to West LA, it was only 2:00 so he stopped at Kelbo's, which was a Polynesian bar and restaurant with a large tower near the San Diego Freeway. He was only ten minutes, max, from his meet up with Kappe.

There were pulleys and barrels, colored glass balls covered in netting that probably served some practical purpose beyond decoration and a diving suit with a huge tarnished brass helmet that looked like it would sink you immediately to the bottom of the briny deep if you put it on.

Twangy, languid Hawaiian guitar music wafted through the restaurant and led him into the bar where there were three large fish tanks filled with colorful tropical fish.

The bartender was a burly man in a Hawaiian shirt with a buzz cut and an anchor tattoo on one bicep and a hula dancer tattoo handed Lester a large menu describing all the Polynesian drinks decorated with cartoons of surfers chasing after bare-breasted Hawaiian girls.

Lester looked around at the other customers, who were drinking their cocktails out of ceramic skull bowls and hollowed out coconuts. "Can you recommend something?" he asked the bartender.

"Depends on what you have planned for the rest of the afternoon," the bartender said.

"I can't get too toasted," Lester said.

"I suggest one of our 'tropkol' drinks with our special blend of tropical fruit juices. I can go light on the rum if you want. Normally you should probably call a cab after having one at full strength."

"Yeah, go light. Surprise me." Lester couldn't see what was going into his drink and was soon handed a drink in a tall brown tiki-shaped glass with a little umbrella hanging perched on top. "So what's this?"

"It's a mystery," the bartender said and then paused. "That's the name of the drink. If I told you what was in it, the boss would have to kill me. Can I get you anything to eat?"

"No, I'm fine," Lester said before taking a sip of the drink through the straw. "Mmmm, that's great. I could see how you could get into a lot of trouble with one of these."

"Getting into trouble's the easy part. It's the getting out that's tricky. We've got a plastic-covered couch in the back for the extreme cases."

"Ain't that the truth. I'm liable to have a long night ahead of me, so I hope you went easy on the lighter fluid. A drink like this and you can't tell you've tied one on until you fall off the stool."

"Don't worry, I went light on the joy juice. You should be good to go."

Lester could barely taste any rum. Mostly he tasted pineapple juice and lime. He sipped the drink and stared at the wild décor. He didn't feel wobbly at all as he walked to his car and was able to get to his rendezvous with Kappe a few minutes early.

He waited in the car for the first ten minutes but when Kappe didn't show up, he got out of the car and looked up and down the block, then down at his watch. The street was quiet except for the sprinklers watering the lawn of a house halfway down the block. It was a quarter after when Kappe pulled up in his car, scraping his hubcaps against the high concrete curb.

"You're late!" Kappe growled as he stepped out of his car and then went over to the curb to check for damage to his car.

"I've been here for almost half an hour," Lester groused.

"Keep your pants on," Kappe said as he looked at the scratches to his hubcap. "You're probably wondering why I've gathered us here today. Well, we've got a meet up with Agent Joe Biggs, one of J. Edgar's finest."

A late-model sedan sped down the street causing Lester and Kappe to jump out of the way. Just as it reached them, the driver screeched to a halt then rolled down his window. "You Kappe from the HBPD?" the man asked. He was dressed in a dark, double-breasted suit and wore a black fedora straight out of the thirties.

"You almost killed us," Lester said.

Agent Biggs scowled and then grinned. "Life's not a bowl of cherries. You want to survive, you've got to have brains and fast reflexes."

"We heard you coming," Kappe said.

Biggs got out of his car without bothering to park it, blocking half the street. Leaning against his car, he unbuttoned his jacket and adjusted his tie.

"What we're going to do is follow this Manny Hess guy, who may or may not be a Communist agent, and see who he meets," Biggs said. "Since he knows you two but doesn't know me, I'll tail him in the deli. When he comes out, you'll follow him in your car and I'll catch up with you. I've got a change of clothes and a couple of disguises so I can go incognito. Since he already knows you, just stay out of sight. I've got a couple of mustaches in the trunk and a wig or two. You'd be surprised what you can get away with. Unless you're a hot chick, a guy isn't going to pay much attention to you at a glance, so if we get into a situation, stay cool and don't draw attention to yourselves."

"We'll use my car," Kappe said.

Lester checked the parking signs on the block to see what the parking restrictions were then locked his car.

"I've got a couple of bags of peanuts in the car in case we get hungry, a couple of canteens filled with fresh water and a thermos filled with Joe," Kappe said.

Biggs got back into his car and drove the couple of blocks past Factor's and was able to park down the street from the entrance.

When Lester opened the passenger door of Kappe's Ford Fairlane, Kappe leaned over and brushed off the peanut shells from the car seat and tossed a newspaper into the back. The car smelled rancid, like someone had spilled some milk and hadn't completely cleaned it up.

Kappe pulled away from the curb as soon as Lester closed the door, did a quick three-point turn and sped down half a block to the corner of Pico Boulevard. The whole time they waited for a break in the traffic so they could cross the street, Kappe swore in German under his breath. When he got his chance, Kappe tore out across the street then found a place to park half a block short of Factor's. They had a great view of the deli's entrance but were far enough away that the chances were small that they would be noticed.

They sat silently for an hour while they waited for something to happen but nothing notable did. People walked down the street. Cars in front of them and behind them and then left. Kappe turned on the radio and they listened to Vin Scully call an inning of the Dodger's game. After another half an hour, they saw Hess stroll out of the deli, picking at his teeth with a toothpick, and walk to his car.

Hess got into his car and drove east on Pico. Kappe pulled out into traffic, nearly causing an accident, and followed Hess. As they passed Factor's, Lester waved to Biggs as he exited the deli. Biggs nodded and jogged backed to his car.

It was rush hour, so traffic was heavy. They never made it through a block without being caught by a light. Fortunately, Hess kept in sight. At Fairfax, Hess turned left and drove north, past the May Company department store, the Farmer's Market and CBS Television City.

Hess parked across the street from Canter's Delicatessen. Lester got out of the car and crossed the street to Canter's as Kappe found parking up the block. As he crossed the street, he saw Biggs drive past and make a U-turn in the middle of the block to snag a parking space near Canter's entrance.

Biggs strode up to Lester, who stood near Canter's entrance. "The mandel bread this place turns out can't be beat," Biggs said. He'd ditched the fedora and suit jacket for a dark sweater and a flat cap.

"What happened at Factor's?" Lester asked.

"He ate a sandwich and talked with his usual crowd. Have you tried their corned beef?" Biggs said.

"At Factor's?" Kappe asked.

"No, here. It's New York good."

"I've never been here," Kappe said.

"You hungry?" Biggs asked.

Kappe shook his head and looked to Lester.

"Sure," Lester said.

"Then put this on," Biggs said, taking a fake mustache from out of his pocket.

Lester pealed the backing tape off the mustache and attached it to his upper lip, using a window as a mirror to make sure it was straight. "How do I look?"

"Your mom wouldn't recognize you."

Lester smiled and had to reattach the mustache, which had come loose on one side. Biggs led them into Canter's. There was a large bakery case just to the left of the entrance.

"Can you see them?" Biggs asked.

"He's in the back with three other guys. They're having soup. Should we get a table?"

"Yeah, hopefully one near enough to catch their drift."

"You think they'll notice us?" Lester asked as they were shown to a table too far to listen to what Hess and his buddies were saying, but close enough to see what they were eating.

Hess was with two other men, both dressed in slacks and white short-sleeved shirts, not ties. They were trying carefully to eat their matzo ball soup, trying not to splatter their shirts and ties with hot chicken broth.

Biggs ordered the corned beef while Lester ordered the pastrami.

"The pastrami's good but you're missing out with the corned beef. You can have some of mine if you want. So, I'll let you in on what we're seeing," Biggs said, sotto voce. "Manny Hess is a smalltime operator, basically a go-between. He's got ties to the mob and to organized labor. Given that the labor he's organizing is Hollywood unions, we're thinking that there might be a connection to the Communists, but we're not sure. He flits about town talking to people, mostly movie people. He shows them papers and they never seem to bite. We're pretty sure it's a ruse, maybe a numbers game."

"Do you think this has anything to do with the murder we're investigating?"

"Well, it may or it may not. It's possible that Shawn was working for the Commies, but it also could be that he owed someone some big-time money."

"He didn't seem to be a gambler or have expensive tastes. His ex-girlfriend didn't think he had any enemies except for maybe at the company he worked for."

"That's where it gets interesting," Biggs said. "Averodyne is a defense contractor, the kind that's got sensitive information that we can't go letting the Communists get ahold of."

"So, you think that Shawn was passing information to Hess?" Lester asked.

"The truth is, we don't know. It could be that they were just friends. But isn't it interesting that Shawn, supposedly an anti-Communist, should be hanging out with a possible Communist, or at least a fellow traveler."

"So, why would they kill him?" Lester asked.

"Who?"

"The Communists, if he was their guy," Lester said.

The waitress brought them their sandwiches, the meat piled high between slices of rye.

"Do you want your pickle?" Biggs asked.

"Nah, you can have it," Lester said, putting his pickle onto Biggs' plate.

"We don't know that he was their guy. Maybe he didn't know that Hess was bent that way or the Commies were holding his family hostage to get him to spy."

"This is pretty confusing."

"Welcome to my world. Can you see what they're doing?" Biggs asked.

"It looks like they are splitting the check."

"Damn, maybe I can get them to wrap up my sandwich. By the way, dinner's on the Bureau."

Lester left while Biggs settled the bill. Hess stopped at the bakery counter and bought three poppy seed hamentaschen while the others went out the front door. Lester didn't know what to do, whether he should stay with Hess or follow the others. Afraid of being spotted, Lester followed the others out the front door. He could see them casually stroll down the street, stopping to peer into a Judaica shop. Kappe was down the block pretending to browse the magazines at the newsstand on the corner.

Kappe nodded to Lester, put the magazine he'd been holding away, and followed the two guys as they walked down the street and got into an old Cadillac that didn't look so grand anymore, with the paint faded and some dents in the bumper. There was no chance of following them and Lester couldn't figure out why they were interested in them in the first place.

"What'd you see in there?" Kappe asked.

"Some guys having soup and talking," Lester said.

"Looks can be deceiving. There are a lot of ways to pass information. Maybe they slurped in Morse code."

Lester was exasperated. "We don't even know if they have any information. They could've been talking sports. They could just be catching up on their families."

"Don't you think it's queer that Hess, who just ate dinner, stops by here too, again, have dinner?"

"Maybe he was still hungry? He just had soup,"

"It was a meeting," Kappe declared, as if that was enough to end the conversation.

As Kappe, Lester and Biggs were talking, Hess walked past them, not noticing them, and stopped at the newsstand to buy a racing form. Kappe and Lester turned their backs to him and walked slowly down the street away from Hess, all the while pretending to catch up on a long-lost cousin. Biggs came up to them and pretended to ask the time but actually was whispering that the other two men worked props at one of the Gower Gulch Studios.

While Hess walked back to his car, which was parked down the street on Fairfax, Kappe and Biggs went to their cars and Lester pretended to tie his shoe. As Hess pulled out and drove up Fairfax, Kappe was right behind him in his car. As they waited for the light, Lester climbed. Meanwhile, Biggs was right behind them in his car.

Hess turned onto Melrose Avenue. When he reached Paramount Studios, he stopped across the street and honked his horn. A good-looking blond in a tight red dress dashed as best she could in heels through traffic and across the street. He turned left on Western Boulevard and then right on Hollywood Boulevard finally parking just off of Vermont Avenue.

From where they were parked, Lester and Kappe could see Hess help the young woman out of the car and lead her around the corner, down the street and into the Dresden, a swank bar and filet chateaubriand and filet mignon restaurant.

"Do we follow them in?" Lester asked.

"Stupid question!" Kappe growled. "Of course we do. I always wanted to go to the Dresden."

"Are we even dressed for it?"

"For the bar, we should be okay."

As they were talking, they saw Biggs pull up in his car and park behind them. "In the Dresden?" Biggs asked when he got out of his car.

"None other," Kappe said.

"Give me a minute," Biggs said then returned to his car. A couple of minutes later, he returned wearing a grey sharkskin suit and a skinny tie.

"Sharp," Kappe said.

"I'm going in. You two wait outside and hold down the fort." Biggs strode down the block and entered the Dresden.

"Class act all the way," Kappe said.

They waited for two hours before Biggs came out of the Dresden. "They're still in there having the time of their lives. They've barely touched their filet mignons. Total waste because the Dresden makes a choice mignon. Meanwhile, I'm at the bar sipping on a beer and eating the peanuts. And they say crime doesn't pay."

"You're telling me," Kappe said.

"Are we chaperoning his date?" Lester asked. "Or is there anything serious going on there?"

Biggs laughed. "She sure doesn't look like his mother."

"Or my mother," Kappe said. "Anyway, it's only just past 9:00. The night is young.

"Look, I can't go in there again or they'll make me. One of you has to go in," Biggs said.

"I nominate Lester," Kappe said.

Lester blushed. "My wallet is getting a little light. How much is a drink going to cost?"

"You can charge it to the department," Kappe said as he took out his wallet and handed Lester a

Diner's Club card. "I'll approve the expense. If you've never had a filet mignon, now is the time to try one. And take off that mustache, it's crooked."

Lester pulled off the mustache and put it into his pants' pocket. Kappe gave Lester a new tie to wear and the double-breasted jacket he'd been wearing earlier, which looked odd with Lester's pants.

"Don't worry about the pants," Biggs said. "It's dark and nobody's going to notice."

Lester strode from the car to the Dresden as if he belonged anywhere he wanted to go. He swung the heavy door open and entered the bar. It took a moment for his eyes to adjust to the dim light. He looked around and didn't see Hess or his girl.

There was a piano player in one corner playing standards trumped up with filigreed embellishments, as if he'd studied under Liberace. Instead of heading to the bar to get a drink, he strode past the tables of sharply dressed couples canoodling over martinis and manhattans to the entrance to the restaurant.

He peeked around the corner and saw a wonderland of suavity. The Dresden's restaurant was exactly the kind of place you'd take Marilyn Monroe if you wanted to impress her and she wasn't on a diet. The restaurant had white leather banquets that enveloped the customers creating almost private spaces. Manny and his girl were at a banquet halfway across the room sipping champagne and eating peach melbas.

They didn't see him, or at least he didn't think so because it seemed they only had eyes for each other. He retreated to the bar and ordered a Tuborg. Normally he didn't spring for imported beers but this night seemed special and it was on J. Edgar Hoover. He sat at the bar facing the restaurant and hoped that there was only the one entrance. The Tuborg tasted nicer than he'd expected and leaps and bounds better than what he normally drank.

By the time he was done with the beer, about half an hour later, Hess and his girl came out of the restaurant. Hess was holding her so close that they seemed to be one person with four legs. Lester figured that they hadn't been going out for too long because of the way they were all over each other. He couldn't help but feel jealous. Mary was very pretty but he'd never seen her dressed so glamorously nor had she ever attached herself to him the way Hess' girl was doing. That level of affection in a public place would have caused Lester to blush. He blushed just watching them and had to loosen his tie.

A second after they exited to the street, Lester got off the barstool and followed them. As he opened the door, he saw them standing just away from the door, embracing and flagrantly kissing. He tried not to stare as he walked past and back to Sam's car, but of course, staring, at least surreptitiously, was integral to his job.

When Hess and his girl drove off, Lester, Kappe and Biggs followed them. Kappe seemed to think that tailing meant being on their tail. Sure, you wouldn't lose them, but then they couldn't miss you. Hess either didn't notice, and with a girl like that what else was worth paying attention to, or didn't care.

They followed Hess through Hollywood and into West Hollywood. Hess pulled into a small apartment building, the kind with parking on the first floor and the apartments above. Hess and the girl got out and managed to make it up the stairs slowly. They were so closely entwined that it was like watching a slow-motion three-legged race.

Once they'd gone up the stairs, Biggs pulled his car up alongside Kappe's and rolled down the window. "Are they in for the night or is he driving her home and going out again?"

"I'd spend the night," Kappe said.

"Are we going to watch them the whole night?" Lester asked.

Kappe and Biggs looked at Lester as if he was a simpleton. "You got a better idea?"

"He's spending the night. I don't want to seem jealous, but my lonely, empty bed is calling my name."

Kappe turned to Lester and scowled. "This is part of the job!" Kappe said angrily. "We follow the leads and go where they take us. Maybe nothing happens. Maybe we're wasting our time, but then again maybe he gets another visitor or he goes out again. You never know what's going to happen. If you're missing your beauty rest, then you can just go find yourself a cab and high tail it back to your car and home. Just don't expect to be anything more than a meter maid."

"Okay, fine, I'm staying."

They stayed the night, the two of them sleeping in shifts. Each time, as soon as Lester fell asleep, he was woken by Kappe. The lights in what they assumed to be Hess' apartment turned off soon after they arrived but were briefly turned on an hour later.

When the sun rose, they got out of the car and stretched their legs. Lester's had fallen asleep. He hadn't gotten more than four hours of sleep and none of it consecutive. He was beginning to smell, but not half as bad as Kappe, who somehow was chipper and seemed refreshed.

Hess left at a decent hour, presumably after breakfast and coffee, with his girl. They followed him as he drove her to Paramount Studios and then went off to his job, at a film processing company off of Melrose.

Over eggs, bacon, home fries and coffee at a coffee shop, Biggs said that he'd continue having Hess tailed and he'd see about tapping his phone. If he found anything, he'd let them know.

As they drove back to West LA, where Lester had left his car, Kappe complained about Lester's amateurism, telling him that he'd carried his water for too long and if he didn't shape up he'd send him back down to writing parking tickets. Lester nodded and took the abuse in silence. He'd only been on the case for four days. He felt like a kid again with his dad pestering him about not doing some chore to his liking.

When he got back to his apartment, he showered, shaved and changed his clothes, then drove to the station. It was hard for him to keep awake at his desk.

☐

Chapter 10

Back at the station, Lester tried to focus on the case but he was so beat and he'd drunk so much coffee that he spent half his time in the john, not relieving himself so much as not having the energy to stand up.

In between coffee refills and long bathroom breaks, he went through the phone book and called machine shops to see if anyone there knew anyone who had made their own silencer or who knew how to make a silencer. He mostly got a pause and then a curt "no." Some of them he had to assure he wasn't pranking them so they wouldn't hang up.

By lunchtime, he'd called all but a handful of the machine shops in the South Bay, from the El Segundo to Wilmington to Hawthorne and Carson. A few took him seriously and said they'd ask around and get back to him or suggested other types of businesses he could call. With the aircraft and now the aerospace industry, there was a lot of call for machinists. It was a giant task.

Even if he called all the possible places, factories such as McDonnell Douglas, Northrop and Hughes had hundreds of machinists and there was no way that he was going to be able to talk to everyone who might possibly know something. Then there were the auto parts places and the specialty shops not to mention Mattel, which must have a machinist or two.

To clear his head, he walked down to the pier to find some lunch. Kappe hadn't shown up and there was no telling what direction he'd send him. As he walked down Pier Avenue and then down the hill towards the beach, he wondered if he was any closer to solving the case. It didn't feel that way. The case felt as clear as the fog that settled in every evening. If there was some obvious angle that he hadn't pursued, he was too thick or inexperienced to recognize it.

Maybe Kappe had a better handle. He hoped that was the case because if they were both lost then the case was never going to close and he was going to be back writing parking tickets. If it came to that, he'd try to find a job at another, larger department or try another line of work.

He thought about the guy with the Union 76 station shirt at the Poop Deck who had mentioned the shop class. There couldn't be more than half a dozen Union 76 stations in a five-mile radius. If he went to each one, maybe he could find the guy and show him the yearbook pictures. If that didn't work, he still had Mr. Connors.

Driving all the way down to Anaheim and back was a slog he wasn't looking forward to. Hopefully, he'd be back in time to go out with Mary, assuming he could set it up. If only they'd hurry up and finish the freeways. There'd be smooth sailing from the desert to the sea and all the rest of Southern California.

He grabbed a burger at the Foster's Freeze down the block from where Shawn had hit the curb. The street wasn't much to look at. There was a small, one-story apartment building and a couple of tiny houses. The blood had been washed away and it looked like nothing bad had happened there.

He walked for a few blocks north on the Strand. Bicyclists rode slowly past. There weren't many people on the beach. The only time the beach was full was on a summer weekend or the Fourth of July. It wasn't ever like the pictures of Coney Island or the Jersey Shore, with people covering every spot from the boardwalk to the waterline. Hermosa was a beach town but not much of a beach resort. Often, there were more people at night, going to the bars and clubs, than sunning themselves during the day. As always, there were surfers catching the modest waves.

Back at the station, Lester compiled all the addresses and phone numbers of 76 stations from El Segundo to Torrance and had plotted them out on a map. With any luck, the guy he'd met at the Poop Deck was working that day and at one of the local stations and not at the refinery in El Segundo, between Manhattan Beach and the airport.

Before heading out, he called Mary. She had just gotten back from school and was fixing herself a bowl of cottage cheese with fruit cocktail. She asked how he was and he told her about spending the night sitting in a car on a stakeout he couldn't say anything more about. She'd gotten a good night's sleep even though she should have stayed up cramming for an Ancient history test she'd had that morning.

"I've got to go down to Anaheim," Lester said, "but I should be back in the early evening. Can we get together, maybe see if there's something on at The Lighthouse? I didn't get much shuteye last night but, hey, isn't that why coffee was invented?"

"I'd love to," Mary said. "I've missed you, but I've got to see how my reading goes and I've got a paper I've got to start on. Come by when you get back if it's not too late. I'm really looking forward to Saturday."

I hope I don't embarrass you. I don't know how good I'm going to be at lawn bowling."

"Just don't mess up the turf. That's all they really care about. Don't wear any shoes with any nubs. You could spill red wine all over some woman's white dress and that would go over better than creating a divot."

"You've got me scared."

Mary laughed and told him not to worry. She was an ace and, as long as he was on her team, he'd do okay. "It's really how you look not how well you do. It's a party, not a tournament. You've got something to wear, right?"

"I've got that covered."

Kappe showed up, shuffling to his desk. His eyes bloodshot and his breath smelling of whisky.

"I've got to go," Lester said quickly. "See you tonight. Love you."

"Love you back," Mary said.

"Yeah, I'm a sight for sore eyes," Kappe grumbled as he stretched and flopped down in his chair. He squirmed around his chair looking pained.

"You okay?" Lester asked.

"Hemorrhoids," Kappe whispered. "Low level. They flare up sometimes. I've got to cut back on Mexican food and stakeouts. Last night was a rough one."

"I'm getting closer to finding out the guy who made the silencer. I'm going to be out the rest of the day. You're not going to need me are you?"

"Unless you've got some hemorrhoid cream on you," Kappe said. He laughed, then grimaced. "I'll be fine. I think I've got some in my locker. Just report back to me tomorrow morning."

Lester was glad to leave the station behind. Before joining the force, he imagined a wonderful camaraderie straight out of a TV show, instead, he'd gotten an angrier and crankier *Dragnet*. *Dragnet* with a sore butt.

When he'd been working as a meter maid, he'd had buddies. He didn't know any of the guys on the day shift well. The two Johns were all right, guys you could have a beer with after work if you didn't work the night shift.

There were a couple of local coffee shops cops hung out at for breakfast but he was usually so bushed he barely made it home in one piece. He'd never been much of a night owl. Since he'd switched to days, he hadn't seen them.

The meterers working the day shift gave him dirty looks, the kind that you get when the girl that everyone likes goes out with you instead of them. It was a how-the-fuck-do-you-rate kind of glare.

It took him an hour to cover the 76 stations from Hermosa Beach, Manhattan Beach and north to El Segundo with no luck. He hadn't spent much time in El Segundo a small town between Manhattan Beach and an oil refinery to the south, the airport to the north, a water treatment plant to the west and Hawthorne to the east. It was a place a lot of people drove through on Sepulveda and never thought of beyond the oil refinery.

He drove east into Lawndale, which was so much like Hawthorne just to the west that you couldn't hardly tell the difference. There were blocks of modest houses a little bit more modest than those in Hermosa and Manhattan. The guy he was looking for wasn't at any of the stations there or in Redondo Beach past the new TRW aerospace facility, which looked like a modernist college campus with a factory attached.

He pulled into a station in Torrance and the attendant who filled his tank, washed his windows and checked his fluids was the guy from the Poop Deck, he was sure of it.

"Do you got a minute?" Lester asked.

"Sure, I know you right?" the man asked.

"Yeah, I'm with the Hermosa Beach police. I talked with you at the Poop Deck."

"Yeah, sure, right? Did you catch the guy yet?"

"We're working it. If you have a minute, I'd like you to look at some pictures and see if you can identify the guy you said made the silencer back when you were in high school."

"As long as you don't mind being interrupted. I've got customers to attend to, so I'll have to fit it in. You paying cash or charge?"

"Cash."

When his tank was filled, Lester pulled over to the side of the station, next to the service bay, and parked. There were a lot of customers, so his conversation didn't go more than thirty seconds between interruptions.

The attendant hadn't gone to Hawthorne high school, but he knew the guy from the rodster clubs that would cruise Hermosa on the weekends.

Lester showed him the yearbooks, but had to flip through the pages because the guy's hands were so greasy. As they went through the yearbooks, he spotted an ex-girlfriend who was still pissed off at him and some buddy who had died crashing his car in some stunt that everyone had tried to talk him out of. When they found the guy he'd talked about it turned out to be Johnny Cheam. Cheam had a huge, I own the world, smile for his senior year picture. The caption underneath said Cheam wasn't going far but would get there quickly.

"You sure it's him?" Lester asked.

"I'd swear on it!" the attendant said. "Everybody in the rodster world knows Johnny because Johnny makes sure you know him. He could teach the devil to brag. Most of what he says people don't take seriously, but then his dad's got money. They're in the selling shit to the government game. That's the game the smart guys are in. Honest guys like me, we just keep our heads down and hope to own something of our own. A friend of mine wants me to go in with him on a Japanese car business. Would you buy a Japanese car?"

"I generally stick to Detroit. But I'd love to have a slick English sports car," Lester said.

"I've seen some of these Japanese cars at a car show. If you ask me, if they can get over their poor reputation they could be as popular as Volkswagens. Their prices are good, but who's going to buy one something with 'Made in Japan' on it?"

"I've got one of those new transistor radios. I like the one I've got," Lester said.

After another couple of customers, Lester got the man's name, address and phone number, Jeff Martino. He lived with his folks in Lawndale, a town next to Hawthorne that even locals weren't too sure exactly where it began and Hawthorne, Torrance and Redondo Beach, ended.

It was a quarter after three when he finished talking with Mr. Martino. The only time he'd driven to Anaheim was when he and Mary had just started dating and he took her to Disneyland. It had taken an hour, but that had been on a weekend. He'd been down to Buena Park, which was just before you got to Anaheim, a couple of times to have a chicken dinner with all the fixings at Knott's. From Buena Park, he'd consult his Thomas Guide after that to get him to the address Connors had given him.

Out past Torrance and into Wilmington, the refineries and vast tank farms reminded him of Taft. Further out, as he passed through Hawaiian Gardens and neared Buena Park and the Orange County line, the farms, but not the new housing tracts, reminded him of the San Joaquin Valley. A guy could spread out in a place like that instead of being all cramped up like the rest of LA.

The California of surfers and movie stars wasn't his California. He was from the California of roughnecks and grape, orange, plum and almond growers where it hardly rained but there was plentiful water thanks to the canals of the Central Valley Water Project. All of that was also why he couldn't wait to leave. He'd gotten tired of the excitement of watching the oil wells bop up. Sure, he'd yet to find a good Basque restaurant but in LA, you had everything else.

Before moving to LA, the only thing he knew about Orange County was that they grew oranges there and Walt Disney had opened up his Magic Kingdom. When it opened, he begged his parents to take him, but he knew that wasn't going to happen. It was too expensive. It was too far.

There were carnivals that came through the area a couple of times a year and then there was the big one, the Kern County Fair. His family always went to that and his dad would buy him and his brother and sister long strips of ride tickets.

People moved out there for the good schools and the fresh air. The air was certainly fresher than the San Fernando Valley but the county was gaining a reputation for super-conservative politics. Behind the Orange Curtain, it was not quite jokingly referred to as. A land of ticky tacky houses on meandering streets that led to nowhere.

Connors' apartment was in an old section of Anaheim. There were orange and lemon trees in people's backyards and many of the houses were not just pre-war but pre-First World War. The building was nice enough. It was three stories and brick. Though it looked solid enough, one good quake might take it down. It wasn't shabby but it certainly wasn't a choice address. It was hard to imagine what had led him out of Hawthorne and down to Anaheim. It certainly wasn't the pay.

Standing outside carrying the heavy yearbooks in a double-bagged paper shopping sack, he buzzed the apartment. Connors came down a couple of minutes later and let him in the door.

"You find it all right?" Connors said. He was dressed for going out, with his hair slicked back. All that was missing was a tie and a jacket. It certainly wasn't how Lester imagined a machine shop teacher would go to work. He was in his mid-forties, tall and muscular. His hair was so closely cropped on the sides that it was hard to tell if he was greying.

"Yeah, I found it fine," Lester said. "The traffic gets worse every year."

"Well, once the freeway system is complete, it'll be a breeze. It's going to open up the whole Southland," Connors said as he led him upstairs and then down a dark hallway. "Sorry for the mess, and I can't talk for long. I've got a date."

"Hopefully this won't take too long."

When they got to the door, Connors paused and said, "It isn't much, but the price is right," before unlocking the door and leading him into the apartment. "I like a place that I can do some work on."

The apartment was large, with a living room, a kitchen in another room and even a hallway leading to a couple of bedrooms. The furniture was so sleek and modern that it looked like he'd bought it in Denmark. If there was a mess, it must be that the books were out of alphabetical order or publication date.

The coffee table was covered in art and design books, and a small table against the wall that a collection of little metal pieces that looked like parts for a motor or some sort of machinery. On the walls, there were photos of classical sculptures, mostly men, and a print of Greek or Roman wrestlers.

"What I'd like you to do, Mr. Connors, is to look through these yearbooks and identify, if you can, the student that made a silencer in your shop class. We're not interested in the silencer, per se, but we are interested in identifying the person who made it. Do you think you can do that?"

"Yes, I think I can. You know, some teachers are real good about remembering their kids' names. I've never been good with names. That sure wasn't me, but I can remember their faces. Before we get started, can I get you something, tea, coffee?"

"No thanks. It's a long drive back."

"Don't I know it," Connors said as they sat down on the sofa and Lester took out the yearbooks from the shopping bag and laid them out on the coffee table.

Connors moved away a stack of Charles Atlas exercise books to make way for the yearbooks. "Just trying to keep in shape. Do you work out? You look like you might work out."

"Just some sit-ups when I get the chance. Okay, let's start with the latest and go backwards from there."

Connors leaned back and started flipping through the book, stopping to comment on the students and teachers in the photos. Lester nudged him along from time to time but Connors would get off course and reminisce. He spoke fondly of his students and teachers and sarcastically about the staff and principal.

"That's the real evil genius," Connors said, pointing to the vice principal, a middle-aged man with a short-sleeved white shirt and a pocket protector filled with pens. "The man behind the mask who's not what he seems."

"Why don't we just continue looking through the yearbooks?"

"And I thought we were having a wonderful time," Connors said liltingly.

Finally, Connors pointed to Johnny Cheam.

"That's the guy!" Connors said excitedly. "Definitely, that was him. I had to throw him out of the class. I've never met a guy so cocky, well, almost never. He acted like he owned the world, always throwing his money around. He had a nice hot rod, something the guys in shop would drool over but couldn't afford on their own. He was a pretty good machinist too. Johnny Cheam, Johnny Wayne Cheam. He was a hundred percent convinced he was the star of his own movie, but really he was just some punk kid with a chip on his shoulder and a dad who could afford a healthy supply of chips."

"Are you sure it was him?" Lester asked, trying to seem excited.

"Damn, sure, if you don't mind my language. Just between the two of us, if you'd just told me that you wanted to pin something on Johnny Fucking Cheam, I could have saved you the drive."

"That's not how we do things, Mr. Connors."

"He was so proud when he brought that silencer in. He did so many things that they all kind of run together like the worst kind of diarrhea. He brought it in and showed it off to everybody, even took it apart and showed everyone how he made it. I took it away from him, dismantled it and threw away the pieces."

"So, he didn't get to keep it?" Lester asked.

"Hell no! I was in enough trouble," Connors said angrily. "The last thing I needed was to have that pinned on me. Get the FBI involved."

"Do you think he made another?"

"Hard to say. If he's got the right tools and equipment; it's not really that complicated a project. He certainly had the know-how."

"Thank you very much, Mr. Connors. You've been very helpful. If we need to talk with you again, can I reach you at the same number?"

"Absolutely. And if you want to just call and talk, please feel free." He stood up and Lester his hand.

"Oh, and there's one other thing," Lester said. "I've got some copies of plans for what we believe is an aircraft part. Would you mind looking at them and see if you can make any sense of them?"

Lester took out the plans from a folder and handed them to Connors.

Connors stared at the plans. They were smaller and less clear than the originals, but the details were still mostly clear. "It's too bad these aren't larger."

After studying the plans for a while, Connors looked up. "They're for a flange for a jet engine, but you can tell that the title of the plans. It doesn't look that special but then I don't work on jet engines. Also, a lot of really special stuff is pretty simple. The hard part is figuring them out in the first place."

Lester looked at his watch, it was about 5:30 p.m. "Anyway, thanks for everything. I can find my way out." He collected the yearbooks and put them back in the shopping bag as quickly as he could. "I'm trying to meet up with my girlfriend. She hates it when I keep her waiting."

"Well, nice to meet you anyway. I'm glad the trip down was worth it," Connors said sadly.

The drive back to Hermosa Beach was long. He went the same way only stopping at Knott's for a chicken dinner. He picked up a couple of jars of boysenberry jam, one for himself and one for Mary's mom. He didn't have time for the Old West Town or any of the attractions like the stagecoach ride or the mine train, but he wished he had. They reminded him of all the westerns he used to watch in the summer at the Fox. He could ride his bike there, escape the heat, and pig out on candy. He liked the singing cowboys, like Tex Ritter and Gene Autry, best.

It was after 7:00 p.m. when he got back to his apartment. He made himself some coffee to try to keep awake. The lack of sleep was catching up with him so he showered cold and changed into some cleanish clothes then typed his notes. He was too tired to go into the station and was afraid that he was going to be too out of it to be much company.

He set up his portable typewriter at the end of this small dining room table. There was just enough space for four, but he only had three chairs and only two of them matched. He tried to concentrate to figure out what to say beyond just typing up his notes.

Maybe it was just a coincidence that Johnny Cheam had made a silencer and had a beef with Steven Shawn. Was it a coincidence? If that was all he had that wasn't going to be enough to hold a case together unless they could find the gun. He hoped that was enough to search Cheam's place, maybe his dad too, but he was pretty certain it wasn't.

The Cheams were bigwigs and if he was wrong it could cause problems for him. He needed more. They didn't even have a motive. They fired him, which was plenty, and maybe they even had a good reason to do so. They could be jerky bosses and Shawn could also have been a bad employee. The two weren't exclusive.

There was also the issue of the plans. If the plans in Shawn's car were secret, he shouldn't have them, especially since he didn't work there anymore. The Cheams didn't seem to know about the plans or they would have been asking about them. They could even be a side project that Shawn was moonlighting on. The spy angle was the obvious angle. He couldn't fault Kappe for that though the stakeout had seemed pointless, but then maybe it was too much to expect to have things fall into place quickly like they did on TV.

He called Mary's house and got her dad, at first, but then quickly Mary took over the phone. "How was class?" Lester asked.

"Good," Mary said. "I'm free tonight. I've done all my homework."

"It makes it sound like I'm going out with a high school student."

"I was a year ago. Are you blushing? I think I can hear it in your voice. But what else am I supposed to call it?"

"Guilty as charged, but don't get any ideas. I'm glad that you're an adult."

"Did you ever read *Lolita*?"

Lester paused, not knowing what to say.

"Hah! I bet you're blushing now," she said triumphantly. "Do you want to go to The Lighthouse? We could catch a set, maybe two if we like it."

"Do you know who's on? I'm pretty bushed. I've been driving all over the place and barely caught any sleep last night."

"I don't know what's on, but why don't you pick me up and we can go down there and see. If not, maybe we can check something out at The Insomniac. You never know what's on there. Or, what about the Surf Music club at the Biltmore"

"That's such a teeny bopper place and I'm not into the new surf music thing, but I'll go if you want to go. I'll keep an open mind."

"What about the Mermaid? We could just get a bite to eat."

"I'll just pick you up and we can walk down to Pier Avenue and see if what's happening."

"I can't stay out too late. I've got classes tomorrow."

"I don't think I could make it that long. I'm leaving right now." Lester quickly changed his clothes, putting on a polo shirt and his cleanest pair of slacks, then rushed from his apartment, down the stairs and into his car.

Driving east on Artesia he hit the sweet spot, making nearly all the lights until he got to Aviation. He wasn't going so fast that he risked getting pulled over. Driving past the high school and then down Gould Avenue into Hermosa, he hit thick fog and had to slow down. It wasn't the thickest he'd ever seen. There was one time that the fog was so thick that he couldn't see the parked cars. He parked around the corner from Mary's house, on a hill, and made sure to curb his wheels.

It had gotten chilly, at least by local standards, and he wished he'd worn a sport coat. By the light of the streetlamp, he double-checked that his shoes shined, that somehow they hadn't gotten scuffed.

Immediately after he rang the door chimes, Mary swung the door open and rushed out of her house. She was wearing a long blue cotton dress and a light, dark blue cotton windbreaker that she'd borrowed from her dad.

"Do you want to come in?" Mary's dad said from somewhere in the house.

"We're running late," Mary called back to her dad.

"I'll bring her back at a reasonable time," Lester called out to Mary's dad. The front door was closed so he wasn't sure he'd heard him.

"I hope you're not driving," Mary's mom yelled from behind the door. "It's too foggy to drive."

"No, ma'am. We're walking" Lester called back.

"Just make sure the other cars can see you when you cross streets," Mary's mom yelled.

"Can we just go?" Mary whispered to him, grabbing his hand and leading him off the front steps and out the garden gate. "They'll suck you in if we don't go right now and we'll never escape the atmosphere."

"Copy, Houston," Lester whispered to Mary. "I'll keep her safe," he called back.

Mary's parents were standing at the now open door. "You're not going to The Insomniac are you? I heard all they do is sit around in a haze of marijuana smoke and listen to bongo players," Mary's mom said. When she got to the words "marijuana smoke," her voice dropped to a whisper.

"No, nothing like that. I'm a police officer, remember," Lester said.

"We're going right now!" Mary insisted as she closed the front door and led him quickly out of the front yard and down the street towards the beach.

As they walked along the Strand, Mary pressed herself against him and stuck her hands under his polo shirt to keep them warm. "You don't mind do you?"

"Your hands are cold," Lester said.

"Cold hands, warm heart, isn't that what they say?"

It was hard to walk that way, so they made slow progress the ten or so blocks to Pier Avenue. Nobody was out and visibility was limited. You could hear the roar and crashing of the surf and not much else because there were so few cars on the streets. Mary talked about school and what she was learning. Lester yawned, but wasn't able to catch it in time.

"I'm not boring you am I?" Mary asked.

"No, it's just that I had a long couple of days. I had to drive down to Anaheim this afternoon and the night before, I didn't get much sleep at all."

"We can do this another time. It's nice just walking with you. I feel like we've hardly seen each other this last week."

"It'll get better after this case is closed. I'm looking forward to the Spring Fling."

"You're going to love it!" Mary said excitedly.

"I hope your friends like me," Lester said bashfully.

"My friends? My folks' friends. Everyone else is just someone I know and grew up with. The longer I'm out of high school and away from them, the more I wonder why I even hung out with them. Do you ever feel that way? I feel like a whole new person."

"Yeah, but I felt that way in high school and I hardly ever go back."

"What would you think if I went away to college, maybe up to Berkeley? You're the only thing that's keeping here," Mary said tentatively.

"You're the reason I'm happy I'm here, but I guess I'd follow you if you didn't think that was weird. I could probably get a job with a police force there."

When they reached the old Biltmore hotel, there were people hanging around, leaning against the low wall that kept the sand off of the Strand. A few teenagers were huddled together against the wall smoking cigarettes. They were all wearing wool Pendleton shirts over jeans, the girls and the boys. They weren't much younger than Lester and Mary, but he felt like they were from a different generation. It had been a long time since he'd just hung out. In Taft, that was just about all there was to do, if there wasn't a movie at the Fox that you wanted to see.

"Bunch of hodads," Mary said under her breath after they passed them. "I bet a lot of them are from Gardena."

The next two blocks before Pier Avenue had a different crowd. In front of the Poop Deck and the hamburger stands and surf mat rental shops closed for the night. It was all guys in front of the Poop Deck. They were mostly in their mid-twenties. Some of them wore windbreakers with rodster club logos, like the Suspended and the Chromeos.

The parking spots around the corner were filled with hot rods in all stages of completion, from rust bucket to show car. Mary clung even tighter to him as they passed. The guys stopped their conversations and stared at them then started up their conversations after they passed.

When they reached the pier, or what was left of the pier, there were even more people about. The parking lot at the Mermaid was full of late-model sedans. Lester had never been in there but it seemed like a fancy steak and potatoes place from the outside.

The parking spaces on Pier Avenue were all filled. Taco Bills burrito stand across the street from the Mermaid there were teenagers, surfers, beatniks and rodsters.

On Pier Avenue in front of the Mermaid, there was a line of bikers standing next to their motorcycles. An older man with a large parrot on his shoulder wandered about. The parrot man was a regular. He never talked to anybody but, occasionally, someone would start a conversation with him about his parrot.

There was a line in front of The Lighthouse.

"Do you want to wait?" Lester asked.

"Bud Shanks playing. He's supposed to be pretty good," Mary said.

"We can wait if you want. Maybe it won't take too long."

"We're been waiting for an hour," the couple in front of them said.

"An hour we won't have to wait," Lester said.

"The line isn't that long," Mary said.

When Bud Shanks' set ended, enough people left for them to be able to go in. Their seats were in the back near the bathrooms, but the club was full and so they were lucky to get in. Most of the audience had stayed for another set. The Lighthouse was a long and narrow club, with brick-lined walls with the bar along one side and the stage directly across the room.

Bud Shank stood in front of his small band, drums, bass, and piano, tenor saxophone in hand. The band was tight and swung intelligently rather than instinctually. It was music to dance in your chair to.

Lester ordered them beers. Mary whispered to him that she wasn't old enough. Lester smiled, put his finger to his mouth indicating her to be quiet and then kissed her cheek and then neck. Mary blushed and leaned against him, tapping out the rhythms with her fingers on his knee.

When the set was over, they strolled out and crossed the street to The Insomniac. "Do you want to go in and get a dessert?" Lester asked.

"You're so sweet," Mary said as she locked her fingers with his.

The Insomniac wasn't as crowded as The Lighthouse. There were a few people in the front browsing the books and artwork. A man sat at a table and would write you a poem for a small contribution. In the back, a young woman strummed an Appalachian mountain song on an autoharp.

"Do you want to try to catch another set?" Lester asked.

"Bud Shank was hard to beat but no, let's share a slice of cake and call it a night," Mary said.

"We should do this again."

"I'd do it again and again. Isn't this why we wanted to be grownups?"

"I can think of a couple of other reasons."

Mary blushed and leaned into him, whispering, "I can too," breathily into his ear.

They shared a slice of chocolate cake and a couple of glasses of milk and left before the end of the singers' set. Just after they walked out of The Insomniac a fight broke out at the end of the block in front of the Mermaid's parking lot between a biker and a rodster.

A couple of other bikers rushed to support their guy but were soon outnumbered by a score of rodsters who came from all directions. Lester told Mary to go back inside The Insomniac and wait for him.

He rushed over to the fight and identified himself as police. John T and Big John came on the scene seconds later with nightsticks and pulled the men away from each other while most of the other rodsters and bikers ran off in every direction.

Half a dozen squad cars pulled up as the scramble ended, including one each from Manhattan and Redondo Beaches. The flashing lights were blinding and the scene had become theater to the beatniks, hipsters and flotsam and jetsam from the dive bars.

Lester rushed back to The Insomniac and found Mary hiding behind a bookcase wide-eyed.

"Are you all right?" Mary asked. "You've got a cut on your eyebrow." She took a handkerchief from her purse and dabbed the blood away. "It doesn't look like you'll need stitches."

"That. . . could have been so much worse. . . if we'd let those knuckleheads get started." Lester was winded and his words came out in gulps. "We could. . . have had a real brawl."

"Is that what policing's really like? They don't show that on *Dragnet*."

"Someone could have had a knife or some knuckle dusters. We're just lucky that we were able to stop it before it got out of hand. We should get you back home, the fast way," Lester said nervously.

John T came up to Lester. "Kappe's been looking for you."

"Can it wait until tomorrow?" Lester asked.

"He said if any of us Clancys saw you to tell you that Hess has gone missing," John T said.

"I'm going to pretend we never met. I'm running on fumes and need eighty winks."

John T laughed, looked around at the squad cars and all the Clancys and said, "No can do."

"Let me take my girl home and I'll be back at the station."

"That's probably a better move," John T said.

Lester and Mary walked up Pier Avenue to Monterey to get back to her house. The fog was still thick and the lights of the few cars out barely lit up the street. They walked too quickly to hold hands and were back at her house in fifteen minutes.

"That's the most excitement I've had in a long time," Mary said as she hugged him in front of her house. "Your cut has stopped bleeding."

Lester handed her the handkerchief, which she stuffed into her purse. "I'll call you tomorrow."

"I've got to help with the Fling thing. I'll see you on Saturday. Probably you should meet me there. You're going to be okay, aren't you? I need to know that you're going to be all right," Mary said as she hugged him.

"I'll be there. I'll be all right."

Mary smiled and kissed his forehead, then kissed him square on the lips. He kissed her back and wrapped her in his arms. She looked over at her house, the lights dark and it seemed that nobody was up. They were out of the glow of the nearest street light and obscured by the fog.

"I love you," Lester whispered to her.

"I love you too," Mary whispered back. Her hot breath in his ears accelerated his desire for her.

"Would you come away with me for a weekend? We could go to Ensenada. We could go up to Big Bear Lake."

"We could go to Vegas," Mary said enthusiastically before changing her tone. Mary pulled back from him. "Don't think I don't want to. Don't ever think that, but you know I can't. You know we can't. Word gets around. My parents would never approve. We can wait, can't we? We can wait a little longer. Memorial Day weekend, they're going up to Frisco. We won't have to go anywhere."

They kissed again and embraced, their hands caressing each other feverishly. The porch light of her house came on and she pulled away.

"I've got to go. You probably should still put a Band-Aid on it. Do you want to come inside and get one?" Mary asked.

"I've got some in the car. I should probably get going. I'll see you on Saturday. I'm looking forward to it."

Chapter 11

Lester tried to keep his mind on the road. The fog was thick enough that the visibility was horrible so Lester drove very slowly to the station. The glare of the headlights reflected off the fog making it even harder to see what was in front and to the side. He could barely see parked cars.

He parked in the station parking lot and sat in his car for a while before getting out. It had been a long day and the more he tried to concentrate on one thing the more his mind veered off, to Hess, to what might have happened to him, to Mary and how she felt in his arms when she said she loved him, to Johnny Cheam and the silencer.

He tried to calculate the number of days until Memorial Day but his mind went back to Hess what, if anything, it had anything to do with the Shawn case. Beyond being acquaintances, there wasn't any evidence of it as yet.

At the station, the biker and the rodster who'd tussled were making friends while they were being booked. The biker had a black eye and the rodster had a bruised jaw and bandaged knuckles, but it turned out that they'd both gone to Bishop Montgomery, the local Catholic high school, overlapping only one year but they knew a few people in common.

Big John was leaning against a wall and picking his teeth with a toothpick when Lester went came into the station. He looked up at Lester and smiled. "Kappe's looking for you."

"Yeah, I heard," Lester said before stifling a yawn. He slowed down to look at the guys getting booked.

"Heard you were part of the razzle-dazzle down by the pier. You need a bandage? I've got one if you need one."

"Nah, I'm fine," Lester said. "Sorry, I'm feeling forty or fifty winks short of a good night's sleep. Do you know what he wants?"

"I don't get into his business, but I'd stop talking with me and go see Kappe."

Lester shuffled into the office and saw Kappe sitting back in his chair with his feet up on his desk, leaning back so far in his chair that one little tremor would cause him to crash down. He was reading the comics and laughing at the jokes.

"You wanted to see me?" Lester drawled as he rubbed his eyes.

Kappe swung his legs off of the desk and spun the chair around to face him. "You snooze you lose. Hess has flown the coop. He didn't show up at work today and nobody's seen him."

"Maybe he's sick. Maybe he's on vacation,"

"Maybe he's a swallow and flown down to Kapistranov," Kappe said sarcastically. "We looked into that. He's not in his apartment. He's not at his girl's place. He never showed up at his delis or work. His girl's scared but she won't talk. She claims she doesn't know anything."

"So what's the plan?" Lester asked.

"We're going up there and checking it out," Kappe said curtly.

"Is the FBI involved?"

Kappe looked at him scornfully. "The FBI is already involved."

"Are we trying to find him or trying to find out where he went?"

"Good question," Kappe said. "If he's flown the coop, there are only a couple of ways out of town. The airport's fogged in, and we've got that covered. They've got agents working the border just in case he went south and agents on the lookout in Vegas."

"What if he goes north to Frisco or up in the hills?" Lester asked.

"If he goes Joaquin Murrieta on us and takes to the hills, it could take a while. Maybe he's hiding out at Santa's Village up in Big Bear."

"But they'll get him eventually," Lester wondered.

"Have no doubt that if the Soviets can infiltrate agents into the country, they've figured a way to get them out," Kappe said confidently

"If he's skipped, then he must have done it or is worried that he's next."

"But why? We may never know the exact reason. Maybe Shawn wouldn't turn over the plans. Maybe it had nothing to do with the plans."

"Have we had someone look over the plans, someone who knows what they're looking at?" Lester asked. "Also, if it was about the plans, then why didn't the killer take them? He'd have to find the car but that wouldn't be that difficult. With any luck, you could do it in under an hour if you hoofed it. Alternatively, the killer could have followed Shawn to his car rather than shooting him in the alley. Maybe he didn't know about the plans. Maybe the plans weren't important."

"Maybe there were other copies of the plans. There's a whole month of maybes on this case. Why don't you have someone look at the plans? It could be that the Commies put them in his trunk as a red herring."

"What do we do about Hess? Has anyone called in that they saw something?" Lester asked.

"Nobody has called in. The FBI's on it as well as the L.A. fucking P.D. I'll tell you something. Those guys won't ever give us small-town cops a scintilla of respect. Sometimes the thin blue line is pretty fucking thin. You can feel the disrespect the moment you come across them. The Sherriff's Department is better. I can respect those guys."

"So what do we do? Are we going up to his place to check it out?"

"No, the LAPD told me to butt out," Kappe said bitterly. "What we're going to do is go up there and see if we can make Gestetner and Brody squeal."

"Isn't it kind of late?" Lester asked looking at his watch.

"Well, we'll probably catch them at home. This is policing. It's not etiquette class. We can knock politely to not disturb their beauty rest if you want or we can surprise them, catch them off guard? We'll take my car."

It was foggy all the way up Sepulveda until they got to Westchester and then it tapered off. They never went above fifteen miles per hour.

Kappe asked Lester about himself. Lester tried to stay awake and pull together coherent thoughts. When he described his childhood in Taft, Kappe said that he'd never been there but heard it was nice, not full of Okies and migrant workers like the rest of the valley. He talked about Mary and the Spring Fling he was going to on Saturday night.

"Watch out for those highfalutin lawn bowlers," Kappe growled. "I'm with the South Bay Shuffleboarders. We've got our club next to theirs down at Clark Stadium. We're a nice family club. We're not trying to make out that we're better or worse than anyone. We're just trying to play quality shuffleboard, have a good time, be good neighbors, et cetera, et cetera. Every year they have their Spring Fling. They never invite us. They take over the parking lot. It's a public parking lot but on Spring Fling night and their Harvest Gala, you can't park within half a mile."

"We've got rights too!" Kappe declared. "Some of us might want to play some shuffleboard under the stars, but they take up our whole court for their shindig. Step one toe on their courts without the proper equipment and some old biddy just this side of the Wicked Witch of the West will come crabbing out of their clubhouse and swear at you with words that'd even make a sailor blush. We used to invite them to our shindigs but none of them ever came. A little beer and weenie roast isn't grand enough for them. A kid like you, from the sticks, they'll eat you alive, even if you're escorted."

"I'll tread carefully." Lester hoped Kappe wasn't right but he suspected there was some truth deep in the bile.

When they got to the first guy's apartment, it was just after midnight. Joe Gestetner lived in Culver City near the Helms Bakery. The whole neighborhood smelled of yeast and donuts. Gestetner's pad was a second-floor apartment in a garden complex with a courtyard in the middle filled with palms and ferns. In a classier place, there would have been room for a pool. Gestetner was on the first floor near the front. When Kappe pounded on the door, there was no doubt that the whole complex was woken up.

"Police, open up!" Kappe bellowed and then returned to pounding on the door.

"Okay, okay!" Gestetner yelled from behind the door. He was in underwear covered by a terrycloth robe. His hair was disheveled, and a girl could be seen in the back of the apartment, clutching her robe closed and cowering as she stood.

"We were sleeping! The whole place was sleeping!" Gestetner cried.

"Can we come in?" Kappe asked. It was more of a demand than a question.

"Can I stop you?" Gestetner said meekly. "Sorry, Shirley," he said to the woman in the bedroom. "I'm sure there's a misunderstanding."

"Actually, there isn't a whole lot we understand. That's the way it is with you guys. Always sticking together. Always keeping the real deal from prying eyes."

"I've got no idea what you're talking about," Gestetner said indignantly.

"I'm talking about Shawn. I'm talking about Hess."

"Where do you want to start?" Gestetner asked.

"From the beginning," Kappe said.

Gestetner sighed. "It's a shame what happened to Steve. He was a nice guy. A schmendrick he was not. Let me tell you. He was shy, but that's because of being a greenhorn and coming from where he came from and going through what he went through. Twice, I might add. The war wasn't a piece of Sacher torte for him and his family, if you know what I mean, and then '56 was like the icing on the shit cake. His brother was captured and killed."

"He comes over here, gets a job, in spite of being a poindexter, and I suppose it was his Hungarian accent," Gestetner said sorrowfully, trying to squash a sob. "The guy had a voice, let me tell you. He could get the girls. He couldn't keep the girls, on account of being basically a poindexter, but he could get the girls. The class of girls he'd get would eventually see through the accent and what they saw as European sophistication, which was partly true and partly an act. We kept telling him to set his sights on a nice girl, a patient girl, and he'd be in the clover."

"His job stank. He hated the company. We thought it was all talk," Gestetner said. "I mean, who doesn't hate their job? I know you think he was a Red, but he wasn't. He hated the Commies and had more reason to than any of us. Why do you think he worked at a defense plant? He could have worked anywhere."

Lights went on in some of the apartments and people stared out from behind their curtains. A small dog yapped and incessantly in one of the units at the back of the building.

"Why did he hate his job?" Lester asked.

"According to him, they were a bunch of crooks, more crooked than a three-dollar bill," Gestetner said. "The details, I don't know. He said they were secret, and he couldn't make me understand if he tried. That was only last week, maybe Wednesday night before he died."

"How did all of you meet?"

"At the synagogue for High Holidays. We were all sitting in the back, Hess, Brody and me, and this awkward guy comes in wearing the worst, ill-fitting clothes. A real greenhorn," Gestetner said. "We felt sorry for him and invited him along to our regular dinners. The other guys, I've known since forever. We all went to Hammie High, though not the same year. Hess is the oldest and he and his brother were kind of famous in school. Well, more his brother. He's a bad actor, if you know what I mean""

"You mean he's connected?" Kappe asked.

"You didn't hear it from me," Gestetner said. "Those kinds of guys don't like people talking about them. I don't know his business, but I know he means business."

"Hess has flown the coop," Kappe said. "Know anything about it? He didn't show up at work. He's not at his roost and he's not at his chick's roost. His car is nowhere that we know of."

Gestetner looked worried. "No kidding. He's amscrayed? Really?"

"Do you think the Commies got him out?" Kappe asked.

Gestetner laughed nervously. "You've got to be kidding. Sure, Hess talked red but that was just because of his Hollywood union buddies. They expect it.

Secretly, he likes Ike and voted for Nixon. I know, because we argued the heck out of it during the last election."

"Do you have any idea what might have happened to him, why he might want to flee?" Lester asked.

"You got all night? He owes a lot of bread to the kind of guys you shouldn't owe anything to. He spends too much and likes the track, but the track doesn't like him. He doesn't believe in much besides himself, girls and money, and he has a way with girls and a way with money and he's a lot more successful with girls than he is with money."

"If you hear anything, call us," Kappe said. "Thanks for your cooperation, as long as you're on the up-and-up."

As they left, they could hear Gestetner's girl yelling at him.

It was a fifteen-minute drive to Brody's place up in Westwood near UCLA. Kappe was livid, gripping the steering wheel like he wanted to wring it.

"If that cocksucker's right, then Hess is in a whole lot of shit. He maybe six foot under or six fathoms under or it all may be a front. His brother's got connections. That's not in doubt. He probably has connections too. You've got a nexus of evil in a Hollywood craft union. You've got Reds working with mobsters collaborating with Pinkos to undermine the morals of American youth all in the name of profit and freedom of speech."

"Maybe it's just entertainment," Lester said. "If he's been knocked off, it could be a hit, and if it's a hit, then I think it's probably not related to Shawn, unless his murder was also a hit. It seems like a hit. It wasn't a robbery, not with a silencer. If it's a hit, then we may never find out what happened. That could be connected to Shawn too, maybe by the same person. How are we going to solve this case if it's an assassination?"

"That's what I'm thinking too," Kappe said. "Not everything gets wrapped up with a nice little bow. We can only follow the leads and follow our hunches. If both were hits, and hopefully they're connected, then if we can find who did the hit, we can solve both. Let's see what Brody has to say."

Brody lived in a small apartment building on a hilly street in Westwood, a few blocks from UCLA. The building had separate entrances for each unit, but you had to walk up a steep set of stairs to get to the apartments. Kappe, winded by the time they got to the top of the top, huffed and puffed, bent over trying to catch his breath.

Brody was waiting for them at the top of the stairs, sitting on a stool in front of his door, smoking a cigarette. "You made good time," he said.

"Gestetner called you?" Kappe asked.

"We prefer semaphore flags, but Ma Bell will do in the dark."

"Don't get smart," Kappe growled.

"I can only promise to try. And I don't know where Paul Hess is. Sure, we get together to kibbitz and I've known him for a long time, but I wouldn't say he and I are really friends. If I had a life, I'd probably never bother with him. I'm in graduate school, economics." Brody paused to yawn and rub his eyes.

"I would say that Paul leans left, maybe far left, if he gave it some thought, but he doesn't really give it that much thought," Brody said. "The union gig is just a way to make some extra bread to keep up his high life. He likes to talk like he has big thoughts, but he's really just into girls. Sometimes it feels like he just meets up with us to have an audience, so he doesn't have to brag into the mirror."

Brody yawned and stretched before continuing. "His brother's the piece of work and I stay clear of him, real clear. He's always asking you if you want a loan, but it's not like he's being a nice guy. If he loans you money, you will never pay it off, not even if you're J. Paul Getty. He will own you."

Brody looked at Lester then at Kappe. "You'd think that Paul would be doing well. The craft jobs pay pretty well even if the work isn't always steady, but the work has been pretty steady. Worse comes to worst, you crew sex flicks under the table. Nobody talks about it, but everyone does it, or at least that's what I've heard from Paul. If there's a market, people will sell it to you. I don't think that he's connected to any Communist plots or underground cells, but then maybe he's just really good. I've known him since high school and he isn't that swift. The way he is now is the way he was then, just with a car and legal booze."

"What about Shawn?" Lester asked. "Where did he fit into your picture?"

"He showed up a couple of years ago at our shul. This was just after the Uprising. And we saw that he was all alone and we just invited him to hang out with us. His English wasn't so good back then and our

Yiddish wasn't much either and the only Hungarian I know is goulash. My parents took him out to Budapest, this Hungarian restaurant on Fairfax. From the first, he seemed nice, even when we had no idea what he was saying."

"My folks speak Hungarian so, they got along fine with him," Brody said. "He got a job. He got an apartment and a car and started seeing some girl from down in the South Bay. I met her a few times, but can't say I knew her. I'd meet up with them for a foreign film and talk about it afterwards at a coffee shop."

"They broke up a couple of months ago," Brody said. "Me, I'm not really surprised. He was unhappy with her and unhappy with work and she didn't seem that into him, last time I saw them together. I don't know whether it was because he'd had it shitty growing up, barely surviving the war and then having to skedaddle out of the country and leave his family behind or whether it was just that he was disappointed that this wasn't the land of milk and honey."

"Was he a Communist? Did he ever talk about Communism?" Kappe asked.

Brody laughed. "He hated the Communists. He said that after the war, they seemed like the only way forward, so a lot of people were for them. Everyone was optimistic because at least it was better than what they'd gone through. Then you had the show trials, the purges, the anti-Semitism. Then, just when it seemed like they could throw the bums out, the bums kicked them in the nuts and shot the loudest complainers."

"Paul would try to say that it was an aberration, that under the real thing, people would be nicer, things would be better, that the working guy in the USA couldn't get much of a break unless he was backed by a union. I used to tell him that a lot of union guys, not in the industry mind you, but in Detroit, in the real heavy industries, are hardcore right-wingers this side of Father Coughlin. Shawn would tell him he didn't know what he was talking about. Then we'd have an argument and the waitress would tell us to pipe down and then we'd order dessert, a slice of cake. A nice night on the town if you don't have anything better going on."

"Do you have any idea why he might have been killed? Did he owe any money, like to Hess's brother? Was someone mad at him?" Kappe asked.

"No, I don't think he owed any money. He barely spent any money, except on that car, not that the car was expensive except to keep running, and when he'd take a girl out. You know how your mom and dad would save wrapping paper to reuse? He was like that to the extreme. He would order half a sandwich, take it to go but then scrounge your leftovers and take those home too. He never ordered a drink, just had the water, sometimes hot water with lemon. He would drink milk even if it had gone bad. The only people who could be mad at him were waiters and waitresses because he barely tipped and didn't order much. I'm not saying that he didn't have some secret life that we didn't know about. Personally, I don't think he had the imagination for it."

"He was interested in just three things," Brody said as he counted them out with his fingers. "He wanted to get married, preferably to a nice Jewish girl who could cook like his mom. He wanted to get his parents out of Hungary. He wanted to have enough money to buy a house in Santa Monica. He'd talk about books and art and culture, but it seemed like he was mostly interested in those things because girls were."

Brody took a moment to consider what else to say. "The last couple of months, he was hanging around the beatnik clubs, The Insomniac down in Hermosa, the Gas House in Venice. I don't know who killed him. It could have been some random thing where the killer thought he was someone else. You see that in the movies and on TV sometimes. Maybe it had to do with his job. Honestly, I have no idea."

"Did you know he was fired the day he was killed?" Lester asked.

Brody was surprised. "I'm not surprised. He was looking for an out. He said they were crooks but he didn't say in what way. It seemed like more than just talk. You know how people talk about work and grouse about things? He was probably relieved to be fired, except he would have worried about not having another job lined up. I'm sure he had the money to ride it out and he probably could have gotten another job pretty easy."

They thanked Brody for his help and drove back to Hermosa Beach on the 405 Freeway until they got to the airport, then took Sepulveda the rest of the way. The closer they got to the beach, the foggier it got and the slower they had to drive.

Kappe talked the whole way back about how he wasn't convinced either Gestetner or Brody were telling the truth, but he couldn't explain why he felt that way other than that, according to him Jews stick together, not that he meant anything bad by it but that was the way he felt it was. Lester didn't want to make a fuss or start an argument. He was so exhausted that he nodded off while Kappe talked and drove not waking up until they got to the station.

It was nearly two in the morning and the last couple of miles had been brutally difficult. They had to inch along at a few miles an hour and pray that they were the only ones stupid enough to be driving. You could barely see oncoming cars. The diffused glare of their headlamps was the only warning.

"I expect you in the station in the morning, regular time," Kappe said as they got out of the car.

"Why don't I sleep in my car. It'll save me the commute. You're kidding me, right? I'm totally beat."

"Then I suggest you go home and get your beauty rest. If you're a minute late, I'll write you up," Kappe said coldly.

"And Merry Christmas to you," Lester whispered to himself as he walked away. The drive back to his apartment took him half an hour longer than usual. The fog belt usually extended only a mile and a half inland, but that night it extended east, far into Torrance and Hawthorne.

Chapter 12

Lester's alarm clanged on the bed stand. The last thing he remembered was driving through the fog and nothing about getting into bed. His head hurt, not from a hangover, but from dehydration and lack of sleep. He stubbed his toe on a chair covered with his clothes when he entered his living room.

After a short, cold shower, he was awake enough to not cut himself shaving and to make it out of the bathroom without injury. His closet was nearly empty. The only completely clean and pressed clothes he had were his whites for the Fling on Saturday. His metering uniform, which he'd hoped never to wear again, was on a hanger still stained with blood.

He cobbled together an outfit, a clean enough shirt, an old tie he hadn't worn in a while and some slacks that he was able to scrape some dried food off of that hadn't stained. He ironed everything so that he'd look presentable. The heat of the iron brought out some unfortunate odors of which he tried to cover up with spritzes of cologne.

The world looked more hopeful after half a night's sleep, a cup of coffee, a couple of English muffins. The sun was shining. His neighbors were leaving for work. A convertible in front of the apartment building was blasting some boss music, which everyone nearby got to hear, whether or not they wanted to. He stopped at a donut shop for a quick jolt of coffee, burning the roof of his mouth.

Kappe was in the office when he got there, looking like he'd stayed the night and shaved in the bathroom. There was a coffee stain on his white shirt and some sort of food stain just below that. He didn't look up when Lester sat down at the desk across from him and wished him a good morning.

"Can I make a suggestion?" Lester said timidly.

Kappe didn't respond or even look up from the papers he was making notes on.

"I was thinking of seeing if I could make anything out of the plans. I can't understand them, except for where it says secret."

"Let the FBI handle them," Kappe snapped, not looking up from his papers.

"Maybe I could get someone who knows what they're looking at to tell me if the plans are anything special, anything that someone might get killed over. I was thinking of going out to greasy spoons near the airport to see if I can find an engineer or jet engine mechanic to have a look at them."

"They found Hess," Kappe said.

"Dead or alive?"

"Alive, but just barely. He was found at a park up in La Crescenta. Some woman was walking her dog and found him. The dog sniffed him out. He's going to need some dental work and he's got a cracked rib and a broken nose. He'd been there all night."

"He didn't fly," Lester said.

"Should have flapped his wings harder," Kappe said then gave a wheezy laugh.

"You think they wanted him dead?"

"Nah, if they want you dead then they kill you good. If you owe someone money, they would rather have you alive even if barely. You can't squeeze blood from a dead turnip."

"Is he talking? Did he say anything?" Lester asked.

"He's not going to snitch, not the way they worked him over. He still could be connected to Shawn. He's still definitely a Red. Even a Red can owe a vig. I can't figure out the angle to the Shawn murder. Maybe there isn't one and maybe there is. It may not be a Red thing or maybe it is and they're trying to throw us for a loop, confuse us. That would be a brilliant plan but it doesn't seem like we need their help."

"Do you need any help checking out the Hess angle?" Lester asked.

"Nah, go check out the plans angle. See what you can find. I'm going to drive out to the hospital to see Hess. Maybe he'll talk and maybe he'll have something to say or maybe his jaw will be wired shut and he'll have to nod," Kappe said despairingly. "Some fresh air could do the case some good. The chief's on my back about the whole thing. He was chewing me out like I was an old soup bone just before you came in. One murder every other year," Kappe said, imitating the chief's voice, "You couldn't find your own asshole."

"Any suggestions on hangouts near the airport?" Lester asked.

"There's the Hangar Inn on Aviation over in Manhattan, then there's the Cooked Goose and the Purple Tern over near Northrop and Coffman's Breeze on Sepulveda near where there's that aircraft school on Sepulveda just north of the airport. There are probably more down near the Long Beach Airport," Kappe said.

"I'm not going to be back until the end of the day. Are you going to want me to work this weekend?"

"I don't think there's the budget for overtime. I know you've got your shindig, Spring thing and you should go to it. I'll see you tomorrow. You look like shit, if you don't mind my saying. Go home and get some cleaner clothes."

"Hey, I cleaned these a couple of weeks ago," Lester said.

"I could smell you coming in."

"Do you think it's okay to show them the plans, not to anybody, but to people who know about jets? Are we going to get in trouble for having them?"

"Hey, we're the police. If you can't trust us, then who can you trust?" Kappe said with a wink. "If you want, you can come over on Sunday and meet the wife. I can cook up a few steaks. You can bring over your girl if you want."

"I'll ask her. What time?"

"How does five o'clock sound? It's fine if you can't make it, just let me know."

"No, I'll definitely be there. I'll have to ask Mary. She may have homework to do. She's in college. I'm not robbing the cradle."

"That's between you and her parents," Kappe said as he wrote down his address and phone number on a slip of paper and handed it to Lester, who folded it up and put it into his wallet.

"I'm just over in Redondo Beach off of Artesia. If it ends up raining," Lester said, pausing before continuing, "it'll be a miracle."

Lester drove back to his apartment and gathered up his laundry and took it to the laundromat and his uniform to the cleaners. Sitting around the laundromat reading the discarded newspapers from the day before, he tried not to think about his case and just read old news but his brain didn't seem to be able to function. It hopped around from the story he was trying to read to Hess getting beat up, to Shawn getting shot to the silencer back, to the day's news and then he nodded off and was wakened by an old lady who nudged him awake and told him he was hogging the dryers. By mid-morning his laundry was done, and he'd changed into clean clothes and had plotted out the rest of his day.

The Hanger Inn was closest, so he stopped there first. It was only a couple of miles away, in one of the new strip malls that were popping up everywhere and just down the street from the new high school. The Hangar had the tail end of a Cessna sticking out of the roof, like it had crashed into the building. Inside, it was your typical bar, with a big television set in one corner above the bar, a couple of pool tables in the back and some tables in the front.

The bar was half full when he went in with a few guys who looked to Lester like aerospace factory workers sitting at the bar eating hamburgers and Reubens with napkins tucked into their shirts at the neck to try to keep their tie-less short-sleeved white shirts clean.

Lester stood at the entrance surveying the crowd, trying to determine which group to approach first, the workers or the office jockeys. He stood too long at the entrance and the bartender, a young woman who was pretty but looked tough enough to handle the antics of any Neanderthal, sighed.

"You buying or browsing?" the bartender yelled to him over the noise of the lunchtime crowd.

"What do you recommend?" Lester asked as he sat down at the bar.

"Pabst and a mushroom burger, side of fries," the bartender said.

"Sounds good, but hold the Pabst. I'm on duty."

"Cop?"

"How did you know?" Lester asked.

"I made you as soon as you stopped in. You're like a virgin stepping into a biker bar."

Lester laughed. "I'm kind of on a mission."

"You're not raiding us are you or a health inspector? I'll get the boss. We're clean," she said coldly.

"No, I'm wondering if anyone here could look at some aircraft plans I've gotten. It's part of a case. We can't make sense of them and my boss asked me to find someone who knew something about jet engines, at least I think it's for a jet engine. Shows you how little I know."

"Most of these guys are building rocket parts or are actual rocket scientists."

"It is okay if I ask them?"

"Sure, let me get your order started."

Lester went around to each table, asking them if they knew anything about jet airplanes and if they could read schematics.

The guys at the bar said no, in unison, while the guys at the table said yes. He showed them copies of the plans and they very quickly told him that he was right that it was for an engine, but that they were electrical engineers.

The burger was great and the fries alone were worth the price of admission. It wasn't the kind of place that he felt he could take Mary to, or at least the kind of place that Mary's parents would be okay with. Maybe once he was more established with her parents if that ever happened.

When he was living back in Taft, there were roughneck bars, farmhand bars, Mexican bars and biker bars. His dad always warned him away from those places. At some point in his dad's youth, before he'd met his mom, he'd been beaten up for going into the wrong bar at the wrong time.

The Purple Tern was a couple of miles north across from the Northrop plant, which stretched several city blocks along the railroad tracks. The siding was filled with a Ringling Brothers circus train that beautified what otherwise was a dismal area. Across the street from the siding and the Northrop plant were blocks of low rent apartment buildings, liquor stores, Mexican restaurants, a strip club and the Purple Tern in a squat building next to an electronics store advertising transistor radio kits.

The interior was decorated with photos of aircraft-manufacturing teams and bowling league trophies. There were dusty but elaborately painted aircraft models hanging from the ceiling, like a crazy miniature dogfight.

The specialty of the house seemed to be chili. Men were sitting over bowls of the stuff covered in cheese. There were about a dozen customers. The place was all guys except for the two waitresses. One of the waitresses, who looked pretty young, came up to Lester as soon as he stepped into the bar.

"You need a table, or you sitting at the bar?" she asked.

"I've already eaten," Lester said. "I'm with the police. I'd just like to ask your customers some questions."

The waitress looked nervous. "Everything's in order. Me and Janice are legal age. We can prove it."

"No, I don't care about that. I'm trying to find an aircraft engine mechanic or someone like that."

"We've usually got some of those."

"Do you mind?"

"You want me to stop you?" she asked incredulously.

Lester stepped to the middle of the room and clapped his hands loudly, but nobody paid him any attention. He then yelled out, "Hey!" loudly, but nobody paid him any mind beyond looking up than looking down. Lester then took out his badge, held it up in the air, and then bellowed out, "Police!" He commanded their attention then. They looked up from the chili and beers, turning their chairs around where necessary.

"I'm looking for someone who knows something about jet engines. Does anyone here know anything about jet engines? You're not in any trouble. I'm just looking for some information!" Lester yelled to try to get their attention.

"Nobody raised their hands.

"Anybody, please."

"I'll do it," a young man in the back of the bar said. He had a neatly trimmed beard and was smoking a pipe. He was alone at his table and had been working on a crossword puzzle. The puzzle was half completed, and the paper was speckled with chili sauce. He wiped his hands on his napkin as Lester walked over to his table.

Lester sat down at the table and took out the photos from the envelope.

"Where did you get these?" the man said as he wiped his hands again on his napkin then picked up and examined the photos. The light wasn't good in the bar, so the man took out a small flashlight in the shape of a pistol from a pocket in his jacket. "That's better."

"I had one of those."

"*Buck Rogers*," they said in unison.

"Loved that show."

"So, let's see what you have," the man said. He looked closely at the plans. "You don't have bigger copies of these do you?"

"They're what I've got."

"Too bad. I'd love to see them bigger. So, do you know what we're looking for?" the man asked.

"No, I have no idea. I don't even know if they're important."

"Well, they are marked secret," the man said pointing to the marking.

"Just look at them and tell me your impressions, if you have any."

"Don't rush me," the man said before looking at his watch.

Lester sat in the other chair at the table and watched as the man took out a jeweler's loop from out of his jacket pocket and examined the plans.

"It's too dark in here," the man said under his breath. He hummed while he worked, jotting notes on a paper napkin. After fifteen minutes, he looked up from the plans and glanced at his watch. "Give me another five minutes."

After five minutes of peering and notating and talking to himself, the man looked up at Lester but then didn't say anything. He put the photos back in order and then into the manila envelope.

"Well?" Lester asked.

"I have no idea. They look fine to me. They're basically plans for a kind of flanged nozzle that goes on a jet engine exhaust. They don't look that special to me, but maybe I'm missing something."

"How much do you know about jet engines?"

"Some, but most of it's theoretical. I work on hydraulic systems."

Lester thanked the man for his help then quickly left the bar and got back into his car. He checked the address for Coffman's Breeze and found that it wasn't too much further. It was on La Tijera Boulevard in Westchester, just north of the airport and not too far from the strip of movie theaters in Westchester.

Coffman's Breeze was in an old, windowless brick building that had somehow survived the earthquakes. It had a neon sign with a biplane and pilot with a long scarf lowing in the wind with the name Coffman's. The place must have been there since the days when LAX was Mines Field. The cars out front were family models, station wagons and sedans, Chevys and Fords.

The place was packed with older guys playing pinochle or bridge and eating club sandwiches, nothing messy like chili or soup, and drinking frosty mugs of Schlitz and Rainier. There was an unplugged and dusty jukebox in one corner near the bar. The bartender was an older Mexican guy with long sideburns and a comb-over on top. The couple of guys sitting at the bar were taking turns working the Herald-Examiner's crossword puzzle.

"Can I get you something?" the bartender asked when Lester approached the bar.

"I'll take a ginger ale," Lester said as he flashed his badge.

"You're not with the ABC are you? I can get the boss on the horn and he can be here in fifteen minutes, tops."

"Nah, I'm just here looking for some info. I'm looking for guys who know their way around a jet engine. You think any of these guys fit that description?

"Mitch, you work on jet engines at Hughes, don't you?"

Mitch was one of the guys working the crossword puzzle. He was in his early forties and wore black horned-rim glasses, a white short-sleeved shirt with a black tie held in place by a clarinet tie clasp, and a pocket protector overfilled with pens and pencils. "Can it wait? We're almost done."

The bartender handed Lester the ginger ale and waved him off when he tried to pay. Lester insisted and put down a case quarter, a couple of dimes and a nickel.

"Can I ask you a question?" Lester asked Mitch.

Mitch didn't bother looking up. "You're going to have to wait."

"It's a police matter."

Mitch looked up and smiled. "I know for a fact that I haven't done anything wrong and if you try to give my car a ticket, a car that is parked perfectly within the lines in a clearly marked space that I've been parking in for the last five years, three and a half months, I'll have your badge."

"Do you mind?"

The other man working the puzzle looked up and scowled. "You're making it take longer. I can't even concentrate."

"He can't even concentrate!" Mitch whined.

"You know we time ourselves," the other man said angrily.

"We can't count this one for the average," Mitch said.

"I think we were on our way for a record," the other man said, "but now it doesn't even matter."

"What is it you want?" Mitch said, exasperated.

"I'm looking for some advice on a jet engine design. Do you either of you know anything about jet engines?"

"We design them for a living," the other man said. "What we don't know about jet engines hasn't been invented yet."

"By us," Mitch added.

"If we haven't already," the other man said under his breath.

"So, if I show you some plans, you'll be able to tell me if there's something interesting?" Lester asked.

"Does it snow in Alaska?" Mitch asked.

"In the winter," the other man added.

Lester took out the plans and laid them out on the bar, covering over the crossword puzzle.

"So, let's see what we've got here," Mitch said as he took the plans.

"I can hardly read them," the other man said. "Do you got any better copies?"

"If he did, he'd show them to us," Mitch said to his friend. "You would, wouldn't you?"

"I'm sorry, this is all I've got for now."

Mitch took out a jeweler's loop from his pocket and fixed it to his eye and peered at the plans all the while humming.

"He always hums like that," the other man said. "I've tried to get him to stop, but you might as well try to stop the movement of the tectonic plates."

"You might order some lunch," Mitch said. "This might take a while."

"What about our lunch hour? There's only sixteen minutes left of it," the other man said.

"If we're late, what are they going to do, dock our pay? We're salaried," Mitch said.

Lester finished his ginger ale and ordered another ginger ale and a plate of french fries. By the time he was done with the fries, Mitch was done looking at the plans.

"Okay, I've got it," Mitch said.

"Got what?" Lester asked.

"Patience," the other man said before breaking out in hysterical giggles.

"As I was saying," Mitch said. "Don't mind him. We only let him out on his better days. As I was starting to say, you see this flanged nozzle. This nozzle flange is supposed to be lighter and more efficient, by five percent, than a standard nozzle. I can see what they're trying to accomplish, but I think that, at best, the effect would be less than five percent, maybe even less efficient, but essentially a wash. It's one of those things that looks better than it is. I bet they really impressed them with this thing. I'd heard that Averodyne was on to something like this and they'd gotten a contract to supply the Air Force, but frankly, I'm not impressed. I can see why this was supposed to be so hush-hush."

"Sorry, but I have no idea what you said," Lester said.

"In layman terms," the other man added.

"I may be wrong on this. I'm just a professional. I think this flanged nozzle that Averodyne is selling is flimflam," Mitch said.

"Flimflam?" Lester asked.

"Bogus," the other man said.

"But don't quote me on this. They may be hiring." Mitch said.

"Can I use you as an expert witness if I need to?"

"Oh sure," Mitch said. "Expert witness. I like the sound of that."

"Do you need another expert?" the other man asked.

"Do you know about jet engines?"

"I'm more of a wingman myself," the other man said.

"I'll let you know," Lester said.

"I can tell you that just because of something that you might not know," the other man whispered. "Anyone can buy a secret stamp and a pad of red ink."

"We used to mark my timesheet secret just to see if anyone noticed," Mitch said.

"And did they?"

"Ssssh, I can't tell," Mitch said, putting his forefinger to his lips. "It's on a need-to-know basis."

That cracked the other man up so much that he spurted his drink out his nose. Lester grimaced and had them write down their contact information then left quickly. As they wrote down their contact information, Mitch did a poor impression of Humphrey Bogart and the other man tried out his Cary Grant, which would only impress a deaf person.

Driving south on Sepulveda, through El Segundo and Manhattan Beach, Lester tried to concentrate on the idea that the plans were either fake or a fraud. At the traffic lights, he couldn't help but think that a week earlier, Shawn had been fired from his job and spent the last hours of his life picking up a girl. He must have been happy, at least at the end. It didn't sound like he'd liked his job and he had a lot of skills, so maybe he was okay with being fired, or at least as okay as you can be. He'd been successful and maybe was taking her back to his place or her place. When he tried to focus on what he'd learned, he had two thoughts. The first possibility was that the plans were fake, and the second possibility was that they were real, but flimflam.

Someone behind him honked. The light had changed and so he went through the intersection but pulled over to get gas at a Chevron station. While he waited for the attendant to finish pumping his gas, he saw that next to the cans of motor oil, they were selling smaller cans of OctaPlux, a gasoline additive that claimed to increase gas mileage while cleaning the engine. He'd never tried a gasoline additive, but he knew people who swore by them.

Kappe was just getting off the phone when Lester passed by his desk. "How'd you make out?"

"The plans are a fake," Lester said. "Either they are a set-up, fake plans, or a fraud. I mean, real plans but for a flim flam product."

"You can't catch a fish without bait. Look at this." Kappe took out a folder from his desk, opened it and showed Lester copies of pictures of a kid dressed in a white shirt and a neckerchief tied jauntily around his neck that somewhat resembled Steven Shawn. "Young Pioneers," Kappe said, stabbing the photo. "Born and bred a Communist."

"Maybe they all had to do it? How'd you get that?"

"Does it matter? Does it really matter? If you want to know, my buddy at the FBI got it for me. This is proof that he was indoctrinated into the Communist ideology and Communist mindset. Maybe he was just a simple refugee or maybe the Reds used the flow of refugees after the Uprising, to infiltrate spies. He didn't become a bus driver. He wasn't a cook. He wasn't just some Ivan Average. Maybe you think it's a coincidence that he worked in a defense plant and that he stole top-secret documents. Me, I've got a higher opinion of our enemy."

"I think it's simpler than that. Would Averodyne hired him if he didn't know his job? No!" Lester said.

"But they fired him," Kappe said.

"They said they fired him because they didn't like him. Mr. Cheam said that he was a good engineer. If he was such a good engineer, then do you think he would be fooled by some faked plans?" Lester asked.

Kappe didn't answer. He looked down at his notes when Lester tried to look him in the eye.

"He wouldn't buy it? Why would he buy that? Maybe he knew that the plans were a fraud, that they were selling hocus pocus and maybe he complained and that was why they fired him. He was going to cook their t and they couldn't let that happen," Lester said passionately.

Kappe wasn't paying attention. He was doodling a hammer and sickle on his notepad.

"So what do you want me to do next?"

Kappe finished his doodle and didn't look up. "Just finish up and go home and get some rest. The bosses aren't keen on overtime."

"Okay, I'm going to call the Defense Department's Office of Inspector General. There must be a local one at the Air Force base over in El Segundo. Then, I'm going home. I can barely concentrate. I'll write up my reports tomorrow. Maybe they'll make more sense then."

Kappe nodded and started on another doodle.

Lester found the phone number for the local Air Force base and after being misconnected and disconnected, he finally found someone to talk to. The guy that he talked said that nobody had filed a complaint at Averodyne and that they were a company in good standing.

Chapter 13

Lester got home and took out a stack of note cards and wrote out what they knew. He stacked the cards into piles of friends, co-workers and suspected Communist agents.

Most murderers killed people they knew. He discounted the ex-girlfriend, Elizabeth Lanz, and the new girl, Beatrice Loehner. Elizabeth didn't seem to have a grudge and Beatrice had only just met him. Shawn's friends didn't seem likely suspects, but then maybe they didn't know their connections well enough. Hess was the only one of them that was shady, but what was the motive? How well do your friends really know you? Lester thought about his own life. He didn't really have any friends, at least not down in LA.

His high school friends had mostly moved away from Taft, but he rarely caught up with the few that had moved down to LA or San Diego. His Army buddies were either still in the service or scattered about the country. With his job metering the night shift, meeting new people was a problem. Beyond Mary, his life was pretty empty. In that way, his life seemed a lot like Shawn's.

Who would want to murder him if few people cared that he was alive or maybe that was the point? Maybe the murder was random and had no connection to Shawn. He shuddered to think that was possible outside of a Hitchcock movie. If that was the case, there would be little chance beyond luck to solve the case. He discounted that for the time being but added it to the list of possibilities.

He called Mary, who he knew was at home and asked her if she wanted to go to a movie that night. Lester suggested seeing, *The Longest Day* over at the Fox in Redondo but she wanted to see *Sundays and Cybele*, a French movie that had won an Oscar, up in Westwood.

"What's it about?"

"It's supposed to be really beautiful," Mary said. "It's about this orphan girl who becomes friends with an older soldier who has amnesia."

"What about *The Longest Day*?"

"But I already know how it ends?"

"We could go see your movie," Lester said reluctantly.

"If you don't want to see it, say so," Mary said, annoyed.

"I didn't say I didn't want to see it. I just don't know if I want to drive all the way up to Westwood. How about we do something more local? We could go to Castagnola's or the Polynesian, or Tony's."

"Isn't that expensive?"

"Okay, I haven't gotten a raise yet, but I've got to be in line for one. I'm working my first real case not just handing out parking tickets, but real policing."

"You know, I'm proud of you. Kisses," Mary said, smooching through into the receiver.

"I know, Hon. I love you," he whispered.

"Me too."

"My boss, Kappe, invited us to a barbecue at his house on Sunday afternoon."

"Don't you not like him?" Mark asked.

"Maybe I don't know him well. It's only been a week," Lester said.

"I'll come if you want, but I really want to see that movie," Mary said.

"How about we see it on Sunday night and that way we can have an excuse to ditch the barbecue," Lester whispered.

"Impressive. Honestly, I don't really feel like going out to a big dinner and all. How about we just meet up, walk along the beach and talk about the future and our place in the world?"

"Only if we can recite poetry and drink tiny cups of terrible coffee."

"So, you do want to see the movie?" Mary asked pleadingly.

"I once saw *The Seventh Seal*," Lester said with a sigh. "I only went because I thought it was a Disney nature picture, about a family of seals. Just kidding."

"But did you like it? I found it really profound."

"I'd have liked a movie about seals better. The only deep movies I like are submarine pictures." Lester could tell when Mary was disappointed with him but he wanted to be honest with her.

"How about we meet at my house and go from there?"

"Let me just go back to my place first and change into something less police-like."

"Don't bother. I like a man in uniform," Mary said seductively.

"I'm not wearing my uniform."

"Even better," Mary said before breaking out in giggles. "I can't believe I just said that."

"You've got me blushing," Lester whispered.

"My parents want me to help out with the decorating but I'm going to say that you're taking me to the library to study," Mary whispered.

Lester straightened the notecards and got dressed to go out. He decided to get a bite to eat. It was just after 5:00 and he figured that if he found a place near Averodyne, he might be able to run into some of the workers.

He drove up and down the streets near Averodyne to find a likely spot. At the end of the long block Averodyne was on, there was a corner place called the Burger Stop.

The Burger Stop had a few seats but most of the people were taking their food and leaving. The guys in front of Lester were a couple of guys in coveralls and a couple of guys in grey pants, short sleeves and skinny ties.

"Hey, you guys work at Averodyne don't ya?" Lester said.

The guys turned around and recognized him and nodded.

"Anybody want to talk with me? I've got a few questions and I'll spot your dinner."

"Sure," the guys in coveralls said.

Lester bought their lunches and ordered a burger for himself then followed them out to a small table.

"If you don't mind. I've got a few questions that have been bugging me."

"Shoot," said one of the guys, who was in his late forties and had a pair of safety goggles perched on the top of his head.

"I'm investigating the. . ." Lester said before he was interrupted.

"Yeah, we remember you," the younger guy said coarsely. "You just talked to us a couple of days ago."

"Okay, I'll cut to the chase," Lester said, not sure what to ask.

"Meanwhile back on the farm," the older guy said before taking a big bite of his burger.

Lester paused and looked down at the ground, thought for a few seconds and then said, "What did you think about Steven Shawn?"

"He was okay, when you could understand him with that accent," the younger guy said.

"He knew his stuff," the older guy said between chews. "He could get in your face and he wasn't always right, but he'd back down when you showed him he was wrong."

"Did anyone have a beef with him?"

"Not in particular. He kind of kept to himself as far as I could see," the younger guy said.

"Yeah, he almost never went out to with anyone. He'd bring his lunch and eat at his desk and read books with a dictionary so he could look up words he didn't know."

"What about the Cheams?"

"Well, they did can him," the younger guy said with a chuckle.

The older guy looked concerned. "Okay, don't quote me or him on this, but the Cheams are nice as long as they are in charge and everything's going smooth otherwise you've got asshole and asshole junior."

"Why do you think they fired him?"

"He was back talking them," the older guy said, "and they don't like backtalk."

"About what?"

The older guy looked around to see if they could be overheard, but there was nobody close by. "Look, Averodyne is a scrappy company. I've been with them since just after they started. We're like a lot of companies. We're living off blood sucked from the big players who are sucking from the teats of the Department of Defense. It's all supposed to help the boys overseas protect us from the Red Chinese and the Russkies. The Department of Defense buys what they can get Congress to approve and we sell them what we can get them to buy. Whether or not it's what they need is beside the point when you're trying to make payroll. I just make what we make and cash their checks which pays for my house and vacations down in Acapulco. You've ever been down there?"

"Not yet, but I've seen the ads," Lester said.

"The girls they've got down there make you wish you hadn't brought your wife along," the older man side with a wide grin.

"So, what was it that started the beef between Shawn and which one of the Cheam's?"

"It started with Johnny," the younger guy said. "There was something about a year ago that Steve tried to change the specs on and Johnny just about blew up. Remember that?"

"Yeah," the older guy said. "You're costing us money was what he yelled at him."

"Steve looks at Johnny and says, coolly, well, that' better than the part failing at Mach 1," the younger guy said.

"Johnny looked at him like he'd take a wrench and beat him upside the head, but Johnny cooled himself down and we re-did everything, and I mean everything," the older guy said.

"But he was right," the younger guy said.

"Yeah, you could say that about him otherwise the Cheams wouldn't have done it," the older guy said.

"Then did anything else happen?"

"Yeah, about a month ago, they were yelling in the big guy's office," the older guy said.

"It was hush, hush," the younger guy, "but, and I've got this from a good source. . ."

"Who?" the older guy asked.

"From a good source, let me just say that. So, the story is that Steven complained to Carlton that something he was working on wasn't up to snuff and Carlton says to him, supposedly. . ."

"Supposedly?" the older guy asked.

"Supposedly. That's what I was told. Carlton tells him, Steve, that if he didn't like it he could leave."

"What was he like the day he was fired?"

"I heard that he kicked Carlton's car," the older guy said.

"I saw him do it. Then he drove off mad," the younger guy said.

"Do you think that they had anything to do with his murder?"

Both guys looked stunned. "Nah, why would they. They'd fired the guy," the older guy said.

Lester thanked them for their help and then ate half his lukewarm burger and threw the rest in a trashcan as he walked to his car. It was not even six o'clock when he drove out of Hawthorne and down to

Torrance. He had no idea whether or not Elizabeth was going to be home but it was worth a try.

As he drove south on Hawthorne boulevard through Lawndale he stopped at a gas station and used the payphone to call Elizabeth. Her mom answered when he called and said that Elizabeth wasn't home, but she expected her within the hour.

"Sorry to bother you again, but I've got some more questions about Steve Shawn."

"It's so horrible what happened to that man."

"Did you ever meet any of his friends?"

"I once met some of the guys he kibbitzed with. They came over for Passover last year before they broke up. They were okay, but not necessarily guys you'd want your daughter to marry. One of them, I can't remember his name, was okay. He was a student. There was one guy, Hess, his name I remember. I didn't like him at all. He was so brash and a big name-dropper. You'd think he knew a lot of people in Hollywood, like he was a big shot, but I could see right through him. They were quite a bunch. The only thing I could figure about why they hung out with each other was that they hadn't settled down, didn't have anything better to do."

"You mean they didn't get along?"

"No, they got along okay. I mean, that they didn't have anything in common except maybe for loneliness. There's a woman for every type, so they say but some guys take more work than the others."

"What about Mr. Shawn? What did you think about him?"

"He was lonely," she said sadly. "That was obvious. Theoretically, he was a good catch. He was good-looking, cultured, with a good job and an interesting accent that was strong but you could still understand him. He'd suffered during the war, as you can imagine, and then after the war. He was tough in a way that you could tell but not in a tough-guy way. He reminded me of my dad and uncles."

"At first, I was glad that they were together," she said, "but after a while, I could tell he'd never found a place in my daughter's heart. You can tell these things. For a while, I thought that maybe they'd grown on each other. He liked her, and honestly, who wouldn't. She's got a good head on her shoulders and she's a looker. We just haven't found the right guy for her."

"Can you think of anyone or any reason that someone might want to kill him? Did he owe anyone money? Was there anything amiss with him?"

"Owe him money? He was careful with his money, but not in a crazy way," she said with a chuckle. "He never wore anything fancy or flashy. He was careful with everything. He'd clean his plate no matter what I cooked, even if I burned it a little, which I rarely do."

"What about Paul Hess?"

"What about him?" she asked contemptuously. "He's a skirt chaser. That's the best I can say about him. He's over at our house, for Passover. Afterwards, Elizabeth tells me that he asked to play hide the afikoman with him, if you know what I mean?"

"Not really, but I think I get the basic idea."

"Steve was sitting right there, almost next to her. That's some chutzpah. I told him, Steve, the next time I saw him, that I'd rather he didn't bring all of his friends next year. I think he understood."

"Did Hess and Elizabeth ever go out, as far as you know?"

"No. I don't think she would. I don't think he's her type, at least I hope he isn't. What kind of a man does that?"

"So, do you think Hess might have held a grudge about it?"

"I don't think he even noticed he was making a pass. That's probably just how he talks to women," she said flatly. "Anyway, if he was jealous there would have been no reason to be. Elizabeth broke up with Steve a couple of weeks later."

"But would Hess have known that?"

"Why wouldn't he?" the mom said. "I can't imagine what else those guys had in common to talk about. Oh, I think Elizabeth's coming in the door. Do you want me to put her on?"

"Yeah, sure." Lester could hear some noise in the background and then Elizabeth came to the phone.

"My mom says you have some questions for me," Elizabeth said.

"Yeah. Sorry to bother you. I'm still trying to make some headway. Did Mr. Shawn owe any money to anyone? Did he have any enemies or someone who might be jealous of him?

"Manny Hess, I didn't like," Elizabeth said scornfully. "He'd make a pass at me whenever I saw him. The other guys are okay. Even his brother Paul is sort of okay, at least in comparison to Manny. As far as I know, none of them had anything against Steve and I don't think Steve owed anybody any money. He liked to take me out and buy me things, maybe a little too often for my comfort. Nothing ever expensive. If we were out at a restaurant and there'd be one of those guys selling red roses, he'd buy me one. I don't even like them. Maybe when I was fifteen, I'd have appreciated it. It's just something else to hold. I've got my purse and now I've got a rose I've got to figure out what to do with and not forget at the table."

"So, you don't think he owed anybody any money?"

Elizabeth laughed. "If you saw him count out nickels and pennies to pay a waiter. No, I don't think he did. What would he have spent it on and besides, I think he got paid pretty well at his job, or at least he should have."

"And you don't think he had anything to do with any kind of spying?"

"For whom?" Elizabeth asked sarcastically. "Maybe it was all a big show, but he really hated the Communists and especially the Russians. And the Germans too. We'd drive past a Volkswagen dealership and he'd say he couldn't understand how any Jew could buy a German car, no matter how good the engineering."

Lester could hear stifle a sob. "What about with Hess, Manny Hess. Did you think he was shady in some way?"

Elizabeth laughed. "Manny Hess is the kind of guy that has to worry about other people, husbands especially."

"So, if you have to guess, and maybe this isn't a fair question, but if you had to, who do you think might have killed him?"

"How am I supposed to know? That's your job. I still can't believe he's gone."

"Sorry, just a few more questions. What about Averodyne?"

"You said they fired him, right?"

"Yes, the day that he was murdered."

"Then why would they kill him? He didn't like working there and I know he was looking for another job. We would talk occasionally. He'd call me and sometimes I'd talk to him. We broke up, but I still. . .I did consider him a friend."

"Why did he want to leave? Did he say?"

"He thought they were crooks, but he wouldn't say why," she said angrily.

"What was he like with other people?"

"He was pretty cautious. You can imagine why. Sometimes I thought he'd go too far with it and wonder if he was being followed or was being spied on. He'd say, 'I love America, but Americans are so naïve.'"

Lester couldn't think of anything more to ask, so he thanked her for her help and told her to thank her mom too. "I'll get back in touch if I have any more questions."

He stopped by his apartment, took a shower then called Mary to tell her he was on his way. He was at her house in twenty minutes. Mary opened the door as he came through their gate.

"My parents are at the club getting ready for tomorrow. My mom's on the planning committee and my dad's roped in every year setting things up. Do you want a drink? I just learned how to make a martini," Mary said.

"A beer would be fine. Aren't you too young to be drinking?"

Mary laughed. "What are you, a cop? Seriously. There's a bottle of Soave in the fridge."

"That would be great too," Lester said as he came into the house.

Mary went into the kitchen, so he followed her there. When he entered, she handed him a glass of Soave and poured one for herself, too.

"I know I'm underage. You're not going to arrest me are you officer?"

Lester put his glass down on the kitchen counter and gently pulled Mary to his side. "I've got you now."

They kissed and as their kisses became more passionate, Mary paused, drank some of the wine in a gulp, and put the glass down on the counter next to his before returning her lips to his. His hands roamed from her waist, up her back to caress her neck and then down her sides just grazing her breasts. She leaned into him and placed her arms around his neck then played with his hair. His hair was too short to run her fingers through, so she just brushed it back and forth as if it was the nap of a camel's hair sofa.

Mary un-entangled herself and stepped back. She reached for her glass of wine and took a long swig. "That's cooling," she said shyly.

Lester took a sip from his wine and said "I've never had Soave. I like it."

"I like you, that's what I'm worried about."

"Is it a problem?" he said, reaching out for her hand.

She took his hand, interlocked her fingers with his, then pulled her hand away. "You were saying something about a weekend away."

"It was just an idea. We could go to Catalina or maybe San Diego or even Vegas."

"I don't think I'm ready for Vegas. But I think I might be some day."

"It's just an idea."

"It's a lovely idea. I think about it. I think about it a lot really. I imagine waking up next to you. I imagine having breakfast in bed. You don't think that's too naughty of me, do you?" She blushed as she spoke and turned her head away from him shyly.

"I don't."

"My parents would never go for it unless they didn't know. I could tell them I was going with one of my friends. Janet would cover for me. I know she would. We could go next weekend. I don't want you to have to wait that long," Mary said bashfully.

"I don't mind waiting," Lester said.

"I know you don't and that's really sweet of you. That's one of the things that I like about you. And that's one of the things that makes it so hard. For me, that is." She leaned into him and enveloped him with her arms, pressing her body against his. "Do you want to see my bedroom?" she whispered in his ear.

"I'd love to," Lester said, his hands roaming up to cup her breasts.

Mary sighed and kissed him, then led him down the hall to her room. "What about. . ." she stammered nervously.

"I think I know what you mean," Lester whispered. "I've sworn an oath to serve and to protect."

An hour or so later, Lester lay on her bed with Mary's head on his chest and her arms around his body, her legs still wrapped around his.

"My arm is falling asleep," Lester whispered.

"I want to stay like this forever."

"Are you okay? No regrets?"

Mary lifted her head up and stared into his eyes. "We need to sneak away for a weekend."

Lester lifted up his head and kissed her. Mary lowered herself on to him and returned his kisses with an ardor he'd only ever experienced with her half an hour earlier.

"I should probably air out the room," Mary said quietly.

"Do you want to get something to eat?" Lester asked.

"I'd love to get something to eat," Mary said dreamily, "but I probably should clean up, take a shower before we go."

"I could join you."

Mary was taken aback. She sat up suddenly and pulled away from him. "No. No, I can't do that," she said as if Lester had asked her to do something unbelievably embarrassing. "I'll be naked!"

"You're already naked."

"Don't remind me," she said nervously. "That's completely different."

"And I'm naked, at least underneath my clothes."

"That's fine for you. I'm not used to it, in fact, could you not stare,"

"Okay, I won't stare,"

"And don't peek."

Lester pulled the covers over his head while Mary got out of the bed and sprinted out of the room and down the hall. With her back turned, he lowered the covers and peeked at her beautiful and naked backside.

"You're peeking," Mary said as she rushed into the bathroom.

"It's all a blur. I don't have my glasses on."

"You don't wear glasses!" Mary called out before turning on the shower.

A little while later, Mary came back from the bathroom, wrapped in a pink, terry cloth robe. Lester had remade the bed, got dressed and was sitting at her desk looking over her textbooks.

"Let me get dressed," Mary said as she clutched the robe tightly around her. "Alone."

Lester smiled and left the room. "We could get a burger and head downtown or maybe some Mexican. You like Mexican."

"There's always something going on downtown, but I can't stay out late, not without telling my parents."

"We could leave a note."

"But then they'd know you were here," Mary said nervously.

"So, you leave a note and just say that I came by to pick you up. Do you still want to go to the movies? It's not too late."

"How about dinner and a walk along the beach? It'll cool us off," Mary said with a sly smile.

Downtown Hermosa was hopping, from Pier Avenue south to the Redondo Beach line and north to 22nd Street and the Green Store, a corner market. It was still early evening. The rodsters were making their circuit through the town, slowly cruising Hermosa Avenue in their fancy cars, their engines grumbling and snorting like bulls ready for a matador. Teenagers waited in line at the Foster's Freeze for burgers and shakes.

The serious surfers were all home in bed, getting their forty winks to face the morning's waves. The hodads and part-timers were spiffed up in their Pendleton shirts and huarache sandals. The girls and the gidgets followed along or led the way. It was hard to tell who was first and which was second. The bikers weren't out yet. The fights hadn't started and the crowd was still largely milkshake and soda sippers.

Lester and Mary went to for some veal piccata and eggplant parmigiana. They were not the only daters dining by candlelight. A man tried to sell them a single red rose, but they waved him off.

After dinner, they walked along Hermosa Avenue towards the Pier. As they stopped at an intersection and waited for a parting of the rodsters, Johnny Cheam pulled up to the curb behind the wheel of a brilliant white Packard with beautifully painted red flames and an exposed, chromed engine.

"Dude!" Johnny called out. "Mary!"

Lester was surprised to see Johnny and that he seemed to know his girlfriend.

"Why walk when you can ride in style?" Johnny called out to them. He was alone in his hot rod but because he was blocking the flow of traffic, the cars behind him began honking vigorously. "Hey, I'll pull over so we can parley."

"I've got no beef with you," Lester said.

"We're just going for a walk," Mary said. "I'll see you tomorrow."

"Tomorrow?" Lester asked.

Johnny jolted through the intersection then parked half a block up.

"At the Spring Fling," Mary said. "His dad is past president of the board of governors. I've known him since junior bowlers. We don't have to talk with him if you don't want to. How does he know you?"

Lester paused and considered what to say. "The guy who died last Friday night worked for his dad's company."

"It's a small world after all," Mary said.

Johnny rushed up to them. He was wearing a red jacket with a white stripe along one side and an Ascot Park racetrack patch. "Didn't know you two knew each other. It is a small, small world."

"He's my boyfriend," Mary said, blushing.

"I can see that," Johnny said. "You guys want to go for a ride. I just finished this one and I need to break it in. It's a beaut', huh? You want to check her out?"

"Sure," Lester said.

"I'd rather not," Mary said, tugging on Lester's shirtsleeve.

"Ah, come on," Johnny said.

"How about just for a moment," Lester said.

Mary frowned, but followed Lester and Johnny back to his car.

"You can't see it so well in this light," Johnny said, "but I've put a lot of elbow grease into this one. She's like my Mona Lisa, my Venus De Milo. You should have seen her when I got her. I've got some pics. The whole process." Johnny opened the door to the car and took out a small photo album. He showed them pictures of the car when he bought it, which was not much more than a rusty shell sitting on blocks.

"That must have kept you busy," Lester said.

"You don't know the quarter of it," Johnny said.

Another hot rod pulled up next to them. The driver whistled to them then sped off. An older guy out walking his Dalmatian stopped and stared at the car's engine. "Nice car," the man said.

Johnny turned from Lester and Mary. "Do you want to see my photo album?"

"Sure," the guy said as his dog squatted to shit.

"We'll catch you tomorrow," Mary said as she pulled Lester away from the car.

Lester looked back as Mary walked quickly away. Johnny was busy showing off his car to whoever stopped or turned around, reveling in the attention. He was like one of those guys you see hanging out with a huge parrot on their shoulder hoping someone some chick-a-dee couldn't resist a guy whose shoulder may at any moment be covered in bird shit, though that never seems to happen, either one, take your pick.

When they were around a corner and halfway down one of the pedestrian-only streets that lead up to the beach, Mary stopped.

"What gives?" Lester asked.

"Sorry. I'm not normally that rude. It's just that he brings it out in me. We once dated, well dated is a strong word for twelve-year-olds. We were officially a couple, a junior bowling team. We won the SoCal Regionals. We went on to all state and could have won, but I couldn't stand him anymore. We'd have gone on to nationals. I could have gotten to fly to Hartford,

Connecticut, but I threw the game. I think he knows I did. I claimed I had a headache. I don't remember exactly what I said. We barely even kissed if you can call him grabbing my face and slamming his scratchy peach fuzz lips against mine and trying to stick his tongue in. I can still taste his tongue because he'd just eaten a whole package of pixy sticks. Then later, I saw him with Sheila Miller. We were never really an item. It was a figment of other people's overactive imaginations including his own. We didn't go to the same high school, so I'd only see him at the club and neither of us spends much time there anymore."

"Do you feel guilty about it, throwing the game?"

"Whew, I'm sorry to lay this on you," Mary said as they reached the Strand and headed back towards the pier.

The Strand was nearly empty. There were a few other people out for the evening, walking along the beach. The fog had rolled in and it was so thick you couldn't see the stars.

"He was even kind of cute back then," Mary said. "All the other girls thought he was, and I guess I did too at first, but then I got to know him and the more I knew him the less I could stand him. It wasn't all his fault. Our parents seemed to think we were the perfect couple and destined to marry, creating some lawn bowling dynasty. I hope you don't think I'm cruel for saying so. He's never done anything wrong to me besides trying to kiss me with a mouth that tasted like grape soda and cherry soda all mixed together."

"Was he violent? I know he was just a kid, but was he violent? Is he violent?"

"No, he wasn't violent, but then I didn't go to school with him. At the lawn bowling club, he's a shining light, especially with his dad on the board of governors."

"What's his dad like?"

"Two peas in a pod. No, more like a puppy that follows you around. That's another thing I couldn't stand about him. That's what keeps him from being who he could really be. Not to psychoanalyze him, but he's got mommy issues and he's definitely got daddy issues. When we lost the tournament, his dad never forgave him. He lost at Southern Cal the next year with another partner and then he stopped entering the tournaments. He's still one of the best bowlers we've got, maybe one of the best in the state."

"Do you think he's seeing someone?" Lester asked.

"Not that I know of," Mary said anxiously. "He's brought some girls around from time to time, but they never seem to last. He's usually hanging out with guys and the last year or so, he hasn't been around much. I guess he's really gotten into this whole rodster thing."

"So, he's not a hothead or a brute?"

"Not with me. Being a clumsy twelve-year-old doesn't count. But I have seen him blow his stack. Even when we lost and I know he knew I'd let him down. Sometimes when he's been drinking and if he loses, he can get pretty belligerent, but then you should see his dad. He's nothing like his dad, in every way. For his dad, everything is personal. He can hold it together most of the time. I guess that's why he gets elected to the board of governors every year plus I think he likes to be in charge."

"So, I have a lot to look forward to tomorrow. I'm not going to have to bowl, am I?"

Mary laughed. "Of course you're going to have to bowl. Don't worry, you can be on my team. Not everyone is any good. Some just come for the fun of it."

"And I have to wear white?" Lester asked to tease Mary.

"You have to wear white!" Mary exclaimed. "And wear some sneakers, nothing that will cut into the grass. You'll be banished and condemned, worse than Hester Prynne."

"What happened to her?" Lester asked even though he knew the reference.

"*The Scarlet Letter*. You must have read that," Mary said skeptically.

"Yeah, of course." He didn't mind that she knew more than he did on most things academic. At his school, they just didn't have the resources or the advantages that some other schools had, but he wouldn't have known the difference if he hadn't scrammed from Taft.

Just before they got to the pier, where the defunct Ocean Aquarium was, its blue stuccoed walls peeling away to expose the wire mesh beneath, they saw a wave of surfers and surfer chicks stomping to the sounds of a band. They were under the pilings of the pier and about halfway from the water's edge to the Strand.

"They shouldn't be there," Mary said. "That pier could fall down any time. That's what my mom says. She's on the committee to build a new one."

"We could go over and tell them," Lester said.

"I'm sure they wouldn't listen, if they could even hear us with that racket," Mary said contemptuously as she swayed with the beat.

"I kind of like it. You can dance to it."

"It is pretty trippy? Do you want to?"

"I'll carry our shoes."

With their shoes off, they went over to the surfers. Mary knew some of them from high school and they nodded to her as they approached. The band was really cooking, the sax player was wailing, and the drummer was driving the kids wild. The dancing was like the Twist, but with less twisting, probably because they were dancing on sand rather than a floor, and with arm pistoning up and down, like he was milking a cow, rather than swinging.

"Isn't this the ginchiest!" a girl dancing next to them exclaimed.

"No doubt," Lester said as he tried to follow the dance and not look like a goof.

Mary was better at the dance, which required her to vigorously shake her rump in the opposite direction as she twisted her torso.

They danced through a couple of tunes before Mary signaled that she wanted to go. They made their way through the crowd, which had grown larger and younger, to the Strand. They brushed as much sand as they could off of their feet, which was never enough, and put their shoes back on.

At Pier Avenue, in front of the Mermaid restaurant's parking lot, several men stood next to their motorcycles. They were cleaner cut than the typical bikers, and their motorcycles were shiny Honda Super Hawks rather than Harleys.

Pier Avenue, from the pier to Hermosa Avenue was hopping. All the parking spots were full. There was a line outside the door of Pio's Italian Restaurant. The wide storefront of The Insomniac was the brightest spot on the block. The bars and The Lighthouse on the opposite side of the street had lines and people hanging outside. Bikers roared up and down the block, making a noisy circuit. Clumps of teenagers strolled about eating burgers and fries out of paper bags.

"I'm not ready to go home," Mary said, putting her arm around Lester's waist.

"We don't have to call it a night," Lester said before kissing her.

"Can we stay out all night? I don't want this night to ever end," Mary said.

"Your parents wouldn't be happy," Lester said.

"My parents, my parents. I'm an adult. I'm a woman. Not a kid. I'll never forget this night. Not ever," Mary exclaimed.

"How about just another hour or two and then we can get you home?"

"Home? I don't need a home, when I've got you." She wrapped herself around him and nearly toppled him to the ground with the forcefulness of her hug.

Mary's ardor was making Lester uncomfortable. He could see that images of wedding gowns, PTA meetings, Thursday night casseroles, and the pitter-patter of the feet of little children were dancing around in her head. He'd only just gotten promoted and it wasn't even official yet. He could slip back down the rungs to metering if they didn't catch the killer. He could quit the force and try another line of work, not that he had any ideas. There was no way that he could support the two of them on his metering salary. Sure, the saying was that two could live as cheaply as one, but that only applied to the rent. He only had a double bed. They'd have to buy a bigger bed and sheets. Sheets were expensive, which was why he only had the two sets.

In front of The Insomniac, near the painter flicking pigments onto a canvas, a young woman with long, braided hair and wearing a purple peasant dress sat at a table shuffling a tarot deck.

"Let's have our fortune read," Mary said.

"I don't believe in it," Lester said as led her to the back, through the tables piled with books. A folk band was playing old-timey music, like something you could square dance to except that instead of calls, they were singing about hard times and life on the road.

"Aren't they great?" Mary said as they found some empty seats. "I just love folk music."

"When I was a kid, we just called it music. My uncles used to play music like this when we'd have a get-together on the weekends."

"Maybe we could go up there sometime. I want to see where you grew up. I want to meet your folks. I want to know everything about you."

Lester grimaced. "There's not much to know. I couldn't wait to get out of there."

"But it made you who you are. I've got to meet your family sometime. I don't want to meet them the first time at the wedding, assuming we get married, which I'm totally not assuming, but we did, you know." She blushed when she said it and looked at him like she was thinking about doing it again.

At the wedding, Lester thought. He liked the sound of the word, wedding, but dreaded all that went along with it, not the before or afterward, just the wedding itself.

"I love this music," Mary said enthusiastically. "It feels so real, not like Bobby Vinton and Pat Boone. It's real music with real feelings about real things. I love it. I wonder if they have a record."

Lester didn't feel that way at all. To him, it was a bunch of country club college kids singing about woes they'd never personally experienced. "I used to watch Buck Owens and Merle Haggard on *Chuck Wagon*. Do you like that stuff?"

"No, sorry, I don't really like country music. I just like folk and jazz." Mary smiled when she said that in the same way as people do when they tell you they've just gotten over a case of poison ivy.

When the set was over a poet came on stage and declaimed a long poem about walking across Texas with only his dog as a companion. Five minutes into the poem, Lester suggested they leave. Mary wanted to hear the rest of the poem, which ended in Oklahoma. The audience clapped wildly, except for Lester, who clapped reluctantly.

"I love this place," Mary said as they left. Her arms were around his waist. She kissed his cheek and neck and nibbled on his ear.

Lester blushed and returned her affection by gently grasping her ass. She pushed his hand away but didn't scold him.

"There are people here," she whispered into his ear before grabbing his ass and then giggling.

They walked through the crowds away from the beach. At the corner of Pier and Hermosa Avenues, Johnny Cheam was getting ticketed for blocking the intersection by Big John while John T waved cars around when the light changed. The blocks before and after were nearly gridlocked, so only a couple of cars made it through. The couple of girls in the back of Cheam's Packard, got out and waved goodbye. Cheam, leaning out the car's window, glanced back at the girls, then returned his attention to the cops.

"Let's walk the other way," Mary said, "along the beach."

The Strand in front of the Poop Deck was quiet but at the corner of the next block, at the Biltmore Hotel, a couple of teenagers duked it out on the beach, their girlfriends looking on in disgust. A larger guy ran over and broke it up, pulling the boy on top off of the other boy, who was protecting his head with his arms from the blows. The rest of the walk was quieter. The fog hadn't rolled in that night so they could see the lights of a couple of oil tankers unloading their cargo just up the coast and as far as the lights of Pacific Ocean Park amusement park just north of Venice.

Mary's parents were home when they arrived at her house. They retreated back around the corner to say good night, hugging each other tighter than they ever had before. They kissed and caressed and molded themselves against each other until they were breathless and had to pull apart.

"I'll walk you to your door," Lester said.

"I can't wait to see you tomorrow."

After Mary opened the door, she turned and waved to him and blew him a kiss before closing the door.

As Lester drove back to his apartment, he could smell her on his clothes. He could still feel her pressed against him. It wasn't very late, so he watched a *Francis the Talking Mule* movie on the late show.

At some point, he woke up on his couch, the TV still on with the test pattern Indian staring in the direction of the clock on his living room wall, then got undressed and into bed.

He had trouble getting back to sleep. Sensual thoughts of Mary, remembering her feel, her joyous exclamations and encouragements, the mess and awkwardness afterward, strayed into thoughts of Johnny Cheam and his hot rod and back to Mary.

He wondered if Cheam did it. He seemed like an arrogant asshole, but could he kill? In the Army, Lester had learned that anyone can be taught to kill. He hoped that Mary wouldn't get pregnant. He'd tried to be careful and she'd said the time of the month was good, but you never really knew. He'd buy some protection before he saw her again.

Why should Cheam kill Shawn? Being an asshole could be enough but was it and could he prove anything? He had to find the gun. Nobody had come forward as a witness. He hoped that Mary didn't have any regrets. Were they moving too quickly?

Chapter 14

It was already after eight when he woke up. There wasn't much in his fridge, so he fixed himself oatmeal, which he ate while watching the *Deputy Dawg* and *The Alvin Show*. After breakfast, he went back to the TV and watched more Saturday morning cartoons until his inner voice, which always sounded like his dad, got on his case for lazing about.

He checked his white clothes to see that they were clean and then pressed them good enough to pass inspection by the nastiest of his drill sergeants. Lunch was a cheese sandwich with mustard, a beer and more TV.

If he solved the case, especially if he beat Kappe to it, that had to ensure a promotion, maybe even help him move to a larger police department. The murder was Shawn's bad luck but his good luck. It didn't seem right to feel that way, but he couldn't help himself. He made himself another half sandwich and took a nap in front of the TV while it played a Western he had no interest in but didn't bother to turn off. There was a book on the nightstand next to his bed that he'd started and never finished and another one he'd bought but hadn't started.

Midday passed slowly into the afternoon without him having accomplished anything his dad would have considered an accomplishment. He re-checked his clothing, made himself a peanut butter and honey sandwich and thought about the case.

The Cheams were going to be there. He wondered if it would be fair to check them out, try to sneak in a few questions when they were relaxed and lubricated. For Shawn's sake, he had to do it, but he could see problems with Mary's parents cropping up if he broke the decorum, or spoiled it, or whatever you did with decorum if you were indecorous.

How far could you throw a lawn bowling ball? Did you toss them like a horseshoe or roll them like in tenpin? Mary had given him a short course once while they stood in line at the La Mar to see a movie, but he hadn't paid close enough attention and it was purely theoretical.

He carefully got dressed, making sure his hands were clean and cleaning them and drying them before putting on each article of white clothing. From his apartment to his car to the Beau Rivage Lawn Bowling Club was only a few miles, but all it took was one mishap to the kibosh on his ensemble. They probably only served white wine and no colas or iced teas. There was sure to be mayo.

His clothing survived the drive to Hermosa and the walk from the station, where he was able to park his car without fear of a ticket. It was only a couple of blocks to Clark Stadium where Beau Rivage had its clubhouse and bowling greens. The shuffleboard courts had been taken over for parking, but that lot was already full.

In the adjacent community center, a rock band, the Plungers, played on the small stage playing slow numbers for the teeny boppers underneath yards of blue pastel crepe paper streamers. The boys and girls were all dressed in white and danced chastely with each other. Grandmotherly chaperones, also dressed in white, stood on the outskirts of the dancefloor, glaring at the moral decay of their grandkids. The kids and the band, who were still in high school, looked like they were driving around with their parking brakes on but ready to floor it if they were left unsupervised.

He didn't see Mary, so he walked back to the bowling green. It was hard to tell people apart, beyond male and female, old and young, when everyone was dressed in white. Groups of players were rolling the black bowls towards the small, yellow jacks. Spectators watched intently from the sidelines drinking white wine.

He found Mary sitting on the sidelines talking with two girls. There were large bowl bags at their feet, each one looking like a vertical carpet bag but made out of canvas. She stood when she saw him, kissing him quickly before introducing him to her friends from the club. The girls were nice and were as happy to meet him as Mary was to show him off. They were blond, tanned and fit and looked like they spent all their spare time at the beach or a pool.

"Is this your first time?" one of the girls asked him.

"Can you tell?" Lester said.

"You don't have your own bowls," she said. "The ones they have in the club are okay. You'll do fine."

"With Mary, you'll probably win the whole thing," the other said.

"Not if they're playing against you know who," the first girl said.

"Don't listen to them," Mary said. "I'm not going to feel bad if we lose. Just roll, but not too hard and concentrate. Just remember that the bowls are weighted and designed to arc. Just relax and don't worry about it. It's not a real tournament anyway."

"Except for being crowned King and Queen of the Fling," one of the girls said. "I remember when you and Johnny first won it and you beat the under-seventeens. Do you remember who that was that year?"

"I'm not even interested," Mary said.

"She's interested," one of the girls said. "If you don't think she's competitive that's because she hides it well. They were only fifteen and he must have been seventeen."

"Jill!" Mary exclaimed, embarrassed.

"You know it's true," Jill said. She looked up at Lester and winked conspiratorially.

"And with that, we bid you adieu," Mary said as she took Lester's arm. "Would you mind carrying my bag?"

Mary handed Lester her bag, which was quite heavy. She asked him if he wanted to practice as she led him to the clubhouse so they could sign in. "You can just use my bowls. There's a practice green if you want to warm up and take a few practice runs."

"Sure, but you're not going to be upset if I'm no good," Lester said.

Mary leaned in and whispered, "I think you're very good," in his ear before giggling and blushing then looking about to see if anyone noticed.

The practice green was filled so they only got a couple of rolls in before their first game. Thanks to Mary's great skill, they easily won their first two games. The third game was a harder win, but Lester had a good enough game that he contributed more than he hindered.

Between their third and fourth game, they had a pause, long enough to grab a bite and relax with a glass of wine, at least for Lester. Mary wasn't old enough so she drank ginger ale.

"It looks like you may be playing against Johnny Cheam," Mary's dad said when he walked by.

Mary looked over at the green and pointed Johnny and his teammate, a girl Mary said was still in high school, though a senior. When they were finished with their game, Johnny brought his partner over to sit with them. She sat silently as she sipped water from a glass.

"We meet again on the field of battle," Johnny said confidently.

"It's just a game," Mary said.

"Said the girl who. . ." Johnny began to say before Lester cut him off.

"I'm not going to let you treat her like that," Lester said angrily.

"I'm just teasing her, razzing her, in a friendly manner," Johnny said defensively. "Can't you take a joke?"

"Take a joke?" Lester said indignantly.

"I can take care of myself!" Mary called out. "Save it for the bowling green, Johnny. We may not take you down. I'm not saying we will and I'm not saying we won't, but we're going to do it with class and grace."

"This isn't the ballet," Johnny's girl piped in.

"How about we keep everything copacetic," Lester said. "It's just a game, however important some of us might think it is."

"Okay, okay," Johnny said. "Point taken. Do you want to go get a beer with me?" he asked Lester, patting him gently on the back.

"Don't get him drunk," Mary said. "I need him sober."

"I'm sure you do," Johnny said.

Mary laughed but the other girl said, "I don't get it."

Johnny led Lester to the clubhouse. Inside, there was a bar with a bartender in a short black jacket, white shirt and black tie shaking a cocktail in a silver shaker. Practically the only people at the bar were men, most of whom were smoking cigars. "Pre-Castro," someone said.

The bartender handed Johnny two beers, one of which he passed on to Lester. "On the house," Johnny said. "It's an open bar if your dad's paying for the booze."

Lester thanked him then followed him outside.

"Sorry we got off on the wrong foot," Johnny said, offering Lester his hand. "She knows I like to tease her. She's used to it. I've been dogging her since we were kids."

"I'd appreciate a hiatus," Lester said.

"I can handle that. It's just a habit and by the way, you and Mary are the only team I don't mind losing to."

"I used to be okay at horseshoes," Lester said.

"I'm sure you are. I'm sure your good at hand-eye coordination, since you're going out with Mary."

Lester reddened and felt like punching him but Johnny just laughed.

"It's all about relaxation. You should take some deep breaths," Johnny said then took a big breath and held it before letting it out slowly then doing it again.

"So, I was wondering, did you always want to be a machinist? Did you ever think about going to college?"

"Nah, college is not for me. I like making stuff. Every day I come into work and I feel like the king of the biggest, baddest machine shop. I could make anything in there. After work, I make parts for the rodster scene, special orders and shit and I've got a car I race over at Ascot Park. I'd like to set up a separate division but my dad says, and he's right about this, that there's no customer as good as Uncle Sam. With the Cold War going on and now the Space Race, if you can make it, they will buy it and their checks won't ever bounce."

"I heard that you almost got thrown out of high school for making a silencer," Lester said quietly.

Johnny smiled proudly. "That's on the up and up. To me, it was just a project. You see those things in movies and they're impossible to get if you're in high school and pretty hard otherwise. I guess I was watching too many spy movies and reading too much Ian Fleming. I found some info on the general principles, drew up some plans and made one. So, like a stupid shit, I bring it into class and show it off. I'm thinking that the shop teacher would be really impressed but instead, he has a cow, really, really goes ape, I mean one hundred percent certified baboon and confiscates it. I was really pissed but I guess I was lucky that it wasn't reported."

"Did you make another one?" Lester asked.

"Seeing as how you're a Clancy, and now you've been promoted to Dick, I'm not saying. In principle yes, of course, I could. They're not that complicated. I think I'll stick to hotrods."

"Just curious. When you made it, could you fit it into anything? I imagine that it's not one size fits all?" Lester asked.

Johnny grinned and downed the rest of his beer. "I sized it for the Luger my dad brought back from the war. Man, he sure was in the thick of it. You should hear some of his stories. Anyway, I thought it would look cool, like something from a spy movie. I wished he'd had a Mauser. That would have looked totally cool."

"Did you get to test it out?"

"Are you kidding me? Where was I going to do that? It's not like I could bring it to a shooting range?"

"What about up in the mountains, Lake Arrowhead or Big Bear? You must have a place up there?"

"Yeah, we've got a cabin up in Arrowhead, but we don't use it much. I have some parties from time to time. You should come up sometime. With the altitude, you can drink half as much beer for twice the buzz."

"Sounds like you know how to have fun."

"Oh, I know how to have fun. I just can't remember afterwards how much fun we've had. I'm thinking of slowing things and leave the speed to my rod."

Their game against Johnny Cheam and his partner went well at the beginning, but Lester muffed a roll, knocking the jack closer to Cheam's bowls. Mary tried to rescue them, but it was a nearly impossible shot. She came close, but didn't end up changing anything. It ended up being a rout. Johnny Cheam grabbed his partner, kissed her and swung her around, let her go and then pumped his arms into the air. There were a lot of unappreciative murmurs amongst the onlookers. Mary bowed and led Lester off the field towards the buffet table.

"He's such a you-know-what," Mary whispered angrily in his ear.

"I'm sorry I lost the game for us," Lester said.

"Oh, it's okay, honey. We did okay. We won the first three."

"Good game," Carlton Cheam said as he joined them in the buffet line. "Try the shrimp before it's all gone," he said, pointing to a tall pile of boiled shrimp that must have cost a fortune. "Hi Mary. I didn't know you two knew each other."

Mary blushed as she put her arm around Lester's waist.

"It's a small world," Lester said.

"It is a small world, after all," Mr. Cheam said. His smile looked forced to Lester, like he was putting on a show past the limit of his abilities.

"Your son is pretty good."

Mr. Cheam glared at Mary, still forcing his smile. "Nearly state champion. He could have gone on to nationals."

"Well, it's just a game," Lester said as he loaded his tiny plate with shrimp. "Hmm, the shrimp does look good."

"Yes, but you have to admit, winning sure beats losing," Mr. Cheam said.

"I think I'll go find us a place to sit," Mary said as she topped off her plate with some Crab Rangoon.

"I'll find you."

Mary hurried off gracefully enough not to spill anything off her plate.

"She's always been a handful," Mr. Cheam said. "One thing about Mary; you can always count on not counting on her."

"That's my girlfriend you're talking about," Lester said sternly.

"Then you know what I'm talking about," Mr. Cheam said. "Oh, I don't mean just her. Take my wife. . .please."

Lester didn't laugh at the joke. Mr. Cheam waited awkwardly for a reaction that never came.

"You know, Mr. Cheam, I had an interesting conversation with your son. He sure is some machinist. Did he ever tell you about how he made a silencer in high school shop class?"

Mr. Cheam scowled. "Braggadocio! That's Italian for he talks too much. You shouldn't listen to everything he says," he said in an angry whisper.

"I'd love to see some of your war souvenirs. I hear you've got quite the collection. My dad worked in an essential industry and my older brothers were too young. Korean War souvenirs just aren't as collectible, are they?"

"I've got a friend who picked up a really nice Tokarev off of a Commie officer. He had to pry it out of his frozen dead mitts," Mr. Cheam said.

"You must have brought something back from Europe," Lester said.

"A guy could make a lot of money back then selling souvenirs to GIs who never saw combat. I knew a guy once who made a lot of dough selling daggers and medals and stuff straight from a captured Nazi depot. It was like minting money. There were crates of them, mint, never issued."

"What about you?" Lester asked.

"Let me just say, that I didn't need to buy my glory. I found mine fair and square," Mr. Cheam said smugly.

"It's good to know that I'm in the presence of a real American hero," Lester said with a smidgen of sarcasm.

"Were you in the service?" Mr. Cheam asked.

"Yeah, but nothing special. I was stationed in Germany and my only worries were paper cuts and the older brothers of some of the Fräuleins."

"When I was there, there was a strict no fraternization policy, but things happened, of course," Mr. Cheam said with a wink at the end of his sentence.

"Well, I best be finding Mary," Lester said as he looked around the party for her.

"With a girl like that, you better keep your eyes peeled out for rustlers. If you've got something good, someone out there is going to want to take it all away from you."

"I'll keep that in mind." He added a couple more shrimp to the pile on this plate and carefully walked through the tipsy throng until he found Mary.

"Every time I think about yesterday, I blush. I can't help it. Do you think anyone has noticed? Do you think I look different?"

"They're only going to notice that you're the most beautiful woman here."

Mary blushed from head to toe.

In the space where the shuffleboard court was, a band wearing matching Hawaiian shirts that began playing Island tunes.

"They're playing a Limbo," Mary squealed. "Oh, come on. You've got to do it with me!"

Lester was reluctantly led onto the dance floor where tipsy revelers were doing their best to slink under a bamboo pole while the band did their best calypso impression. Mary was easily able to slink underneath the pole no matter how low it got while Lester and most of the others fell to the ground or knocked the pole out of the hands of its two merry minders. One of the dancers looked very much like Beatrice Loehner, the woman who was with Shawn the night he was murdered. Lester only got a glimpse of her.

Johnny Cheam joined in after the first couple of rounds and lasted longer than most of the other guys, not counting the little kids for whom it was easy peasy. The last surviving dancers were Mary and two teenage girls who surely must have been gymnasts, perhaps champion gymnasts. The pole was so low at the end that an average-sized dog wouldn't make it yet somehow Mary made it under while the two gymnasts didn't.

Mary bounced up after passing under the pole, pretended that she'd thrown out her back and then knocked back a glass of champagne offered to her by Mr. Cheam, who'd taken over the microphone from the MC.

Lester looked about for Beatrice but didn't see her in the crowd and he began to doubt that he'd seen her at all. She wasn't dressed as a beatnik. Nobody would wear basic black at the Spring Fling. That would be like declaring your Communist sympathies at a Baptist church.

"Let's hear it for the multi-talented Mary Nix!" Mr. Cheam drunkenly bellowed out. "I'm sure I'm not the only one who's not surprised that she's so limber, except for maybe my son and some other lucky ones out there."

Mrs. Cheam blushed and rushed up onto the little stage where Mr. Cheam was standing to tug on his jacket.

Mr. Cheam looked down at his wife and said, "Enjoy it now guys, after twenty-five years and a kid or. . ." He wasn't able to finish the sentence. Mrs. Cheam yanked the microphone from his hands while several older men tugged him off the stage.

"What my husband meant to say," Mrs. Cheam said, gamely attempting to hide her embarrassment with a broad and toothy smile, "is that we're all happy for Mary and are impressed along with everyone else."

"Can we go?" Mary said, handing Lester her half-full champagne glass.

"If you want," Lester said before finishing off the champagne in one gulp.

As they walked back to his car, Mary fumed about what an asshole Mr. Cheam was, especially when he was drunk and what a competitive jerk Johnny was. Lester tried to calm her but she was too riled up. When they got to his car she got in, closed the door and cried.

"Do you want to go somewhere? We can just sit here as long as you want to," Lester said.

"No, let's go for a drive. Let's drive up to Palos Verdes and maybe just drive around. I feel like parking," Mary whispered.

They drove through Redondo Beach past the Hollywood Riviera, a collection of swank shops and restaurants on a bluff above the ocean that was more pleasant than the real Hollywood. Skunk was the dominant smell of Palos Verdes, at least around Malaga Cove a fake, but still beautiful, Mediterranean-ish shopping center with the fountain of Neptune. The higher up the hills you went the nicer the houses, but they stuck along the coastal road, Paseo del Mar, where the houses were up to the edge of the high cliffs.

"Park near the Dominator," Mary said, referring to the wrecked former Liberty Ship, the SS Dominator that ran aground in the fog carrying a load of beef and wheat from Vancouver. You could see the wreck, almost intact from the bluffs above the cliff. The night was clear enough and the moon full enough that they would have a good view of the ship's silhouette.

Mary didn't want to talk, not about the Cheams nor about anything. She wanted to snuggle up against him in the back seat feel how much he wanted her.

"Somebody might see us," she whispered as he unbuttoned her blouse, but she didn't stop him.

The car's windows steamed up and as their breathing got hotter and heavier. With his mouth ranging across her neck and breasts, he unbuckled his pants.

"We can't. Somebody might see us," she said, pulling herself out from under him. "I want to. I really want to, but not like this," she said.

"What about my place? We could do it at my place," Lester said desperately.

Mary pressed him close, crying on his shoulder. "I can't. Don't be mad, but I can't. I shouldn't have yesterday, but I couldn't wait, not with you. My parents would kill me, literally kill me if they found out."

"I don't mind. I do about the killing. We can drive home." He pulled a handkerchief from his pocket and handed it to her, then buckled his pants up.

Chapter 15

As they drove back to Mary's house, she cried most of the way and wouldn't explain why. He didn't know if she was mad at him, mad at herself, embarrassed, or if something else was up with her. He walked her up to the door. The porch light came on. Mary put her arms around Lester and melted against his chest. "I love you," she whispered through her tears. "I hope you love me back."

"Of course I do," Lester whispered into her ear as he ran his fingers through her hair then took out a handkerchief and gently wiped her tears away. "I'll pick you up in the afternoon, about 4:30. We don't have to stay long, just long enough to eat and for me to have a beer. We could do something afterwards, maybe catch a movie. I'll see anything you want to see."

"*Sundays and Cybele*?" Mary asked. "I can't stay out late. I've got classes on Monday.

"Whatever you want," Lester said.

He had to get the promotion, a real promotion with a real pay raise. On his current salary, he could never support the both of them and he didn't want to take a charity job with her family's supermarkets. If he solved the case, they had to give him a raise and if they didn't, he'd just find another department. There must be at least forty departments in the county including the Sheriff's Department.

When he got back to his apartment, he sat in front of the TV watching *The Late Show*, a monster movie with a giant insect, and thought about the Cheams.

Why would Johnny freely admit that he'd made a silencer if he'd recently used it in a murder? Either he didn't kill Shawn or he was super cocky. Was anybody that cocky? Mr. Cheam was even worse. He was an aggressive drunk and pretty aggressive when he wasn't drunk.

The angry scientist in the movie, who'd turned into a bug during a failed experiment, was killed by his assistant and the assistant's girlfriend. As he died, he turned back into a human and repented all his bad mutant bug deeds as he died.

He woke up on the sofa sometime before 5:00 a.m. He'd managed to turn the TV off before he went to sleep, though he didn't remember doing so. He was still in his white clothes. The bottom of his pants was stained with dirt and grass. He took them off and put them on top of his laundry bin, laid his shirt on top and got into bed. The next thing he knew, it was after 9:00 a.m. and his phone was ringing.

He expected it to be Mary, but it was unlike her to call so early on a weekend.

"It's Sam. We arrested Cheam, the dad, last night for drunk driving but let him out on his own recognizance after his lawyer made a huge stink about calling the mayor and the chief of police. When he got out of the car, he threw up on his shoes and fell over. Damn, I wish I'd been there to see it. Just because the mayor and half the city council is part of that damn club, which is on city land by the way, he thinks he can kick around us shuffleboarders like we were dirt on his sparkly white, white shoes. And when we want to through a party, and not with a band that's going to keep half the city awake, it's no way Jose'. We have to have ours over at the Elks Lodge in Redondo, not that they don't put on a good spread."

"Do you want me to come down there? Maybe we can search his car or something?" Lester asked.

"Nah, by the time you get here he's probably going to be bailed out and get a slap on the wrist and the keys to the city. I'll see you tonight?"

"Yeah. Wouldn't miss it," Lester said.

He pulled together breakfast, scrambled eggs, toast and coffee and sat around in his underwear putting his case notes in order. He'd read a lot of mysteries and the detectives either made lucky guesses or were somehow smart enough to figure out what picture all the pieces of the puzzle would make. Maybe if he had a sidekick who'd accidently say just the right thing that would turn on the lightbulb over his head and the pieces would fall into place. He felt like he had a jumble of pieces from several different puzzles.

They had two tracks, the spy angle that Kappe was keen on but seemed a stretch and his angle that didn't seem a stretch but didn't have any evidence. There was also the possibility that they weren't smart enough to figure it out.

The Cheams had a motive. Keeping it under wraps that his prize product was a cheat, seemed enough of a motive, but then would he really do it? Also, was the product really bogus. He'd fired the guy, so anything Shawn said would seem like it was sour grapes. Johnny Cheam seemed like the real hothead of the family, at least until old Mister Cheam tied a big one on, but he had less of a motive than his dad did. Sure, the company could go under, but how liable was he? It seemed like he had the machinist chops to get another job pronto.

The key might be the silencer. It's not like they were common but then if you were going to kill someone out in the open. Nobody had come forward to say that they'd seen anything. There had been plenty of people in the area. If it was Johnny, then he'd have the opportunity. He was always down in Hermosa cruising and it was possible he'd known Shawn was a regular at The Insomniac. If he wanted to kill him, all he'd have to do is bide his time. If his dad, Mr. Cheam, did it then how would he have known that Shawn was there?

As he laid out his notes on his desk and put some order to them, he thought about how he used to be consumed by baseball statistics.

He went and picked up a pepperoni pizza from Piece O'Pizza on Artesia and brought it back to his apartment for lunch. He'd ordered a large, thinking he'd save half of it for another meal but finished it off. That and the beer knocked him out the rest of the afternoon. He listened to Vin Scully call the Dodger's game not able or wanting to get up or bend his torso. After the fifth inning, he fell asleep. The game had gone into extra innings and was still on when he woke up.

He put on an old pair of jeans and the red checkered shirt he'd bought when he was on leave in Garmisch. His buddies had sprung for lederhosen, but that had been a step too far for him.

"You couldn't have worn something nicer?" Mary said when he picked her up. She was wearing a nice floral sun dress with a cute contrasting scarf around her neck.

"I know, I'm sorry. It's just a barbecue."

On the short drive east to Redondo Beach, Lester asked Mary if she thought that Johnny Cheam could be violent.

"You mean like kill somebody?" Mary asked, shocked. "He's a jerk and I could see him dusting someone that got in his face but no. I've tried not to know him since high school and generally I've pretty much succeeded. I'm sorry about yesterday and the whole lawn bowling party. Things always get out of hand once the hooch starts flowing. When I was a kid, it just seemed like what adults did. Maybe having kids and supporting a family does that to them. I sure hope not. I don't want to be thirty-five or forty-five or fifty-five and having to explain to the kids why their dad's driving license was suspended and where his black eye came from."

"I gotcha!" Lester said.

"And keep your eyes on the road," Mary said after catching Lester peaking at her cleavage.

Kappe's house was in a neighborhood between train tracks and a grassy powerline right-of-way. The streets had aspirational names, like Vanderbilt, Carnegie and Rockefeller which emphasized the modesty of the houses. They were single-story, stuccoed ranch houses many with laundry hanging on umbrella clothes lines in the back yard and large television antennas on the roofs.

Kappe's house was set back from the street. In the front yard, he had a picnic bench and large grill billowing smoke. Kappe was wearing Bermuda shorts and a Hawaiian shirt covered by an apron with "The Cook is King" and a cartoon of a chef with a large twirly mustache on the front and a billowing chef's hat.

They parked in front of the house and walked through the front gate rather than by the driveway. Mrs. Kappe exited the house with a tray of glasses and a pitcher of lemonade.

"Glad you could make it," Kappe said with a big smile.

"Can I get you something to drink?" Mrs. Kappe said. "I just made the lemonade." She was a shade taller the Kappe and looked tan enough that she could be Mexican. "I'm Philomene," she said with a shade of a French accent that hadn't been apparent previously.

"That's a nice name," Mary said.

"My people are from Louisiana, near New Orleans, originally," Mrs. Kappe said with a big smile as she poured them lemonades.

"Get the guy a beer, will you," Kappe said. "He doesn't want a lemonade, do you?"

"I like a good lemonade," Lester said.

"My wife, she makes the best damn lemonade, pardon my French," Kappe said enthusiastically. "How do you like your steaks? Bloody, rare or crispy?"

"Well-done," Mary and Lester said in unison.

"The beers in the cooler next to the table," Kappe said.

"Do you want me to show you around?" Mrs. Kappe said to Mary who nodded and followed her into the house.

"Great, her spoon collection will keep them busy for a while," Kappe said. "Anything new?"

"So, Cheam got arrested for drunken driving?" Lester asked.

"He'll get off, but it was great watch him taken down a peg. After he threw up on himself we just left him there in a cell to dry out until his wife came to pick him up. She didn't come."

"I think Johnny Cheam may have done it, killed Shawn. He's got a gun. He made a silencer, once. He hangs out down there near around Pier Avenue with his rodster buddies so he probably had seen Shawn hanging out there."

"Why would he do it? I don't get the angle," Kappe said.

"Hear me out. I checked up on those plans, the ones we found in Shawn's car. The best that I can tell, Averodyne has been selling snake oil to the United States Airforce. Their main product, which is some sort of flange thing for jet engines, is worthless, humbug. You might as well put a good luck charm on the rearview mirror."

"It's all we've got right now. I haven't made any headway with the spy angle," Kappe said reluctantly. "You got to figure that they'd keep their lips sealed and their legs crossed. It could have been a mob hit. They take them out like that but then I couldn't get a handle on a motive. Sometimes they don't need a motive. They whack somebody as an initiation. How'd you like to join that club? Nabbing a Cheam, even if it's just little Johnny Junior would be a treat, though they're kind of like old Jedediah Smith. They seem to find a way to survive. You watch your front and back with them, especially if you don't want to get blackballed from Hermosa Beach. They've got that kind of power and not even your girlfriend's dad can save your job. We've got to be absolutely sure."

"How are we going to do that? It's just an idea that I have and the only one that fits," Lester said.

"Let's go with the silencer angle. Johnny Cheam lives in Manhattan Beach, in an apartment. I know some guys over in the MBPD who can give us hand with a raid. They'll figure it's us, the Cheams will, or you at least. If he's got a silencer, even if he hasn't used it, he's going to be in a heap of trouble. Meanwhile, we can check if he has any weapons and if any of them have been fired recently."

The women came out of the house, carrying a bowl of salad and ears of corn for roasting on the grill.

"She has quite a spoon collection," Mary said to Lester. "My aunt Bertha would probably be jealous."

"Oh, it's just things I've picked up over the years," Mrs. Kappe said bashfully. "Wherever we go, I just stop in at the curio shops and see if anything strikes my fancy."

"We bought the first display," Kappe said proudly, "but the rest of them I made."

"They all looked great to me," Mary said.

As they waited for Kappe to cook the steaks, they sipped beers and ate potato chips dipped into the dips Mrs. Kappe had laid out, a confetti dip with a variety of finely chopped vegetables, a Braunschweiger and onion dip and a sharp cheddar cheese dip that she warned was quite sharp.

"The Braunschweiger was my mom's recipe," Kappe said. "She used to bring it to some of the parties we used to go to up in Hindenburg Park before the war. It was a different world. In some ways, I think it was safer. Now with the Communists, especially so close in Cuba. . ."

Mrs. Kappe interrupted, "Maybe we can talk about something else. It's nice that we finally have a real baseball team. Have you been to the new stadium yet? I know there was a lot of hue and cry when the built it, but you should have seen the living conditions up in Chavez Ravine. It was scandalous."

"But that's how they live," Mr. Kappe scolded. "We should never have let them come up from Mexico."

"A lot of them have lived here since the time of Pio Pico," Mary said. "Do you think they like being poor? They had a community. They were happy. They were told that they were going to move into new buildings. We'll see if that ever happens, but it isn't looking good."

"Part of it isn't their fault. That's for sure," Kappe said, waving his half-empty beer bottle about as if it were a wand. "At least the Catholic Church keeps the number of Communists down, not that they did such a good job in Cuba. If you want to talk injustice, let's talk about Cardinal Mindszenty over in Hungary." Kappe's face was getting red and he nearly hit Lester in the face with the beer bottle.

"Kappe, check on the steaks. It smells like you're burning them," Mrs. Kappe said severely.

Kappe, glaring at his wife, got up from the picnic table and checked on the steaks, which were fiercely sizzling on the grill.

"I'm sorry. Sometimes he gets very passionate. He cares so much about people," Mrs. Kappe said.

"People are all we've got, and all people have got is their individuality and their God-given right to freedom. That's all I'm saying," Kappe said. He was in tears as he said it, though it was difficult to tell how much that was because of sentiment and how much was because of the smoke that was blowing in his eyes.

During dinner, Mrs. Kappe talked about her favorite acts on *The Lawrence Welk Show* while the rest of them chewed their beef. When she was finished, Kappe picked up the conversation and took into the bushes of solo debate on the relative merits of the Indian Guides over the Boy Scouts.

When Lester and Mary were left with just the fat to chew, Mary nudged Lester under the table with her knee. When he didn't respond, she kicked him in the shin.

"It's been a very nice evening," Lester said.

Mary smiled at him and gently stroked his arm.

"Please stay for dessert," Mrs. Kappe pleaded. "I made a Jell-O, lime with pineapple."

"That sounds great," Mary said, "but I'm just so stuffed. The steak was great, but I'm falling asleep."

"I probably should take her home. We were out late last night," Lester said, trying to sound like he truly had a reason to be concerned about Mary's well-being. "Maybe we can have some to go?"

Mrs. Kappe brightened. "I can put some in a Tupperware!"

"As long as he brings it back," Kappe said.

"I can bring it in tomorrow. It'll be spick and span, not sticky at all."

"I made a lot."

As they drove away, when they were two blocks away, Mary turned to Lester and pretended to throw up. "I can't believe you have to work with him."

"I think he was in the Hitler Youth when he was younger," Lester said.

"No way!" Mary exclaimed.

"At least the American version."

"Do you think they spiked the Jell-O?" Mary asked.

"You can do that?"

"Yeah. I was at a party once in high school where they had them, spiked with vodka or something like that. The parents thought it was so sweet, until things got messy and sticky."

"Where I lived, we'd just go into the fields away from town where nobody would bother us, except that every year we always went to the same field and it wasn't like it was a mystery to anybody where we were or what we were up to."

"No," said Mary emphatically, "I mean a real mess. The curtains were torn off the rods. The sofa was stained with throw up. The toilets got clogged up and overflowed. The walls were sticky and had pieces of Jell-O on them."

"Did you want still want to go to a movie?" Lester asked.

"I'm still digesting that steak and it's making me sleepy. You don't mind, do you? We can maybe meet up later in the week. I've got a paper due and with the Spring Fling and all, I've barely started it."

Lester drove her home then drove down to the beach and walked along the Strand. At first, he was going to walk north to the Manhattan Beach Pier just to think and to walk off the beef. Instead, he walked south to the Hermosa Beach Pier. It had been one week since the murder and he felt that he was closer, hopefully, closer to solving the case. There were just some holes in the story, assuming that the pieces he had were actually part of the story.

If Johnny Cheam did it, then why did he do it? He was aggressive and a jerk but what was Shawn to him? They lived in different worlds only connected by Averodyne. Also, the Cheams had won. They'd kicked him out. The same went for his dad. The only thing he had to worry about was Shawn contacting the Defense Department's Inspector General or someone who would investigate them, but who would believe the guy who got fired? They could lose their Defense Department contracts, their business could go under and they could go to jail. That had to be the motive, assuming it was them.

The fog hadn't come in yet so the stars were shining brightly, reflected on the ocean. The moon was waning or waxing. He saw it so rarely that he never really could tell, but it was shining on the ocean too.

If they were going to kill him, then why even fire him? Why not. It was like losing your virginity twice. Or maybe like having your cake and eating it too. He couldn't figure out how they would know where he was that night unless they were following him, or they somehow saw him and they took their chance.

Would they really wander around Hermosa Beach in the middle of the night with a gun in their pocket? Johnny Cheam was often there, showing of his hot rod. It didn't seem like he would leave it parked and walk away from it because it could get scraped. Rodsters weren't the type to leave their babies unattended.

Carlton Cheam didn't seem like he would just wait around in an alley behind The Insomniac on the off chance that he'd run into Shawn coming out the back. How would he even know Shawn was there or not somewhere else? They'd worked together for a couple of years and Shawn was a regular, so it was likely that he'd talked about it. It was also likely that Johnny would see him. They knew the lay of the land. He was going to have to get a photo of the two of them and ask around.

They had to know what Shawn's car looked like. They'd seen it every day. If, while driving around Hermosa or walking around, they'd spotted his car, it could be a pretty good guess that he'd be at The Insomniac. They could follow him out of the building and shoot him or maybe they were just lucky to be in the right place at the right time with the right weapon. You'd think they would ransack his car. It would be easy to break into, but then they couldn't know that he'd keep the plans there.

He knew that Johnny Cheam lived in Manhattan Beach, just a mile north, but where did Carlton Cheam live? You didn't have to live in Hermosa to be a member of the lawn bowling club. It was such a rookie mistake, he told himself, to not find out where Carlton Cheam lived. He would find out in the morning.

He'd reached the pier and walked down the alley where Shawn had been shot. You could still make out the blood stain on the pavement. There were a couple of boys hanging out in the shadow of the Biltmore Hotel smoking something that didn't smell like tobacco. They skedaddled when they saw him, calmly walking in nonchalantly as fast as they could without running in every direction but towards him.

He identified himself as HBPD and asked them if they were regulars at the Biltmore. Both of them said yes and looked nervously to each other. They were at the most seventeen and barely had chin whiskers, just faint mustaches. They were wearing plaid flannel shirts not tucked in over white jeans.

"Honestly, we're just hanging out. We've already done our homework, mister," the short one said.

Lester laughed at them. "Sorry, but I'm just checking if either or you were there last Friday night and heard or saw anything?"

"Yeah," the short one said excitedly. "We wanted to get in and see some bands but neither of us had any money, so we just hung out and talked to some girls we know that were in line."

"I heard someone got shot," the tall one said.

"Heard or heard about?" Lester asked.

The boys looked to each other as if for permission.

"Heard as in heard," the short one said. "We were standing in line and then there was a lot of fuss and then a lot of fuzz showed up." When the boy said fuzz, he got really nervous. "No offense."

"None taken. Did either of you see anything or anyone who might be suspicious?" Lester asked.

"Nah, not that I really could say," the tall one said looking down at his friend, who nodded. "Once there was the scream, everyone went running to see what   happened."

"Except for the people who took off in the other direction," the short one said.

"And who was running in the other direction?"

"Like half the people, man," the short one said. "We weren't scared or anything unless it had been some bikers showing. Man, those guys are trouble."

"We heard this girl scream," the tall one said, "and we went to see what happened and the police and everyone were surrounding it and we couldn't really see anything, so we just bugged off. And the chicks wanted to get back in line and see the show."

Lester thanked the boys for their help and wondered if it was worthwhile to see if anyone else saw anything. He kept on walking and went up the hill to the police station. There were only a couple of people on duty, preoccupied by a drunk guy throwing up his three squares from the last twenty-four hours. He found the stack of phone books and found the white pages that covered the South Bay. Cheam, Carlton was listed as living on Circle Avenue, between Monterey and Manhattan Avenues, a ten-minute walk from The Insomniac. He also got a copy of Cheam's mug shot. It wasn't the best picture. He looked wrung-out and lost.

Instead of walking directly to the address, which was on the way to where he'd left his car, which was parked near Mary's house, he walked back down to The Insomniac.

He timed how long it would take if he took the most direct route to Cheam's house. It took eleven minutes at a moderate pace, and this way was uphill. If Carlton Cheam was the killer, he would have walked downhill so maybe it would shave a minute.

Maybe Beatrice Loehner had called him. There was a possibility that she knew them, assuming he'd actually seen her at the Spring Fling. Maybe it was Johnny and he had followed Shawn. Maybe neither of them had done it. The key was finding the weapon. He could have thrown it away. He would have chucked it into the ocean off of a pier, but to do that, they would have to go to the Manhattan Beach Pier because the Hermosa Beach was closed off and scheduled for demolition.

The Insomniac was hopping. There was a poetry reading in the back, an older guy with long white hair, balding on top, and a black-dyed Van Dyke. He held a book in one hand and gestured with the other, like he was conducting his oratory. The front of the house was filled with book browsers and beatniks more interested in beauty in the flesh than the rhyme of this ancient maroon.

He showed the mug shot around to the staff but none of them recognized him. A square over forty would stand out like a palm tree in Alaska.

Lester made his way past the juice and coffee bar to the back where the bathrooms were. There was a pay phone back there. He wrote the number down on the back of a receipt. Beatrice could easily have called one of the Cheams. She wouldn't even have to tell them where she was. They've be able to figure it out from the background noise. All she needed was a thin dime to find someone who cared.

They had to interview Beatrice again. Maybe she was supposed to be meet up with one of the Cheams. Maybe she set up Shawn for an ambush.

He walked past the Carlton Cheam's house on the way back to his car. The house had a grand view of the Pacific Ocean, a blinding view ever fog-free sunset. The windows on the beach side were darkly tinted. You could tell that someone was home but nothing more than that.

Half an hour after he got back to his apartment, Kappe called him and told him he'd set up an early morning search of Johnny Cheam's apartment.

Chapter 16

Lester woke up to his alarm. He was so exhausted; he didn't want to get up. Switching from nights to days was hard. A cold shower and a cut on the back of his neck while shaving woke him more than his coffee. It was a shitty start to a day when a styptic pencil to a shaving cut woke him more than coffee.

Kappe didn't show up until almost 6:30 a.m. and immediately went for coffee at the Hill Top Café making Lester tag along and wait while Kappe wolfed down a cruller and a cup of joe.

"Do you think that Cheam, the dad, has something on the side, a girl, a woman?" Lester asked.

"Why?" Kappe asked. "Because he's a drunk asshole who thinks he's better than us. You know, he's friends with the mayor, which is why he's going to get off this latest charge."

"When are the Manhattan Beach cops raiding Johnny's place?"

Kappe looked at his watch. "Any time now. Do you want to go down there and watch how it plays out?"

"Sure," Lester said, as he tried to adjust his underpants surreptitiously.

"You okay?" Kappe said before finishing off his coffee. "I've got some talcum powder in my locker if you need any."

Lester blushed and quickly said, "Do you want to take my car or yours?"

"We can take mine," Kappe said.

The drive to Johnny Cheam's apartment took only ten minutes and the MBPD were already there going through the apartment. It was only two blocks north of their police station.

Johnny Cheam was standing by the curb in front of his building glaring at cops. "I'm going to fucking sue you!" he yelled at the detective in charge of the search. "I'm going to sue you too, you fuck!" he yelled to Lester as soon as he spotted him. His face was red and sweaty. His work short, with an Averodyne patch on the breast, was sweated through.

"We're almost done," the MBPD detective said. He was tall and blond and looked like a lifeguard, with deeply tanned skin.

"I'll have your badges! You'll be directing traffic at Disneyland!" Johnny yelled.

An older detective exited the building and asked Johnny if he could give them the combination to his gun safe.

"I'd rather not say out loud," Johnny said calmly. "If you want, I can come in and unlock it for you?"

The older detective looked to the detective in charge, who nodded. Johnny Cheam entered his apartment followed by the two MBPD detectives.

"Just wait out here," the blond detective said. "I'll let you know if we find anything."

"Look for guns recently fired or cleaned," Kappe said.

"I know the score," Lester said.

"They know the score, so watch them fuck it all up," Kappe whispered to Lester.

"They seem professional," Lester whispered back.

"Let me tell you a little secret," Kappe whispered back. "In small towns like ours, ones without a lot of crime, real crime not drunks or wife beaters, or disorderly conduct, we don't get a lot of practice. By the way, the chief asked me the other day if you were doing a good job, holding your own. I said that you were good police, green, but with a lot of potential. He says, that he's going to bump you up, get you out of metering permanently."

Lester was too tired to do more than smile. As he waited for the MBPD to finish with their search, he calculated how much a week he'd net. Hopefully it would be enough to maybe even move into one of the new apartments going up along Pacific Coast Highway. The views were great and you could walk to three supermarkets. It might not impress her parents, especially since they owned a local chain of supermarkets.

"Earth to Lester, earth to Lester," Kappe yelled.

"Sorry, I'm just trying to take it all in, pay attention" Lester said, embarrassed to be caught daydreaming, like he was in high school.

The older detective came out the apartment holding a Luger through a handkerchief. "I think we've found something," the cop said. "Recently fired and he didn't even bother to clean it."

"I never fired that!" Johnny yelled out. "I never fire any of those. They're just collector's items from my dad's time in the war. I don't even know that I have any ammunition for it. Most of my guns are 38s and 45s, not 9 mm."

"Here, smell it," the cop said to Kappe and Lester who took a whiff of the barrel.

"Naughty, naughty!" Kappe said to Johnny. "When we get to the station, you can tell us all about it while we wait for the ballistics test to come back."

Lester laughed and stepped up to Johnny. "So, where's the silencer?"

"I didn't do it!" Johnny yelped. "I haven't seen the silencer since my shop teacher gave it to my dad and he destroyed it. Why would I want to kill him? My dad fired him. He was hasta la vista! I want a lawyer. Call my dad!"

"You'll get a chance once we get you to the station and book you," Lester said while taking out his handcuffs from their holster.

"Send that to forensics!" Kappe said to the MBPD cop. "The Sheriff's Office, not LAPD. They'll sit on it until we kiss their asses."

"I don't know," the older detective said, "they've always come through for me."

"If this gun is the gun that killed Steven Shawn, it's not going to look good for you," Kappe said to Johnny Cheam as he yanked on his cuffs and lead him to his car.

"There's no way!" Johnny cried. Tears streamed down his cheeks. "I didn't do it. No way!"

Lester thought it odd that Johnny didn't seem to expect any of this or he was a very good actor. Maybe he'd compartmentalized it. But then, his only experience with perps was giving out parking tickets.

All the way to the station, Johnny alternately cried out that they'd really fucked up this time and that he was innocent.

"Explain the gun!" Kappe yelled back, his rage burning through his shirt collar, his face nearly purple.

When they got to the station, Johnny was handcuffed to a chair while they took a statement. He called his dad first and then his lawyer. Lester and Kappe bet which one would get there first, the dad or the lawyer. Lester won with the lawyer. While they waited, Johnny was all mouth.

"I've got the Monitor and Merrimack of alibis," Johnny boasted. "I was at Ascot Park with my sprint car. A couple of thousand people can vouch for me."

"I'm sure you were the belle of the ball," Kappe said.

"Your crew and everyone can vouch for you?" Lester asked.

"I was there the whole night. Ask anyone," Johnny said smugly. "I was in the program."

"Maybe you were there all night," Lester said, trying to figure out a scenario that could stick. "Maybe you skipped out for a while. Ascot's pretty noisy. You can hear it all the way down here at night. Who's to say you didn't do that? And even if you were there the whole night, what about the gun?"

"I don't know about anyone firing it, but I was there the whole night. Careful you guys don't choke on how much you've bitten off," Johnny said confidently.

"So, you can prove that you were at Ascot the whole night?" Lester asked.

"I can't be in two places at one time," Johnny said smugly.

"You're under a helmet," Lester said.

"I was racing against Jimmy Davies and Shorty Templemen. You think I'd miss that? Do you think I'd let anyone else drive my rocket?" Lester said sarcastically.

"How'd you do?" Kappe asked.

"Not so well. I was having engine troubles. Nothing really bad. I've got to rebuild the engine. For a hundred-mile race, it matters. I was fifth," Johnny said sadly.

"Does anyone else have a key to your place?" Lester asked.

Johnny was about to answer, but paused. "I'm going to have to talk to my lawyer."

"So, somebody else has a copy of your keys," Kappe said.

"I'm done talking," Johnny said.

They could see that Johnny Cheam was worried and trying to think things out. He closed his eyes and grimaced. Beads of sweat appeared on his forehead. They sat there staring at him with him averting their gazes. A bead of sweat dripped from his brow down his nose. Cheam tried to wiggle then shake it off without success.

"I bet you'd like a handkerchief," Kappe said.

Johnny shook his head.

"Does it feel hot in here to you?" Kappe asked Lester.

"I'm fine," Johnny said.

"Do you feel like a tall glass of cold water?" Kappe asked "I bet that'd feel nice just about now. Lester, why don't you get a couple of glasses of water."

Lester got up, went to the cooler and came back with two small conical paper cups of water and handed them to Kappe, who drank both of them without offering any to Johnny Cheam.

"Let's see, who could possibly have a set of your keys," Kappe said. "One of our neighbors has a set of our keys. When we go away you just never know what could happen. I had a neighbor once who didn't leave his keys with anyone and his water line broke and did beaucoup damage. It was running out the front door when he got home. His front door was rotten. His carpets were moldy. His water bill was sky high. Like I said, a lot of problems."

"A girlfriend?" Lester asked.

"That would be naughty and he seems like such a choir boy," Kappe sneered.

A short grunt of a laugh escaped from Johnny's mouth.

"A guy," Lester said.

"That would explain a lot of things," Kappe cackled.

"His dad," Lester said.

"Maybe even a sugar daddy," Kappe said.

Johnny grimaced and hung his head down. His head was beginning sweat with the perspiration falling from his hair onto his lap.

Lester leaned over to Kappe and whispered into his ear. "We can't let his dad know that we suspect him. He's going to ditch the evidence."

"If he hasn't already," Kappe whispered back. "I'm sure he has."

"I need to make a phone call," Johnny demanded.

"You'll get your chance," Kappe said. "If you'd been a little bit more cooperative, we might also be more cooperative. As it happens, my partner and I get the feeling that you don't really like us much."

"What time did the race end? Maybe you had enough time to come back?" Lester asked desperately.

Johnny smiled like he'd lapped them, they'd run out of gas and blown out a tire. "Late. Very late. I took my crew out to Bob's Big Boy for burgers. Check with them. I've got nothing better to do. Take your time."

"Yeah, we intend to do that," Lester said, trying to sound tough.

"Can I see you for a moment?" Kappe said to Lester. "We're going to step out or a cup of coffee. How do you like yours?"

"Black, two sugars," Johnny said.

Kappe led Lester out of the police station and into the parking lot. He looked around to see if anyone could listen in.

"We're double fucked and he knows it?" Kappe said.

"What do you mean?" Lester said indignantly. He took out a handkerchief from his back pocket and wiped the sweat from his forehead. "If ballistics comes back and this is the gun, then I'd say that he's the one who's bending over."

"He's got an air tight alibi. After the race, he's got to take his race car back to his garage. That's his baby. He's going to make sure it's got everything it needs before he goes to bed. His crew will vouch for him. Plus, he's got no motive beyond being an asshole."

"When wasn't that enough? Shawn was going to call them out. That was going to be his insurance. That was going to be his revenge," Lester said.

"If you ask me, even if we can find out who had another key to the apartment and knew the combination to the safe, he's never ever going to tell us.

Unless we can find that out we're not going to have a case," Kappe said angrily.

"The weapons were his dad's. He's got to know the combination and he's probably got a key, too. Or, he could have left the safe open and the apartment unlocked."

"Assuming that's the weapon, his lawyer's going to say that there was no way for him to know that the gun was going to be used in a murder. We can't prove that someone didn't come in and take the gun, that he left everything unlocked, no matter how unlikely that is. We're going to have a hard time proving that his dad knows the combination, unless Johnny cries like a baby, that's a dead end for us."

"What about his dad?" Lester said, his eyes gleaming. "I'm pretty sure I can connect his dad with the beatchick Shawn picked up. She was at the Spring Fling. There's a link. I'm sure of it. Plus, there's a phone back near where the bathrooms are in The Insomniac. She could have called his dad and set Shawn up."

"He does live only a couple of blocks away. It wouldn't take him more than ten minutes to get down there, but he has to have the gun and he has to know that Shawn's there."

"We've got to bring him in and search his place before he gets rid of anything," Lester said nervously.

"Carlton Cheam's the kind of guy who knows when to flush. No chance he'd be shit-stupid enough to keep anything incriminating."

"And if the gun's wiped clean?"

"No fuss, no muss, no fingerprints? Maybe, but he didn't clean the gun so maybe we'll get lucky." Kappe said dejectedly. "Unless we can find a witness, we can't prove anything either. It used to be his gun, so there's going to be his prints on it."

"We've got to try. For Steven Shawn," Lester said.

"His house and Averodyne," Kappe said.

"How fast can we get this done before his dad finds out that his son isn't showing up for work?"

"Hermosa, the house, no problem. I've got a buddy over at Hawthorne PD. I'll get them to saddle up if you take his house?"

"And we've got to get warrants first," Lester said anxiously.

"Okay, why are we talking?" Kappe bellowed.

An hour later, after getting a search warrant, Carlton Cheam's lawyer let Lester into Cheam's house.

The lawyer was an older guy trying to look younger than he could manage, with a slim light-blue sharkskin suit over a gut that flopped over his trousers.

The house was neat except for the dirty breakfast dishes in the sink. It was a new two-story house, very modern with no yard but a roof deck. The house was only a few feet from its neighbors with the garage in the alley. There was a photo of the Cheams including the Mrs. and Johnny in the hallway taken at Johnny's high school graduation. War memorabilia were everywhere and carefully dusted. There were German and Japanese helmets with bullet holes, a civil war sword hanging from the coat rack, and various odds and ends like artillery shell casings and framed campaign maps.

In the bedroom, the bed was neatly made but the bathroom was a mess. It hadn't been cleaned in far too long and there were heavy calcium stains on the fixtures, gunk on the bottom of the bath and red mold in the toilet and sink.

In the master bedroom, the clothes were stuffed into the drawers except for a few nice suits hanging up in the closet still covered by plastic from the dry cleaners. The other two bedrooms were empty except for beds covered in some dust that looked like they'd never been slept in and a second bathroom that was spotlessly clean except or a bottle of girly shampoo and a single toothbrush standing upright in a juice glass.

It didn't look like a woman lived there which meant that Mrs. Cheam had left. Lester made a note to ask Mary if she knew anything about the marriage. At the Spring Fling, it was obvious that Mrs. Cheam wasn't happy with her husband. If she didn't live there, they'd have to search her place too.

It took them a long time to go through the house. There were boxes of business documents and tax returns. If they were auditors, they'd be in the honey. The whole while, the lawyer sat in the kitchen and made himself a cup of coffee without offering any to Lester.

They found no weapons and definitely not a silencer or anything but messes that needed to be cleaned. The trash can was filled with empty beer cans and empty Chinese food containers. There was a box of machine shop projects, including a small steam engine.

At some point the lawyer went down the street for some lunch and brought them back sandwiches and sodas. When they were done, the lawyer asked them if they'd mind putting everything back. Lester wondered if they really had to. They'd spent most of the day and only found out that not all wealthy people live glamorously.

"Where are your manners?" the lawyer asked as Lester left the house without putting anything back in place.

"Do you really think he'll notice," Lester said, while looking to the other policeman, who shook their heads.

"I don't know where you grew up, but my mom always taught me to clean up after myself," the lawyer said coldly but with a smile.

On the short drive back to the station, Lester hoped that Kappe would have better luck than he had. The only thing he'd found was dust and silver fish.

Not long after they got back to the station, Kappe walked in with Carlton Cheam. Cheam was smug and chatty, like he'd won and was going to continue to win. Kappe talked about how the bowling alley up on PCH next to the Lucky supermarket was trying to snag a spot on the pro tour.

"They're toast if they don't," Cheam said. "I go in there and there's nobody there most nights. It's a big beautiful place with lots of potential. There's always an open lane. You ever bowled there?"

"Once or twice when my wife and I were in a league," Kappe said.

"It's the new generation. But they're good kids. They'll turn out all right. They're clean-cut and respectful. That's what you need in a kid, respect, that and hard work. My boy's got that in spades."

"Yeah, well he's got a pretty good alibi too. What about you? What were you doing on Friday night?"

"I was watching a show. My wife likes *Sing a Long with Mitch*, but I can't stand that show, especially since *Route 66* is on at the same time."

"Do you know what your son was doing and where he was on Friday night?"

"He's got this racing thing going. A money pit, that's what it is, but it keeps him off the streets," Cheam said guffawing at his joke. "You've still got my son, don't you? I'm sure he didn't do it. I didn't raise him that way."

"You can never tell," Kappe said.

When Lester came up to them, Carlton Cheam offered his hand. When Lester shook it, Cheam gave him a bone crushing shake, smiling like the Cheshire Cat."

"We're waiting on the ballistics report," Lester said.

"You know, there's no earthly reason for Johnny to kill him or anyone," Cheam said coolly. "And Shawn, you fire someone and you think they're out of your hair and they come back to haunt you. No offence intended."

"We've established that you've got a set of keys to your son's apartment," Kappe said.

"And why wouldn't I? His mom's got a copy too," Cheam said.

"Do you know of anyone else who has a key?" Lester asked.

"You tag teaming me?" Cheam asked. "Look, my son's business is my son's business. He can give out keys to whomever he wants. As long as it's on the up and up and they don't get stuck into a situation, if you know what I mean?"

"Boys will be boys," Kappe said.

"You know they will. He could have stayed with us, but of course that doesn't offer the freedom a young man needs, plus his mom wouldn't allow it," Cheam said.

"And you do?" Kappe asked.

"Out of sight out of mind," Cheam said confidently. "He's his own man. When we were his age, we were in the service making the world safe for Democracy. Am I right?"

"Can you explain why a gun that he owns, that it's an a safe in his house was fired recently even though he doesn't have any ammunition for it?" Lester asked.

"I wouldn't know. I wasn't there. You can buy ammunition at a sporting goods store. Those guns were mine, but I didn't have a place in my house for it and he wanted them so I gave them to him a couple of years ago. I just know, and a dad knows these things, that my son is a good kid. I don't know what he might have gotten mixed up in, assuming there's a match. His only fault is that he's too trusting. I've told him over and over again that the world is a hard place. You were in the war. You know what I mean. It's a hard place and you can't trust everyone who flashes a smile and says nice things about you."

"Why did you fire Steven Shawn?" Lester asked.

"I probably should wait for my lawyer, but I've got nothing to hide," Cheam said calmly. "What I went through at the Bulge in the snow, what I've done for this country."

Lester could see and hear Cheam's indignation rising.

"So, what did you fire him for?" Kappe asked.

"I should have fired him a long time sooner, once I suspected. I wanted to be sure. I wanted to give the guy a break. That's the kind of guy I am. I did him a favor hiring him. I've got a lot of qualified guys that come looking for jobs. He'd escaped the Commies. What the Hunyocks have had to endure, especially Cardinal Mindszenty's got to endure holed up in the embassy. He seemed like a nice guy and, well frankly, I just wanted to do my part, however small. It was my patriotic duty. He was insubordinate."

"We should have taken the Communists out at the end of the war," Kappe said, "Once we got done with the Japs. We could have dropped just one bomb and saved ourselves a whole lot of trouble."

"We just wanted to go home. Return to our normal lives," Mr. Cheam said.

"Look how many boys we lost in Korea," Kappe said.

"It's not if, it's when. And they're crafty. They know what they're doing, and they think we're too weak to put a stop to them and maybe we are, but I'm not one of them. Not me!"

"Yeah, we should have taken them out. I've got buddies who would be alive if we hadn't gone into Korea," Kappe said

"So why did you fire him?" Lester interjected. "How was he insubordinate?"

Cheam whispered, "What we do is secret, a lot of it is secret at Averodyne. It's for the safety of our country. When I got an inkling that he was taking plans home with him, making copies of things, asking too many questions. . .and then the accusations." His voice grew louder as he continued. "I began to think; why do I need this? He could go to one of my competitors. He talked back a lot. And then I began to think, maybe he's a threat to national security. I'm just a guy who knows how to make things. That's all I am. I could be making anything. My son wants to make crazy stuff for the rodsters and the racers. Me, I like airplanes, always have and always will. I had to let him go. It's not like there's a union or a contract or anything. I had ample reason. It's all legit. After that, I thought I was done with him, but no. He's come back like a bad bowl of chili."

Kappe and Lester knew they were empty handed. Johnny wouldn't say who had a key to his apartment and knew the combination to the gun safe.

They let Johnny Cheam and his dad go home. Johnny looked ragged and hungry, like he'd been washed and not dried. His dad looked calm and poised, like he'd been pressed and starched when.

"It could be that the gun was put into the gun safe after the murder, as a way of hiding it," Lester said as he stood next to Kappe's desk.

"If that's true, then it didn't seem like Johnny was in on the joke," Kappe said leaning way back in his chair.

"There's another thing that has been nagging me, two really," Lester said. "The first is that I don't think that Mr. Cheam is still living with Mrs. Cheam. I can't say for sure or even if this is a recent thing. I want to see if I can find out something more. My girlfriend's parents know the Cheams. Maybe they have an idea. The other thing is that here may be a connection between the girl, what's her name, who was with

Shawn the night he was murdered and the Cheams. I'm pretty sure I saw her at the Spring Fling."

"Beatrice? How many people were at the Fling?"

"A couple of hundred."

"It's a small town, even if you include Manhattan and Redondo. She's a pretty girl. Girls like that get invited to Flings to pretty things up. It's a better investment than a punch bowl."

"Can you get the phone records from a pay phone?" Lester asked. "Because if you can, I'd like to pull them for the pay phone at The Insomniac. It's in the back near the bathrooms. Beatrice said that she went to the bathroom before leaving with Shawn. Maybe she made a call."

"We can check on that. I've got a friend who works for Ma Bell. By the way, the chief said he's making your permanent."

They said their goodbyes for the day and instead of driving home, he walked over to Mary's house. If she wasn't home, he planned to walk down the hill to the Strand and have bite somewhere on Pier Avenue. It didn't seem like the fog was going to roll in that night, or at least not early on. He passed by Cheam's house. The lights were on, but the curtains were drawn and he couldn't see in.

Mary wasn't home when he showed up but her parents let him in and told him she was expected back from the library any minute.

"Do you want me to get you a drink? Scotch?" Mr. Nix asked.

"I'd love to but I'm afraid that'll knock me out and you'll find me on your sofa when you come down for breakfast. I got promoted today out of metering."

"Well, congratulations," Mrs. Nix said cheerfully. "Mary's going to be very happy."

"Thank you, very much. By the way, and I don't mean anything by this, but how well do you know the Cheams, especially Mrs. Cheam?"

Mrs. and Mr. Nix looked at each other. Mr. Nix started to answer but only got as far as opening his mouth.

"She's a trouper. That's all I want to say. I wouldn't have put up with half as much as I would have. But it's nice that I don't have to," Mrs. Nix scowled.

"He can get a little off if he's had a few," Mr. Nix said.

Mrs. Nix scowled. "How many times does he have less than a few. I don't know why he gets re-elected to the governing board every year."

"I'm not running," Mr. Nix said quickly. "I've got enough on my plate as it is."

"They should let the women run it," Mrs. Nix said.

Mr. Nix grinned and said nothing.

"I'm serious!" Mrs. Nix said.

"I'm sure you are," Mr. Nix said, winking to Lester mocking his wife's suggestion. "Nobody'd ever get drunk and we'd be having cottage cheese and salad."

"Do you mind me asking about the Cheams?" Lester asked timidly.

Mrs. Nix rolled her eyes and said, "That's exactly why," under her breath.

"What happens at the Fling stays at the Fling," Mr. Nix said.

"Are Mr. and Mrs. Cheam still together?" Lester asked.

"I haven't heard that they've gotten divorced," Mr. Nix said.

"They don't like to talk about it and it's really their business," Mrs. Cheam said, "but they've been separated ever since they built the house in Hermosa." She whispered Hermosa as if that was a secret.

"That's what I sort of understood." Lester yawned and apologized. "I probably should head back home. Tell Mary I'm beat and I'll catch up with her tomorrow."

When Lester got back to his apartment, he soaked in the tub with a glass of lemonade perched within reach on the closed lid of the toilet. He hadn't been soaking long when the phone rang. He didn't want to get it, but the water had grown cold, his skin was wrinkled, and you never knew if it was important.

After the second ring, he climbed out of the tub, splashing soapy water into what was left of his lemonade. With water soaking into the bathmat, he grabbed a towel and wrapped himself in it as he scurried to the phone. The person had hung up by the time he'd reached the phone, after the fifth ring.

He dried himself off, drained the tub and put the lemonade glass in the sink then tried to watch some television but couldn't concentrate. He tried falling asleep but couldn't help wondering they'd be able to prove that one of the Cheams was the murderer. The phone rang again waking him.

"It's me," Mary said brightly.

"Sorry, I just woke up. What time is it?"

"It's just before ten. I heard about your promotion. We could maybe get together tomorrow night?"

"Tonight is always okay. We could get a bite to eat if you're hungry. Just give me time to get dressed and. . ."

"I'll come over."

"We could go to the 'Wich Stand. I've been there a couple of times now and it's pretty decent."

Mary had picked him up and they went out to dinner. She congratulated him on his promotion and they snuggled in a booth. Lester tried to stay awake and pay attention to what Mary was saying about her classes.

Chapter 17

Lester woke before 5:00 a.m. He was on the sofa dressed in his underpants, a t-shirt and a short-sleeved shirt. He stared at the clock on the wall and out the window for the sun to come up.

On the way to the station, he stopped for a bear claw and a coffee, extra cream at the donut shop next to Ralph's Market on Aviation Boulevard. He finished them off as he leaned against his car in the parking lot of the donut shop on Artesia. He licked the sugar coating from his fingers instead of going back in and getting a napkin.

The two Johns were leaving as he was coming in the door. "The sun must be hurting your eyes," John T said, blocking the doorway.

"They should issue you sunglasses since they brought you out of the darkness," Big John said.

Lester tried to think of a response but nothing worthwhile came to him.

"I see he can take it but can't dish it out," Big John said.

"A delicate soul," John T said.

"The flower of his mother's blind eye," Big John said.

"I'm not in the mood," Lester grumbled.

"That's what my wife always says," Big John said.

John T cracked up and Lester couldn't help laughing too.

"What's that sound?" Big John asked.

"The sound of ice breaking," John T said.

Kappe wasn't around and there was a message on Kappe's desk for him to call the crime lab at the Sherriff's Office. He thought about calling them but left it on Kappe's desk. Instead, he called the phone company and checked to see if he could get the phone numbers and times of all the calls made from the payphone at The Insomniac.

The first operator didn't know if she could do it so she transferred him to her supervisor. Her supervisor was agreeable, but the problem was that the person who normally handled these things was honeymooning in Puerto Vallarta, but her supervisor should be in, so he transferred Lester. The supervisor was in a meeting, but his secretary took a message.

Half an hour later, Lester hadn't gotten a call back and Kappe hadn't shown up. He looked over at the note on Kappe's desk and considered calling the Sherriff's Office just to feel like he was making progress.

He couldn't help himself. He had to know. It was like an itch that he really couldn't not scratch. The moment he dialed the Sherriff's number, his phone rang on another line, so he hung up on and took the call. It was the secretary of the supervisor from the phone company he'd left a message with. She said that her boss wanted to know what he wanted.

"Can I just speak with him? I'm with the Hermosa Beach Police and it's an urgent matter."

"I'm sure it is, but Mr. Moreno is busy," she said.

"I'm investigating a murder. I have the phone number for a payphone and would like to know what calls were made from that phone on a particular night during just a few hours. Is this something you guys can do?"

"Us guys and gals," she said indignantly, "are quite capable of doing a lot of things."

"But this particular thing, can you do this particular thing?" Lester said sweetly.

"Give me the number and times and we'll get back to you. It's not like we're magicians."

"I don't expect you to be magicians," Lester said impatiently.

Lester gave her the phone number, the date and time and she said that she'd call him back when she had something for him. "Can I have your name and number?"

"I'm sorry, but I'm married," she said brusquely.

"No, I mean in case I have to call you back," Lester said apologetically.

"We're the phone company. We'll call you back," she said brusquely.

Lester sat at his desk, leaned back and twiddled his thumbs. Staring at the phone waiting for it to ring he tapped his pens on his desk in a poor imitation of Shelly Manne until the scowls of the other detectives caught his eye. He got up and went to the water cooler but the cup dispenser was empty. Instead of returning to his desk, he stopped at Kappe's empty desk and wrote down the phone number of the Sherriff's Office.

Back at his desk, he looked at the clock and looked at the door for any sign of Kappe but there was none. His curiosity was beginning to overcome him which made him feel that it was a failing, perhaps even a sin on the level of gluttony. His hand shook and sweat dripped down from his forehead and onto his nose as he dialed the Sherriff's Office number. Was it going to be a moment of truth, like when you ask a girl to dance with you with the possibility of failure ballooning above the possibility of success? He dialed the first three digits, TWinbrook 8. . ., paused, looked to see that Kappe was still not there, and then he got a call on his other line.

"Hi, it's me," Mary said.

"Hi," Lester said, nervously.

"Are you okay? You were pretty beat."

"I fell asleep on the couch. Can I. . ."

"I can call you back if you're busy," Mary said.

"I'm not really supposed to take personal calls. Can I maybe meet you for dinner? I'd like to do lunch, but I can't promise that I can make it." He hung up on his other line.

"I'd love to."

"Me too." Lester was going to say more, but his other line lit up with a call.

"Wherever you want to go?"

"We'll try to make it special," Lester said quickly. "Can I get back to you?" He didn't wait for her answer before he hung up on her and answered the other call.

"Michelle Cervantes here from the phone company. Is this Lester Patterson?"

"That's me," Lester said anxiously. "Did you get the information?"

"No, apparently it's not possible, but Mr. Moreno said that if you could wait a few years, maybe we could. Is there anything else I can help you with?" she asked.

"No, you've been a big, big help," Lester said dejectedly.

It felt like a big heavy door, had shut blocking him. He looked up Cheam's phone number in the phone book and wrote it down, then went over to the water cooler again. It was mid-morning and Kappe still wasn't there.

Back at his desk, he didn't look about. There was no sign that Kappe was coming in. He should have been worried about him, but he only cared about finding out about the gun.

He dialed the Sherriff's number. One of the lab assistants answered the phone then put him on hold while he went to find the case file. Lester rocked nervously back and forth in his chair while he waited. He held his breath and counted to ten and then continued on to twenty, thirty and past forty.

"I've got your info if you're ready for it," the man said, "but your colleague has already picked up a copy. I can continue if you want?"

"I'd like it now if that's okay." At least he knew where Kappe was, Lester thought.

"You guys have the patience of a gnat," the man said. He then didn't say anything for a few seconds. "I'm just messing with you, here's the info. In regards to case number blah, blah, blah, it is the opinion of this lab that the gun, a 1938 model Luger, is the same gun used in the murder of Stephen Shawn. I can get you another copy of the report if you want to come over and pick it up."

"No, I'm good." He was more than good.

It was as clear as the sky above the Mojave Desert that Carlton Cheam had shot Steven Shawn with a pistol owned by his son. It was possible that he was tipped off about Shawn's whereabouts by Beatrice Loehner, otherwise, how could he have known where Shawn was going to be? Another possibility was that he'd gone for a walk and seen Shawn, got the gun, either from his house or from his son's. He could connect her, possibly, to the Cheams. He realized that he may never be able to prove it but it was worth a try.

Another possibility was to get Cheam's wife to testify against her husband's alibi but getting a wife to testify against her husband, even if they were separated might be difficult. All she needed to do was at the last minute confirm his alibi and that would be it. It wasn't enough to know. There had to be proof. There had to be punishment. There had to be justice.

Lester looked through his notes and found Beatrice's home number. She wasn't there or at least she didn't answer the phone. He called her work and she was on the line immediately.

"ManageTech, Beatrice Loehner speaking," she said.

"This is Lester Patterson, HBPD, I've got a couple of questions if you've got a minute."

"I'm kind of busy right now," she said curtly.

"Or I could come by your office, make a fuss, talk to your boss."

"I think I can fit you in," she said reluctantly, "as long as it doesn't take long. I really am pretty busy. We've got a report going out today and I've got to finish typing it."

"Depends on how helpful you are," Lester said coolly.

"Shoot. Maybe I shouldn't have said that," she said nervously.

"The only one who should be offended is dead," Lester said.

"I'm sorry, it's just what I always say," she said, embarrassed.

"Before I get started, did I see you at the Spring Fling last Saturday night?" Lester asked.

"You were there too?" she said very surprised. "Are you a member? That's a good shindig."

"Are you a member? Do you know Carlton or Johnny Cheam?"

"No, I'm not a member. I don't have enough lettuce in my garden, at least not yet. I know the Cheams, more his dad than the son," Beatrice said sounding alternately confident and unsure. "His son doesn't like me."

"Did you make a call to anyone from the payphone at The Insomniac the night Steven Shawn was murdered?"

"You think I warned someone? Why should I do that? I didn't even know the guy. He seemed really nice, my type, cultured, not like the jocks I used to date in high school or the sparrow boys that usually hang out at The Insomniac. They think that because they've memorized some Rimbaud, have a goatee and look like they subsist on cottage cheese and oatmeal I should fall all over them. The fluttering of a butterfly could blow them over."

"So, did you call anyone?" Lester asked.

"Wow, this is getting pretty personal," Beatrice whispered. "I've got a reputation to uphold."

"It's not my place to judge you," Lester said apologetically.

"That's what all you guys say until we don't want to go out with you anymore," Beatrice said angrily. "Look, I really liked the guy, not that I knew him. He seemed okay. He had a cute accent and was cultured. You never know if a guy is a creepo or alright. So, if I'm going to be spending some time with a guy, especially one that I don't know, I usually let one of my friends know, just in case I don't call them in the morning. You've got to be careful."

"So, you called a friend?" Lester asked.

"I did. Is that all right?" Beatrice said defiantly.

"Was that friend Carlton Cheam? I ask because someone called Cheam's house from the payphone in the back of The Insomniac where the bathrooms are." Lester knew that he couldn't back that statement up and hoped she wouldn't call him on it.

"Wow, I didn't know you could check that," Beatrice said very nervously.

"So you called Carlton Cheam. What did you say?"

"He wasn't happy," Beatrice said. "Nothing unusual about that."

"What did you tell him?" Lester asked.

"I told him not to expect things he didn't have any right to expect, if you know what I mean. I don't want to have to spell it out."

"So, you have some sort of relationship or understanding with Carlton Cheam?"

"Had is too strong a word, but try telling that to him. He wasn't expecting me. I count him as a friend. Nothing more, but he can be overly protective."

"What did you tell him?"

"I told him that I wasn't feeling well and that he'd have to take a rain check," Beatrice said cautiously.

"What did he say?"

"Well, he wasn't happy. I'm sure he could hear the music on in the background. He called me lots of things that reminded me why I didn't ever want to see him again."

"But you went with him to the Spring Fling?" Lester asked.

"Unofficially. I was his guest, so to speak. With his wife there, I knew I was safe. I had so much fun the last time that I couldn't resist and I tried as best as I could to avoid him. He cornered me when he was halfway to drunksville. He was like an octopus but without the suction cups. I skedaddled and lost myself in the crowd until I amscrayed back to my humble abode, alone if you're going to insist."

"So, you've known him for at least a year?" Lester asked.

"Give a girl some credit!" Beatrice exclaimed. "I met him last year ago at a club and I gave him my phone number. He was very persuasive even though I turned him down half a dozen times."

"So, he didn't know you were ditching him for another guy."

"I can't say he didn't suspect," Beatrice whispered. "But I wouldn't put it like that."

"Where were you going?"

"Do you get out much?" Beatrice said indignantly. "I wasn't going to have him stay at my place, not with Carlton possibly on the warpath. I figured that if we parked my car there, he'd think I was at home. Shawn would follow me home in his car and then we'd take his car back to his place that way it would look like I was home in bed just in case."

"In case of what?" Lester asked.

"In case snoopy came a snoopin'," Beatrice said.

"What kind of work did Steven Shawn do?"

"Honestly, I don't remember him saying. I could tell that he was gainfully employed and he seemed A-Okay," Beatrice said.

"Did you tell Mr. Cheam anything about him when you called him?"

"Why would I do that?" Beatrice said, annoyed. "The less he knew the better. I just wish he didn't know where I live."

"Why didn't you call him earlier and tell him that you weren't going to meet him?"

"I should have," Beatrice sighed. "I was hoping that he wasn't at home. We didn't have a date or an understanding that we were dating, though Carlton probably thinks differently."

"Do you think that Mr. Cheam knew Steven Shawn?"

"A million guys in the city, and he's going to know one of them I met practically at random? That would be long odds," Beatrice said sarcastically.

"But not completely at random."

"Well, I'd seen him at The Insomniac before. I wouldn't say that I'm a regular but the place is a hoot and I'd rather meet a guy who at least knows who Rimbaud is than go out with a guy who's trying to recapture his youth."

"Who's Rimbaud?"

"A poet, if you're into that sort of thing. Usually, the guys memorize something by Sartre, say it like it's something they thought up and think you won't notice and be impressed."

"So, why not completely break it off with Cheam?" Lester asked.

"I'm sorry, but the guy's got a temper and with guys like that I don't tell them no directly and then I hope they find their honey in someone else's beehive," Beatrice said coldly. "Don't ever treat anyone like that."

"I try not to. That's not the way I was raised," Lester said.

"Your mother must be a real sweetheart. Your girlfriend is a lucky girl."

"Yeah, we've been going out for six months," Lester said happily.

"And things are going well between you two?"

"Yeah, I think so. I hope so," Lester said hopefully.

"Then put a ring on her finger. What are you waiting for?" Beatrice exclaimed.

"I. . ." Lester stammered.

"Don't get cold feet. A girl isn't going to wait forever."

"I know. I just wonder if I'm good enough for her."

"Confidence and desire, that's what's going to win her over. When are you seeing her again?"

"Today, probably," Lester said bashfully.

"Call her now. Take her out to lunch. Surprise her!" Beatrice urged.

"I'll do it now!" Lester exclaimed.

"Go get him, tiger," Beatrice said.

Lester thanked her for the help, hung up and then immediately called Mary's house. His heart was pounding and as he dialed the number. He tried to calm himself by holding his breath. Mary answered the phone and was happy that Lester wanted to meet her for lunch.

"Wherever you want," Mary said.

"Well, I shouldn't take that long for lunch, so how about we meet at Steve's across from the old aquarium, unless you want to go someplace nicer. Why don't we go to someplace nicer?"

"How about Pio's or the Mermaid?"

"The Mermaid. You can park there and they have a lunch special."

"I'll probably just walk. It's not that far. I'll see you there at noon."

Lester looked at his watch. It was only 10:00 a.m. He looked down at the notes from his call with Loehner. When he looked up again, Kappe was standing over his desk with a frown.

"He did it. There's no doubt about it, at least in my mind," Kappe said coldly.

"Cheam. The dad," Lester said.

"The gun matches!" Kappe bellowed.

"I just got off the phone with Beatrice Loehner, the beatchick Shawn was with. She knows the Cheams, the dad. She even called him from The Insomniac that night to tell him that she wasn't going to see him that night."

"Do you think she set him up?" Kappe asked.

"I don't think so. If she did, I don't think she'd ever say. We could press, but I don't think she's going to pop. That would leave her open as an accessory.

Also, she says that she doesn't even like Carlton Cheam, so if that's the case, then why would she help him snuff a guy she'd just met? There was no motive unless she was doing Carlton Cheam a favor. Maybe she didn't know that Carlton was going to murder him. That seems farfetched. What is in it for her? According to her, they were going to Shawn's place."

"She'd have to be a real empty-headed ditz to tie herself to that sinker. Johnny couldn't have done it. He's got an alibi."

"V8 and super-charged," Lester said. "Carlton's wife and him are on the outs and she probably wasn't there to give him an alibi. Believe me, I'm sure she doesn't even live there. Where ever she's living it's probably their old house over in Hawthorne. We should be able to check that out. We could even ask her."

"I'm sure they're on the outs, but we can't count on her testifying. He'd go bust and she'd be out on the street," Kappe said.

"What about calling the Air Force's inspector general?" Lester asked.

"You mean on the whole engine thing? Call them out on it?" Kappe asked.

"Yeah, that's the motive, isn't it? That and jealousy," Lester said, frustrated.

"Money and jealousy, a potent mix. It's not a murder charge. It's just fraud, if we can get them to bite."

"Why wouldn't they?" Kappe asked.

"So, maybe he gets fined. Maybe he gets some minor time," Lester said.

"It's better than nothing!" Lester said indignantly.

"Not if you're Shawn. For Shawn, it's not justice. It's not put to rest," Kappe declared.

"So there's no justice?" Lester asked.

"We'll know," Kappe said.

"But will he know that we know?" Lester asked.

"He'll suspect. He's got to know."

"But he'll know pretty quickly that we can't prove it and then once he's figured that out, he's going to be pretty smug. He's not going to suffer. He's not going to pay a price, except for his soul, which he probably auctioned off a long time ago."

"But he's going to worry if he thinks we're not giving up," Kappe said.

"I'll never give up," Lester said adamantly.

"And he'll know that and worry."

"This isn't making me feel better. So, he has some sleepless nights but gets on with his life. That's not much justice," Lester said.

"There's always the Pearly Gates."

"The jazz club over on Pico?" Lester said with a wry smile.

"We can try bringing them in and seeing if we can get a confession, but we don't have much."

"What about threatening to arrest Johnny?"

"He's got an alibi. He's just going to claim that someone set him up. His dad's going to claim that he was at home and unless we get an eyewitness, and nobody's come in so far, we're not going to be able to get past a reasonable doubt. Unless Miss Loehner says she saw him, and I don't think she saw him. The murderer was behind her. I don't think, and I don't see how we could prove it if it were true, that she led him like a lamb to the slaughter. Don't feel bad kid, you're not always going to come out a winner. You've been a good partner and I'm going to make sure you don't get bumped back to metering."

Lester thanked him and promised to do better in the future. They left it at that. The gun was clean. No prints. The only thing left was taking a stab at wringing out a confession, but both of them knew it was a waste of time.

At ten to noon, Lester rushed out of the station and walked quickly down Pier Avenue to the Mermaid just before the decrepit pier. A surfer rode up the hill on his bike, his surfboard attached to a trailer. His flannel shirt was tied to his waist and flapped against the back wheel of his bike. He wiped the sweat from his brow with a handkerchief as he stood in the parking lot. Mary was waiting for him in the parking lot, sitting on the low wall that separates the parking lot from the Strand. The morning fog was just lifting.

They embraced and kissed until Lester was overcome with self-consciousness and pulled away to stare into her beautiful eyes, took her hand and led her into the Mermaid. The dark interior of the nearly windowless restaurant was a contrast to the beach outside. A waitress led them to a booth and they chatted about nothing while they waited for their orders. Lester had a cheeseburger and onion rings while Mary had cottage cheese and a side salad but still ate half of the onion rings. Mary chatted about them trying to get away for a weekend like they'd talked about but that it would have to be when her parents were going up to their cabin in Big Bear.

Lester played with his food. Picking up one of the smaller onion rings, he toyed with it his hand wondering whether he should or shouldn't act. Meanwhile, Mary was slurping up a spoonful of cottage cheese.

"You seem kind of down. Anything wrong at work?"

"No, nothing's wrong. It's just that I've got a lot on my mind."

"Do you want to talk about it?"

Lester shook his head.

"Or you can't talk about it," Mary said sympathetically.

"Mary, I was wondering," Lester said nervously.

Mary looked up and smiled, the kind of smile that had melted him the first time he'd seen it, the night he'd bashfully handed her a parking ticket.

"Mary, now that I've gotten a promotion, now that I've got a real job and my salary's increased, or is supposed to increase because we haven't done the paperwork yet," Lester said bashfully. He looked at his lap rather than Mary as he spoke. "I shouldn't have to pinch pennies so much anymore, not that I'm rich, but I'll be able to manage, get a better apartment, save up for a house."

Mary smiled and took his hand.

"I know that I'll never be able to give you the kind of life that you grew up with, but I hope that. . ." Lester said, his voice trailing off as he caught her broadening smile.

"You know I don't care about all that."

Lester lifted up her hand and then placed the onion ring on one of her fingers. "Mary, would you marry me?"

"Of course I would!" Mary exclaimed, beaming as bright as a flashlight in the eyes of a couple parking up near Malaga Cove.

Lester couldn't believe how happy and relieved he felt, which made him feel guilty that he'd failed Steven Shawn. Maybe he didn't have what it took. Maybe they'd send him back to metering, though he didn't think so.

"I love you. Lester," Mary whispered in his ear.

Lester paused, tried to accept this moment without any of the rest of his life which swirled around in his brain, but found that he couldn't. "I love you too," he said in a way that felt perfunctory, which he hoped that Mary wouldn't notice.

Mary pulled back and looked at him and wiggled the onion ring around her finger. "I guess this took a lot of planning. I'm glad we didn't go for Italian."